Praise for RETRIBUTION by Anderson Harp

"Tense and authentic—reading this book is like living a real-life mission."
—Lee Child

"Want to see what the military's really like? Harp knows his stuff. *Retribution* proves that the scariest story is the true story. Here's the real intelligence operation."
—Brad Meltzer, bestselling author of *The Fifth Assassin*

"I seldom come across a thriller as authentic and well-written as *Retribution*. Anderson Harp brings his considerable military expertise to a global plot that's exciting, timely, and believable. His characters are exceptionally well-drawn and convincing. If you like Tom Clancy's work, you'll love *Retribution*. Anderson Harp is very much his own man, however, and to say that I'm impressed is an understatement."
—David Morrell, *New York Times* bestselling author of *The Protector*

"Anderson Harp's *Retribution* is a stunner: a blow to the gut and shot of adrenaline. Here is a novel written with authentic authority and bears shocking relevance to the dangers of today. It reminds me of Tom Clancy at his finest. Put this novel on your must-read list—anything by Harp is now on mine."
—James Rollins, *New York Times* bestselling author of *Bloodline*

"*Retribution* by Anderson Harp is an outstanding thriller with vivid characters, breakneck pacing, and suspense enough for even the most demanding reader. On top of that, Harp writes with complete authenticity and a tremendous depth of military knowledge and expertise. A fantastic read—don't miss it!"
—Douglas Preston, #1 bestselling author of *Impact*

"*Retribution* by Anderson Harp is a fast-paced, suspenseful thriller loaded with vivid characters and backed by a depth of military knowledge. Top gun!"
—Kathy Reichs, #1 bestselling author of the *Temperance Brennan* and *Tory Brennan* series

The Will Parker Thrillers by Anderson Harp

NORTHERN THUNDER
BORN OF WAR
RETRIBUTION
MISLED
KILLING MERCURY
NOVEMBER 400CP IS MISSING

November 400CP Is Missing

Anderson Harp

LYRICAL UNDERGROUND
Kensington Publishing Corp.
www.kensingtonbooks.com

LYRICAL UNDERGROUND BOOKS are published by

Kensington Publishing Corp.
119 West 40th Street
New York, NY 10018

All Kensington titles, imprints, and distributed lines are available at special quantity discounts for bulk purchases for sales promotion, premiums, fund-raising, educational, or institutional use.

Special book excerpts or customized printings can also be created to fit specific needs. For details, write or phone the office of the Kensington Sales Manager: Kensington Publishing Corp., 119 West 40th Street, New York, NY 10018. Attn. Sales Department. Phone: 1-800-221-2647.

Lyrical Underground and Lyrical Underground logo Reg. US Pat. & TM Off.

First Electronic Edition: May 2021
eISBN-13: 978-1-5161-0978-4
eISBN-10: 1-5161-0978-3

First Print Edition: May 2021
ISBN-13: 978-1-5161-0982-1
ISBN-10: 1-5161-0982-1

Printed in the United States of America

"Hunger, love, pain, fear are some of the inner forces which rule a man's instinct for self-preservation."

—Albert Einstein

Chapter 1

The sound of the helicopter came long before he saw it appear above the palm trees. It reminded him of another one on the other side of the world.

I hope this one does better. Charles Hedges rubbed his arm. His left forearm had suffered a bad compound fracture when the Marine CH-53 tore into a hillside just outside of Camp Leatherneck in the Helmand Province of Afghanistan. A sudden sandstorm had blinded the pilots. He was the only survivor, who had, some would say, the luck of being thrown out of the plunging machine and into the rocky hillside. More bones than his arm had been broken, but the arm would always hurt. It reminded him of his fellow Marines who didn't survive the fireball that engulfed the wreckage.

Operation Khanjar finished off Chuck Hedges's Marine career after several months in Bethesda and a medical board that didn't agree with his argument that he could still carry a combat load on his back. He left the Corps as a major and Executive Officer of 2nd Battalion, 8th Marine Regiment. As a leader of 2/8 in a third combat tour, he was destined to be a colonel and possibly much higher. But he had a sterling record of getting the job done and employment opportunities started calling once he hit the door.

"Come on, Chuck. It can't be that bad." The leader of the Chevron expedition never served. He went straight to work with Chevron's exploration team after leaving the University of Michigan.

"What?"

"You have that worried look again." The engineer lit another cigarette as they stood in the field deep in the heart of Sumatra.

Chuck Hedges pulled up the shoulder strap of his backpack in demonstration of ignoring his boss's comment.

"This is your last haul. You've been worried about this one more than I have ever seen." The Chevron engineer smiled at Chuck as the two stood on the edge of a clearing surrounded by a forest of palm trees. He pulled another drag on his cigarette. A small white metal Butler building was just inside the grove of trees and had been their home for the last several days. The engineer led a small team of three plus the security officer, Chuck Hedges.

"We needed to leave a week ago."

Chuck had been worried. Sumatra was turning back toward a place that should cause one to worry. The island had been a hotbed for fundamentalist Muslims before the Great Sumatra fault just to the west had split open a decade earlier. It caused one of the most devastating earthquakes to strike Southeast Asia. Far deadlier, a tsunami quickly followed the quake and struck the coastal towns and cities with a wave that came in at two hundred miles an hour. The wall of water was well over a hundred feet high. The northern coast of Sumatra became, for a flash of a moment, something out of a Hollywood disaster movie. The death count was well into six figures. In all of the bad news, there had been one piece of good news. It had broken the back of the Muslim fundamentalist groups. Sumatra and Indonesia had been quiet now for a decade. But time had allowed the disaster to become a footnote. Trouble was brewing again.

"Time to get out of here." Chuck had the respect of the chief engineer and the other bosses at Chevron Pacific. He was a wiry, medium-built man who barely reached six feet, with a black curly beard and cold brown eyes that could push a stranger back if one stared into them. The broken bones had only made him stronger, more determined to be fit and capable of his job as head of security for the Sumatra exploration team. His workouts were well known by the Chevron staff, two hundred sit-ups every morning. He found a crossbeam in the building they camped out in and used it for his fifty pull-ups. He also carried, under his blue Chevron polo shirt, tucked in a holster in the back of his 5.11 combat pants, his Glock 23.

"Last one before corporate." The chief engineer had helped Chuck's Chevron career, as had others. Chuck was leaving the field to head up Chevron's security system. For the first time in his two careers, Chuck Hedges was going to spend more than a few nights at home, in bed with his wife, and playing ball with his two young sons.

"We aren't there yet." Chuck turned his back to the Chevron Sikorsky 76D as it gently touched down in the grass of the clearing. The men grabbed their bags and backpacks and ran to the aircraft as its blades continued to spin. The helicopter had the full fittings of an executive machine with leather seats and dark wood paneling. Chuck was the last one on board, making sure that all were secure and safe.

The aircraft rose up, turned to the south and accelerated over the acres and acres of palm trees. After several miles, Chuck watched the terrain change. The palm tree groves gave way to a spiderweb of oil rigs that covered the valley as far as he could see. The oil fields of Minas were the richest in all of Indonesia.

Since the 1940s these fields gave up enough black gold to provide nearly half of all the oil produced in Indonesia. It was the largest producer of crude in all of Southeast Asia. But it had a problem. It was giving out.

Chuck pulled out his iPad and pulled up the most recent threat brief from the Department of State and the Central Intelligence Agency. Chevron Pacific Indonesia's security officer had been given special access to the daily intelligence briefings on Indonesia. The agencies limited Chuck's access to Southeast Asia, but it had been a good source of warnings. It only confirmed what he was worried about.

"Damn," he said to himself. A police station in Kuala Lumpur had been overrun by a terror group that had killed five officers. As a security officer, he didn't like the feel of the country.

The other men started to doze off with the hum of the turbines. They had lived on cots for most of a week, eating rations carried into the backcountry but supplemented by several ice chests full of Anker beer. The beer had to be brought in on their Chevron aircraft, as it was getting rarer for alcohol to be found in the Muslim island of Sumatra.

Chuck continued to stare out his window. His boss tapped him on his knee.

"Time to go into town and get a shower?" The man shouted the words over the roar of the engines.

"No." The former active duty Marine shut down the thought with one word. "Straight to the bird."

"OK." The engineer didn't fight the order. "Honolulu then." He looked at his watch. "I'll get our pilot to call the bird and get it warmed up." He turned to the two up front, tapped one on the shoulder, leaned over and told the man something only the two could hear. The response was a thumbs-up.

Chuck knew that the mission they were on needed to be reported back to corporate headquarters as quickly as possible. For the same reason, it was important that the team leave not only Sumatra, but Indonesia as well.

The Sikorsky started to descend from its altitude just as darkness was setting in. Chuck stood up in the cabin, looking over the pilot's seat to see the green, white, and red glow of the instrument panel and, beyond, the lights of Sultan Syarif Kasim II airport. The city of Pekanbaru was off to one side of the airfield in the distance.

Chuck adjusted the Glock as he sat back down when the aircraft started to bank into its landing. He looked out on the airfield and in the low light saw the shape of Chevron's Gulfstream G650ER. Their mission was important enough that corporate had provided one of its primary executive airplanes that could easily reach Hawaii with its Mach .9 speed. There was activity around the Gulfstream, crew moving quickly to ready the aircraft to pull back for takeoff.

The Sikorsky landed just to the side of the Gulfstream and as Chuck heard the turbines of the helicopter wind down, the engines of the jet started to overtake the noise. A ground crew worker pulled the door open and grabbed the bags of several of the men.

"See you onboard. The ice is waiting!" The engineer slapped Hedges on his knee.

"Got to make a call. Be right there." Chuck held up his satellite phone. He looked at his watch and calculated the time zones. She wouldn't be there, with her job, but he just wanted to let her know that the journey home had begun.

The phone went to voice mail.

"Hey, gettin' on the last ride. They want us to stop in Honolulu but should be home by Tuesday. Love you. Tell the guys to get their gloves ready." At Annapolis, he'd lettered all four years on the Navy's baseball team. He wanted his kids to have the same skill set, but time was running out. They would be well beyond the coaching stage if he delayed much longer. Chuck had thought long and hard about this transition in his life.

He stepped onto the tarmac and stepped around the puddles left by another thunderstorm. Rain happened on a daily basis. The Gulfstream's tail number N400CP stood out on the white, glistening body of the aircraft.

"Get some sleep on this bird," he said to himself. The seats were large, leather, and soft and would lay out flat. The Gulfstream would quickly climb above the weather, settle down at something above forty thousand feet, and the first cool air in several weeks would quickly put them all to sleep.

"Ready to go, sir." The man standing in front of him had on a Chevron shirt and dark pants.

"Where's Guppa?" Chuck stared at the man for a brief second.

"Out sick."

The engineer was waving at the door to the aircraft.

"Let's go!"

Charles Hedges ran to the door. He should have gone with his instincts.

The Gulfstream's male steward closed the door as soon as Chuck came through it. At the same moment, the aircraft started to taxi, and in no more time than it took Chuck to sit in a seat and put on his seat belt the engines spun up and the airplane was airborne.

The engineer sat across from Chuck and raised his crystal glass in a toast. "Ice and bourbon. Life is good!"

"Yeah." Chuck waved at him. He noticed the steward headed to the back, where the restroom was in the rear of the aircraft. Chuck loosened his seat belt, sat up, and pulled the Glock with its holster from his belt, setting it on a side table. Sleep came quickly as he knew he was safe and the jet climbed above the thick cloud cover.

The fall from the sky came quickly.

Chuck saw his Glock float up in the air then fall away from him, as if it was a fastball thrown by a major leaguer. The jet was in a deep dive. The masks came down from the overheads as a loud scream of noises rose through the aircraft. Chuck, still restrained by the seat belt, reached out and grabbed the engineer's arm. The man's eyes were as wide as saucers, his face was pale white, and he had the look of pending death and fear.

"You're not going to die." Chuck knew an important clue. The steward had not come out of the bathroom. "Listen to me! Tell them nothing! If you do, they will kill you! Nothing!"

"What?"

"Your life doesn't mean anything to them if you tell them why you are here. Got it?"

"OK."

The aircraft pulled out of the dive at less than fifty feet above the water. The lights had been cut off and the Gulfstream traveled for some time in complete darkness. Chuck wanted to reach for his Glock but every time he stood up, the airplane made a giant swing as if to put him back in his seat. Finally, he gave up and pulled his seat belt tight.

"They are going to run this into the ground." He said the words, but no one was listening. They were all praying to their God and working their cell phones. It wouldn't matter. Chuck pulled both his cell and his satellite phone from his pockets, but both were out of commission. Whether it was the speed of the aircraft or the low altitude, the phones had no reception. Chuck figured out what the pilot would do. The plane would stay low to the end of its journey, then slow down with full flaps, but not rise up, and run into the water or the ground. The airplane would stay well below radar for the remainder of the trip. "Keep your head down to your legs as long as you can."

The engineer shook his head and tucked down. He didn't have to hold the position long.

Chuck remembered hearing, at the beginning of the end, the wings clipping the tops of palm trees, then seeing, as if in slow motion, the aircraft being shredded by the crash. It all happened in an instant and then blackness overtook him.

Chapter 2

Will Parker hadn't planned to be in Alaska for more than a month. He had returned from his lodge in Georgia to get in some flying. Alaska offered the opportunity to fly like no other place in the world. He often had to set his airplane down on a river shoreline, or with pontoons on an isolated lake, or at other times, land on ice. He loved it. Alaska was the last, great frontier. It required the best of a pilot and mistakes rarely were forgiven.

Where are they? he thought as he followed a river up through a valley where one lake was connected to another. Two hunters from the lower forty-eight had called in an emergency. Their guide, who promised a hunting trip for bear at a very low rate, turned out to be an alcoholic. Once he finished his last bottle, he went into the d.t.'s and they woke up a long way from any civilization. They had gotten what they had paid for.

Will's Turbine Maule single engine airplane was made for the wilderness. It was built like a tank and could make a landing on any surface if given enough room. He slowed the aircraft, dropped some flaps and cruised the circumference of the river valley.

Got to be on this one. Will had covered much of the river above where the hunting party had been dropped into the wilderness. The hunting permits for nonresidents were for Game Management Unit 19D, which helped narrow the search down, but a poor guide could have taken them much farther from the drop-off spot. This was their ninth day and supplies would be low. But the Maule's fuel was getting low as well.

"November 156 following the Kuskokwim River passing Vinasale Mountain. Making one more lap up the river." Will's radio report helped those back at the airfield keep track of the effort. The late spring sunlight gave him several more hours to search than a month ago. The hunters had a radio and had reported in, but the guide was unconscious and of no help. Will had been told that they had been dropped off, hiked for several days, and had no sense of where they were. The country had an ample supply of nine-hundred-pound grizzly bears who could turn the hunters into those being hunted. One bear in the area had come in at over thirteen hundred pounds with claws on its front paws that could shred the body of a pickup truck. And it would be a mistake to run. Jesse Owens would not have escaped a hungry brown bear.

Will's aircraft banked hard to the left in a turn and looked for any sign. Vinasale Mountain jutted up from the river valley. The Maule circled the point of rock.

"Roger, November 156, better bring it on in before we are looking for you."

Will recognized the voice. The brotherhood of bush pilots watched out for each other. Will turned the Maule back to the south.

"Another night can't be good. One more pass." Will had seen the weather reports and more thunderstorms were expected. He guessed that the men thought well of themselves as being expert hunters, but Alaska could wear you out quickly. And desperation would set in. A hunter in the lower forty-eight could always walk out of a bad situation. If he followed a river downstream in the West, it would lead to something. In Alaska, it led only to more wilderness.

As Will turned to the south, he saw something near the bank of the Kuskokwim River.

A sliver of white smoke rose up from the woods on the far shore of the lake. *Got 'em.*

"November 156, hunters on the Kuskokwim just southwest of Vinasale Mountain." Will loved the Maule. He had bought the single engine taildragger aircraft on this trip to Alaska. It could carry four in tight quarters and land on nothing more than fifty yards of flat riverbank. The turbine engine had more power than needed even with a full load. It was the Porsche of bush pilots.

He banked the aircraft again, going slow over the river and picking out the spot of sand and smooth river water. It was no more than fifty yards from the spiral of smoke.

Will made the final turn into the wind, dropped some flaps, and slowed to a fast walk. The large donut tundra tires rode gently over the sand and rocks. As the turbine spun down Will was greeted at the nose of his aircraft by two men who looked very ready to head back to civilization.

"You guys OK?"

"He's dead." The taller of the two had sloped shoulders, gray hair tucked under a well-worn Orvis hunting hat, and a week-old beard. His companion stood just behind him, a foot shorter, but just as worn out. Their clothes were wet and covered with a layer of mud.

"Your guide?" Will was asking the obvious.

"Back at our lean-to." The taller one spoke.

"You sure?"

"We are both doctors. He's with MD Anderson." The smaller one took over the conversation. "We were residents together at Mayo."

Will had heard of the famed Houston cancer center and Mayo Clinic. It sounded like an often-used line that certainly would impress many in the lower forty-eight. Here in the Alaska wilderness it fell in the category of not a "need to know."

"When did you last eat?"

"Ran out of everything four days ago. Didn't even see a chipmunk."

This land wasn't covered with chipmunks, but the lack of game probably began when they lit their fires. Hunger was setting in with the two lost hunters.

"Let's get you out of here."

"Just need our rifles."

"Sure, I'll call the AWT. They'll get a helicopter out here at first light." Will knew that the Alaska Wildlife Troopers, or game wardens, would want to investigate a death and get the body out before the wildlife had it for dinner, but they wouldn't go into the wilderness with the sun going down. Looking for a dead body in the dark could lead to more dead bodies.

"Thanks." The taller one stuck out his hand. "We owe you one."

Will laughed at the comment.

"Happy to help. Get your stuff and let's go."

The Maule lifted off with ease, turned to the south and headed toward the closest airfield. The men had a hefty bill to pay. They would carry the price of others who had diverted from their own hunting parties to help in a rescue. With a hunt in Alaska costing $10,000 or more, the bill for a rescue wasn't cheap. Several airplanes had flown on the rescue mission, but the two doctors from Houston wouldn't mind paying. The fear of the wilderness could make any man humble. But Will knew one other thing about this rescue. It was far more important that nothing was said that would get back to Texas. Anyone who traveled to the backcountry of Alaska had his pride.

The two hunters climbed out of the Maule at the airfield. The older, taller one turned back to their rescue pilot.

"Can't say thanks enough."

"No problem." Will didn't need any more thanks than the fact that the two left the backcountry of Alaska alive.

"Didn't get your name?"

"Just a rescuer." Will didn't need a gift package later on.

"OK, rescuer. Thanks again." As the hunter walked away, he stopped and turned around. He dropped his backpack to the ground, struggled with one of the side pockets and pulled out a business card. "I owe you a steak. If you ever get to Houston, call!"

A truck pulled up with a tank of fuel on a trailer. The driver attached a hose to the airplane and hand-cranked the pump. Soon the Maule had been topped off.

"The state's got this." The driver pointed to a uniformed figure who had walked up to the airplane.

"I'm heading back," said Will. The man who had controlled the rescue effort stood in front of Will. He was dressed in the uniform of an Alaskan game warden and stood at the wingtip of the Maule. "Their guide's body is a quarter of a mile down the Kuskokwim just below Vinasale Mountain."

"Thanks for your help." The game warden stuck out his hand.

Will shook it.

"We got some steaks on the grill. Don't you want to join us?"

"Thanks, but the air's calm, there's plenty of moonlight and I need to get back."

Will's airplane slipped off the runway and climbed out over the forest. It soon gained altitude and once his altimeter showed four thousand feet, he knew he was clear of any of the small mountains between him and his home field. The full moon cast a light that reflected off the rivers below. Will had flown over this territory many times and the illumination of the light as it struck the water and the twists and turns of the rivers gave him his bearings. The green glow of his instruments also confirmed his direction. The moon, the stars, and the hum of his engine reminded him why he had come to Alaska to fly.

Will thought this was his last rescue mission for the year. He would be wrong.

Chapter 3

The two men walked past the gold sign attached to the bleached-white wall that surrounded the building on Jalan Ampang Hilir in the suburb of Kuala Lumpur. They stopped at the front gate, then moved on quickly. One spat on the sign as they moved away: the Embassy of the Republic of the Union of Myanmar.

A few minutes later a white Toyota pickup truck roared down the quiet street. It turned suddenly into the embassy, crashing through the gate. Neighbors could hear the sound of automatic rifle fire followed by an explosion. Then there was a second explosion. Sirens began to wail as both the police and military descended on the building. Smoke could be seen rising up from the structure.

A day later the Malaysian military unit VAT 69 quietly surrounded a hut near the small village of Kuala Berang on the east coast of Malaysia. The repeated thuds of silenced automatic rifle fire could be heard by the villagers. The weapons all carried the suppressors used by special operations units.

An officer with a sand-colored beret walked up to the hut as the blood-drenched body of a young man was being dragged out. He was still alive, but mumbling words. His legs had been shredded by the gunfire and hung loosely, like a racehorse with both legs broken.

"Is this all?" the officer asked of the man who led the raid, who still had his HK automatic rifle slung over his shoulder and his face covered in a mixed camouflage of green and black paint.

"Yes sir."

"One less wolf pack." The officer kicked the man. "Rat pack is what we should call them." He bent over the man. "How is your salvation army now?"

He was referencing the most recent Malaysian terrorist group to surface—the Arakan Rohingya Salvation Army. Their attack on the Myanmar Embassy the day before resulted in a swift response by the 69 Commando unit, or VAT 69. It was the most elite of elite units, with an acceptance rate of one out of ten. Of six hundred applicants, only sixty were accepted. The first two weeks of training started with the candidates being dropped off deep in the jungle with no food or water. Those who came out of the brush were covered with dirt and insect bites and begging for water. Thereafter, the training only got worse.

Another man, dressed in a loose-fitting shirt, slacks, and sandals, stood near the VAT 69 colonel. He too stared at the bloody man on the ground.

"Does this help?" the colonel asked the stranger.

"Yes." The man was the aide to the ambassador of the Myanmar Embassy.

"Sir, here are some of their papers." The leader of the raid handed them to the colonel. "And we got several phones."

The colonel first handed them to another officer of the VAT 69 standing there. She, too, was dressed in the camouflage utilities of the unit with a sand-colored beret. The woman's caramel hair, tucked under the beret, and soft brown eyes were nothing like the men of the unit. In fact, nothing of her appearance other than the uniform made one think she was a member of an elite special operations unit that had been trained to kill without hesitation. She ran through the papers and looked at the cell phones.

"This is our intelligence officer." The colonel pointed to the woman.

"It is a pleasure." The aide extended his hand. "I'm Saw."

She didn't respond.

"We don't give out our names. Too much often needs to be done without others needing to know who you are. Too much risk they follow you home." The colonel was brisk, but in as polite a manner as he could be.

"May I see the papers?" the aide asked.

"Yes." The colonel took the papers from his junior officer and handed them to the guest.

He leafed through the pages. They spoke of the persecution of Rohingya Muslims in his country. They were correct. The Muslims often had been pursued and beaten in Myanmar. Since well before Burma changed its name to Myanmar, the minority group of Muslims had been chased and killed, and many disappeared in his country. So they brought their hatred to another country. The embassy was a likely target.

But VAT 69 would pursue any attacker in Malaysia to the very end. For more than a decade, since the great earthquake and tsunami, terrorism had been quiet. Now, it had started to raise its ugly head in an assortment of splinter groups or wolf packs that were springing up everywhere.

"Your men did a great job." The aide handed the papers back to the colonel. "And woman. I will report this to the ambassador."

"Yes. We will stop this." The colonel saluted the aide.

"One last question. Where were they from?" The aide needed to report this back to his higher-ups. He was asking whether they were all Malaysians.

"This one was their ringleader. He is Malaysian. Raised in Banda Aceh. He had a Filipino with him and two from your country."

"Two from Myanmar?"

"Two."

"Muslims from our country?"

"I would think so. Rohingya Muslims." The colonel handed the papers back to his sergeant.

"We don't use that word."

"Sorry?"

"Rohingya." The aide stood there with his arms crossed. "They are Bengalis." He was talking of the hatred the majority of Myanmar citizens and Buddhists felt for the minority. It went back decades. Over one million of the Muslims tried to leave Myanmar only to be turned back, over the years, by bordering nations. They held no rights of citizenship in Myanmar despite being there for well over five hundred years. The people were truly stateless. And their plight caused a brewing hatred. It was a boiling pot and the steam was flowing over to other nearby nations, including the colonel's.

"Yes. I understand."

"Best watch out." The aide was predicting the future.

Chapter 4

Will passed over the last ridgeline north of his cabin as he started the descent. The river he had followed twisted around the peak of the hill mass and headed straight toward his camp. With the moonlight, he made the last turn to the landing strip. His runway was an old Army airfield he had improved and was constructed of concrete, unusual for the backcountry of Alaska. Many of the runways in the backcountry were gravel, which could tear up a propeller or jet engine with one rock. This runway protected his aircraft.

The concrete also caused the runway to stand out in the moonlight. Will lined up the aircraft with the landing strip and as he slowed down, he clicked his microphone on a special frequency that lit up the runway even further. With the moon's bright illumination, he didn't need the runway lights except to make sure that a moose or bear had not stopped in the middle of the landing strip. Just to be sure, he flew low over it and circled around for the final landing. There was no wind. The wheels barely squealed as they settled down on the concrete. It was past midnight when he parked the Maule and tied it down.

The cabin was pitch-black as he used his flashlight to come in and start a fire in the fireplace. It was another cool night which, for now, kept the insects at bay. The smell of burning wood soon filled the cabin and the crackle of the wood helped Will fall asleep in his chair. He kept his Heckler & Koch automatic near his side more out of habit than for any specific danger.

The rescue of the doctors helped Will sleep. It was a tonic for the years of living on edge. It required the best of his flying and, equally importantly, gave him a reason for the life he was now living.

Soon, daylight came through the shuttered window. As he was sipping a coffee, his cell phone began to ring. Few people had the number. He looked at the screen and instantly recognized the caller.

"Hey, what you up for?" The voice was someone he knew well.

The call was from Andy at TEMSCO. The letters all had meaning— Timber, Exploration, Mining, Survey, and Cargo Operations. If translated to practicality, TEMSCO used helicopters to move nearly everything in Alaska. Tourists enjoyed riding to the top of a glacier on TEMSCO helicopters. And work crews on the pipeline would occasionally need ferrying to a work site. But this call was about another mission.

"Just got back from up north." Will stood up, glancing out of habit at the Maule, making sure it was still secure just outside his hangar.

"I heard. Good job. They are going to call you the doctor savior."

Will heard the comment followed by high-pitched laughter.

"Yeah, what you got?" Will figured Andy had a reason for the call. It had been a few weeks since he'd heard from him.

"Sorry to put you back on the road."

Will knew that meant one thing—a search and rescue operation. It had to be something unusual for TEMSCO to be calling and for them to be calling right after his return from another mission.

"Must be special." Will made the comment, waiting for the reply.

"Right up your alley."

Will took a sip from his coffee as he walked outside to his front porch and sat down in a rocker. The day was crystal clear, and after a full moon, it didn't seem like there could have been a bad airplane crash. At least not in this southern part of Alaska.

"And what is up my alley?"

"Thought you might say that." Andy seemed to have fun pulling his chain.

"And?" Will asked it again.

"A climber is missing on Denali. Winds are coming in. Appears the missing person broke a leg and was last seen at nineteen thousand feet." Andy's voice took a more serious tone.

"No climbers around who can help. Their party was fighting for their own survival." Andy was describing a bad situation. "Weather is moving too fast. Up there it is howling."

"What about the Guard?" Will had worked with the 212th Rescue Squadron of the Alaska National Guard. The unit out of Fort Wainwright not only had some excellent pararescue specialists, but also a CH-47 helicopter that could reach higher altitudes than most.

"Their copter is down. Problem with maintenance. Expect to be back up soon, but may be too late for this guy." Andy was making his case.

"So what's the plan?" Will took another sip, leaned back in the rocker and turned toward a sound. An A-Star B3e helicopter did a fast bank over his cabin, stopped in midair and slowly descended to the runway directly across from the cabin.

"Got some more coffee?" Andy shut down his turbine and hung up his cell phone.

Will stood on his front porch as the pilot walked up to the cabin. He had a TEMSCO flight suit on with a Chicago Cubs baseball hat.

"I like those A-Stars." Will pointed to the helicopter pilot's ride. It was one of TEMSCO's newer helicopters.

"It's the three." Andy was describing the newer model more technically called the Airbus AS350B3 or model 3.

"What's its max altitude?"

"The book says twenty-three thousand." Andy was proud of his new transportation.

"McKinley is twenty thousand and the man is at nineteen thousand?"

"Yes, sir."

"So you need me?"

"The climber's alone, had a broken leg, been at altitude for at least twenty-four hours and the winds are kicking up." Andy sat down on the lip of the porch. His long legs stretched out in front of him. The ball cap covered the bright blond hair that matched his eyebrows. The others called him Dutch, as Andy had followed his love for flying to Alaska from the Netherlands. He had been flying the bush and Denali for nearly a decade and had been involved in dozens of rescues.

"What about the other SARS guys?"

"They are good but you are better for this one." Andy used his arms to support himself. "The top of this mountain. A hurt climber who is lost." He was giving more than a recruitment pitch. The pilot needed to believe in his crewman. And for this, Andy trusted only Will Parker.

"Not sure about that." Will stepped out beyond the porch and looked off to the mountains nearby. He could see a whiff of white blowing off the peaks in the distance.

"Who's at Kahiltna Glacier?" Will was asking about the base camp where the climbers all started from.

"It's busy, but they are bringing everyone down as quickly as they can."

"So the weather isn't getting better up there." Will had climbed Denali and remembered it could be a very cold mountain. Even in the middle of summer the mountain could be well below zero. At its worst and with heavy winds, it had been known to go as far down as over one hundred degrees below zero. In the wrong weather and with high winds, the top of the mountain could mean death in a matter of minutes. The wind was never a friend on the mountain or to its visitors.

"You sure he's still alive?" Will's question was cruel but accurate. Mount Everest was covered with the dead, most of whom were amateurs who wanted to add to their brag sheet before they had the capabilities to handle the dangers.

"The last call was two hours ago. But the radio is getting weak."

"Let me get my gear." Will needed to plan for something more difficult than just an in and out. It was the ins and outs that cost lives. One had to plan for the worst. It was a lesson Will learned in combat some time ago.

Andy's A-Star stopped at TEMSCO's camp to refuel. They had the SARS contract with the National Park for such rescues. And the contract paid well. But the flight up the mountain required a special pilot. When the bird reached the heights where the air was thin, the blades would lose their grip. As the density of the air lessened at higher altitudes, the helicopter lost its lift. And with the loss of lift, a helicopter became as fragile as a baby trying to take his first steps. Without lift, a sudden gust of wind could put the blades into the mountain. A downed helicopter at nineteen thousand feet meant zero chance of survival.

"We can have another rescue team climb up there, but it will be too late. The weather is closing in quickly. One team couldn't find him." The team manager for TEMSCO was giving them the most up-to-date brief.

"When was last contact?"

"Faint signal about an hour ago."

"We need a screamer suit?" Will asked both of them. The PCDS or personnel carrying device could easily be wrapped around an injured climber without trying to tie him into a harness. It kept the man in place as the hoist brought him up to the helicopter.

"Got it," Andy responded.

"What about an emergency shelter if we can't move him in these winds?"

"I got one we can drop." Andy had thought this out.

"Nifedipine?"

Andy looked at the team manager.

"Got it in the medical tent." They all knew the drill. "Plus some oxygen."

The drug could provide some help to a man drowning in his own fluids from pulmonary edema.

"And where was he last seen?" Will had climbed the mountain some time ago in his early trips to Alaska.

"The climber was heading down from the summit and toward the football field." It was a location on the mountain most climbers knew of. "But that was before the fall."

"What's it look like for the next twenty-four?" Will looked over the team manager's shoulder and studied the radar on an iPad that he was holding. The weather was moving quickly from left to right across the mountains.

The manager looked at both Andy and Will. "Best to do this now if you are going to do this."

A life was at stake. They were not turning back.

"Let's go." Will pulled up the zipper on his jacket. He was suited up for a high-altitude climb carrying ropes, a backpack, and another sling bag.

The two didn't say anything more.

The A-Star quickly lifted off from the base camp and started its climb up the face of the mountain. The raging winds rocked the aircraft as it pulled itself higher. They would go into clouds and then suddenly appear on the other side. For another pilot, this would have been deadly. But Andy had a feel for both his machine and its capabilities. And he knew where the mountain was as he continued to reach higher.

As they cleared eighteen thousand feet the weather suddenly broke to reveal a white expanse. The winds, however, pushed the ship from side to side. Will had to hold on, as the gear would jump when they got a sudden updraft. The A-Star's warning horn started to sound.

"Not going to make it much higher," Andy shouted to the back. "Got to give up."

Will leaned forward.

"This is good enough." He pulled the door open. "That flat spot below the outcrop." He pointed to the left and below. The helicopter was over the football field and well above seventeen thousand feet.

"Got it."

Will threw out a rappel rope and grabbed on. The aircraft stayed steady for a moment. As it did, he tossed out the gear and then slid out on the helicopter's skids.

"I'll call you on the radio if we can use the screamer."

"OK." Andy gave a thumbs-up. He would quickly descend to an altitude that the A-Star could handle. The helicopter pulled away from the mountain and disappeared into the howling wind and blinding snow.

Will hit the snow hard. He rolled so as to absorb the impact, but stopped short of a drop that would have taken him down more than a thousand feet. He stood up, getting a feel for his directions, and walked a small half circle until he hit the other supplies that were dropped. Will headed toward the summit walking a set pace, turning and retracing his steps. By some good fortune, on the third lap he almost tripped over an object—a person huddled in a fetal position.

"Climber!"

The person didn't reply.

"Climber!" Will hugged the person in a bear hug, trying to get his attention. "You there?"

The climber turned to him, pulled down the goggles and gazed into his eyes.

Will was startled by what he saw.

"You OK?" He looked directly into her blue eyes.

"I guess so." She coughed and a frothy pink saliva covered her lips.

"What's your name?" Will held her head with his two gloved hands.

"Robyn."

"OK, Robyn, we need to get you out of here."

The weather had gotten worse. He brought the supplies back to her and turned her torso. She had buried herself in a sleeping bag, which probably saved her life, but the right leg was bent in an odd shape and at an odd angle.

"Got to splint it." Will used a splint kit from his backpack and stabilized the leg. She was moving her hands without moving her fingers. He put her hands into the interior of her jacket and then bound another wrap around her. Will fit her into the screamer suit and used it as a makeshift toboggan.

"Take this." She seemed on the border of delirious. He gave her the drug for pulmonary edema, then fit a mask on her. Will applied the small oxygen bottle.

"Hold on." He slowly started the move to the football field. The progress was slow, with every step made as if he was walking through a minefield. It took every piece of information he knew and had taught his Marines at Bridgeport and in the Arctic Circle. Will's skill set for survival in this environment gave both of them one chance to get out of this alive.

"Rescue, are you there?" The radio cracked. It was Andy somewhere down the mountain.

"Got her."

"God damn!" Andy's excitement spoke through the radio.

"Moving down."

"Bad news. Not a chance of getting to the football field."

"Thought so." Will didn't expect an A-Star to handle these winds. They were only building up to a greater roar. "She's not going to make it much longer."

"We are working on it."

"Going to keep heading down." The wind and ice shards cut through every gap in the wrap around his face. His hands were getting colder by the minute. But Will had a sense of the topography and with that feel he could move forward slowly but safely. Their movement was the only hope that she had of staying alive.

Chapter 5

He touched his head with his hand and felt the sticky, dried molasses that covered his face. Chuck Hedges tried to focus his eyes as he stared at his hand. It was covered with blood. Thirst and a pounding headache made him nauseous. Chuck moved his arm and then his other arm. He slid his right arm down his body and then to his legs one at a time. He tried to sit up, and in the dark started to make out the shapes of the wreckage of a torn-apart Gulfstream.

"Hello?" Chuck called out, not expecting a reply. There was silence.

"Hey?" he said again.

"Oh." A voice came from his left. It was the team leader.

"You OK?" They had just survived a high-speed airplane crash. Chuck realized how silly his words were.

"Yeah."

"OK, let me see what I can do." Chuck pulled himself up. He was still seated and buckled in. The rigid structure and padding of the seat had probably saved his life. He was covered with wiring and a window that had been sheared out of the airplane. The former active duty Marine pulled himself upright, cleared away some of the debris, and stood up.

I thought Fallujah was bad. His duty as a young lieutenant in the Iraq war had been in the worst of a battle. Operation Phantom Fury had cost the lives of several of the men in his platoon. It was the first time that Chuck had faced death. But Fallujah made him stronger when faced with adversity.

"We need to get out of here." Chuck worked his way over to the team leader. He pulled the man out from under some of the airplane debris and used his hands to feel down his legs.

"What hurts?"

"Everything?"

"What of the others?" Two of the Chevron team had sat in the back as well as the missing steward who was last seen in the rear of the airplane. The rear of the aircraft was gone. As Chuck's eyes adjusted to the darkness, he realized that only the forward cabin of the aircraft was intact. He heard the lapping of waves coming from where the back of the aircraft had been. The Gulfstream had crashed into a jungle, but had hit the water then plowed into a tropical forest that had stopped the wreckage with its vegetation. The rainforest had been silent, but now the whirling sound of the insects came alive.

The others were gone. They were the only survivors. Chuck thought it was a blessing. It was a gift that they had survived the crash, but there seemed to be no purpose to the terrorist grabbing a Chevron jet and plowing it into the ground.

"Let's get out of here." The smell of jet fuel was overpowering. He pulled his teammate out of the rear of the wreckage. They stood, torn up but alive, on the sands of a beach. He breathed in the salt air, then turned to how to survive.

"We need some water." Chuck sat the man down near an outcrop of rocks and headed back into the wreckage. He had no flashlight and had to brave the smell of jet fuel, feeling his way by his hands, slowly to avoid the shards of aluminum. He found a seat at the very edge of the severed body of the airplane, and tucked in the side pockets of the seat were several bottles of water.

Things are looking up. The two swallowed the bottles of water. Chuck went down to the shoreline and used the warm salt water to wash his face. The salt burned the cuts, but they were only lacerations.

"How you doing?" Chuck walked back out of the water line and leaned against the rock next to his teammate.

"Feel like a linebacker took me out with a blindside hit." He laughed but smiled. "But damn, I walked away from an airplane crash!" His voice was as excited as if he had just survived his first parachute jump.

"Yeah, we had some luck."

It was then that their luck changed.

Chuck didn't see the man until he felt the AK-47's barrel pointed in the center of his back. He stiffened up as the rifle pushed into his upper back. Soon several men emerged out of the jungle and the dark. The rifles all pointed at the two survivors of the crash.

The engineer fell to the ground.

Chuck went to help him up, and the butt of a rifle struck him on his shoulder blade. He went to his knees, still holding on to the engineer.

"Remember what I said. You say anything about why you were here and we are both dead. Nothing. No matter what." Chuck whispered the words on the hope that none of his capturers spoke English. It was a good bet.

The two were dragged to their feet and another man tied their hands behind their backs with some bamboo strips, which were pulled tight and cut.

A leader emerged and pointed them back toward the jungle. The rainforest was as black as a night could be, forcing him to extend his hand out to feel where he was going. The two captives couldn't use their hands and ran into the slap of vegetation as they tried to follow the trail with only their feet.

As they entered the jungle, Chuck took one last look at the wreckage. Others from the party were dragging cut palms and covering the aircraft from one end to the other. One wing stood out near the beach and several men were covering it with sand. He took one last glimpse out into the water and saw no evidence of the remainder of the Gulfstream. Somehow it had been shredded enough that there was no sign that a multimillion-dollar aircraft had set down in this remote part of the world.

"Shit." Chuck spoke the word to himself. The men on the beach, the controlled drop from the sky, the specific location that was chosen—all added up to a plan that had been long in the making.

The man behind him hit him again with the butt of his rifle. He shouted words in his language.

It was the one regret Chuck had in agreeing to take this mission. He didn't know the language.

Start now. His survival instincts kicked in. He would work on small words and small phrases, trying to learn the language and more of the men.

The trail seemed to continue for several miles, crossing through a pass in a small mountain range. On the far end of the hills they came to a well-established camp with several huts sheltered under some overhanging rocks. Campfires were also tucked under the rocks, but in such a way that the smoke would climb up the edge of the overhang, go into the palm trees, and disappear as it rose.

"Good job." Chuck said the words to himself. It was a brilliant plan that would disguise their presence from even the best satellites, if they even knew where to search. He worked the math in his head. The jet didn't make the journey over the water at such a low altitude at max speed. It would have flown at 300 knots at best, and as they were over water on the eastern shore of Sumatra, the bet was they had flown north. With the time that passed from the hijacking to the crash, he best-guessed that they were north of the Sumatra island. But he didn't see any shipping in the Malacca Strait.

"What would account for that?" he asked himself again in a whisper. Again, he received a blow to his shoulder. Chuck didn't know the language but felt fairly certain that he was being cussed out.

At the end of the encampment the leader of the group stood next to one of the small fires. He had a brutal face that was amplified by the flickering light of the fire. The man's black eyebrows nearly crossed his entire face. A scar on one cheek extended from his brow down to his chin, as if someone had tried to fillet him like a fish. The scar was white in contrast to his dark skin.

He wore a mishmash of a black tee shirt and camouflage shorts held together by a leather belt, which carried a long scabbard and blade.

The man pointed to a post in the back of the overhang. It was deep inside the rocks, almost like the beginning of a cave. The two prisoners were chained to the post and allowed to slide down and sit on the rocks.

"Water?" the leader asked the two. It was the first English since the crash.

"Yes, please." The engineer's voice was a plea more than an answer.

The leader turned to another, yelled something in their language and watched as one of the men entered another hut and came out with two large bottles of water.

"Thank God," the engineer mumbled.

Their hands were not loosened from the chains. The man unscrewed the tops and held them as he poured the warm liquid into their mouths. Chuck tried to gulp as fast as he could, hoping to consume every drop possible.

And then his heart stopped.

He glanced at the bottle being held by the guerilla. It had the label and markings of the red-and-blue logo of a "wau kucin" or moon kite. Chuck knew the logo well for two important reasons. He had purchased two of the kites when they first arrived in Pekanbaru and Sumatra for his two sons. Somewhere in the wreckage of the Gulfstream on the beach were the two gifts.

But it was the other place he had seen the wau kucin before that made him struggle with the shackles around his wrists. The logo was known around the world when it appeared on the tail of another aircraft.

Chapter 6

The night came late on the mountain. The sun extended its light well into the early summer evening, but it didn't help on top of Denali. The winds tore across the peak picking up snow but from above and from the snow pack, causing a brutal, blinding force of nature that moved like a blowtorch through anything alive.

"He won't make it. They won't make it." The rescue team leader looked out from the tent on the glacier.

"Bullshit!" Andy wasn't prepared to tolerate the comment.

"I understand."

"I didn't bring him in to get him killed." Andy wanted to make another run with his A-Star but visibility was gone, the winds would have pushed the helicopter over—and all that had to be overcome to even have a chance at finding him.

"Kahiltna Glacier, this is Polar Bear Six."

The two men glanced at each other. A helicopter could be heard beyond a hill mass to the southeast. Soon, a Chinook CH-47 appeared and circled the camp. It had sleds instead of wheels, as it was made for this country.

"Yes, base camp here."

"Can you pop a smoke and signal best landing spot," the radio crackled.

"Where's a smoke?" Andy shouted to the rescue team leader.

"In the tent. A case of them."

Andy ran into the tent, resurfaced, and scurried to the end of the glacier near where his A-Star was located. The glacier was solid there and they would know it by seeing his helicopter on the ground. He popped the red smoke and it quickly rose into the wind, giving the men from the 212th a guide as to where to land. The large Chinook settled to the ground, blowing more ice and snow as its blades churned the air. An airman came out of the rear of the aircraft and walked over to Andy.

"Hey, I'm your chief mountaineer."

"Thanks for coming." Andy had a smile a mile wide across his entire face.

"Nice night for a rescue." The man's words gave Andy what he wanted to hear. Neither the weather, nor the winds, nor the nightfall would slow them down.

It was on the patch on the man's jacket. It said it all. We never give up.

"I'm with TEMSCO. Flew him up in the A-Star."

"Yeah, we worked together last year. The rescue near the pass." The airman walked to the tent.

"Yeah, the man that didn't make it." Andy remembered their efforts well. It was a couple from Germany. The man had gotten lost in the blinding snowstorm, stepped the wrong way, and fell over a thousand feet.

"Who do we have here?"

"A climber broke a leg coming down from the summit. Our rescuer was dropped off at the football field."

"You got a man to the football field in the A-Star?" The airman asked the question with a tone of respect. The football field was well above Camp Four.

"It got worse. Hoped to get him in, find the climber and get them out, but it got crazy."

"Yeah, we got an update on the weather report. Not pretty."

"What's your thoughts?" Andy asked most of the questions as the rescue team leader stood in silence. As they spoke outside the tent, several other airmen joined the group. The 212th Rescue Para Jumpers, or PJs, and mountaineers knew Denali as well as anyone in Alaska. Too many rescues required both the A-Star and the heavier Chinook. This Air Force bird had been amped up for high-altitude missions and could hold itself in much stronger winds than the A-Star.

"We go out an hour before first light and try to get to Camp Four. From there we head uphill."

"Sounds like a plan." Andy liked the fact that there was no reservation in their efforts.

The Chinook's turbines broke through the darkness well before the sign of first light. The night had continued to howl at the glacier with winds, which meant that the wind speed would only have been tripled up the mountain.

"Do you want to go with us?" the airman looked at Andy.

"Hell yes." He hadn't bothered with sleep. It would have been a waste of time.

"Can you handle the altitude?"

Where they were going was well beyond where the air had much oxygen.

"I climb on off days as well." Andy wasn't going to miss this no matter what. He put Will in this situation and had promised to come back for him.

"Let's go."

The Chinook held a team of four mountaineering airman suited up for a climb like an assault on Everest. Andy had also carried a parka, and the full outfit for arctic conditions.

"You stay in the helicopter."

"Yep." He worked his way up to the cockpit and shook the hands of the two pilots. They had their shoulder patches from the 212th, which owned the bird.

"You need to strap in." The lead airman tapped Andy on the shoulder. "Going to be rough."

The helicopter lifted off the glacier and quickly rose into the air. It passed through clouds with no visibility and then broke out into open air. The sun's light was piercing the sky and gave brief glimpses of the mountain. Andy felt the vibration of the two turbines as he sat in the seat, held in place by a web belt. The air would lift him up in his seat and then throw him down like a parachute drop.

The aircraft weaved back and forth as the pilots seemed to run a channel like in a high speed boat. The air became brutally cold, their breath blowing a white fog with every spoken word. Andy felt the cold from the metal come through his gloves.

And then the helicopter seemed to stop. It hung in the air as a crewmember dropped the tail. The rescue mountaineers stood up, scrambled to the rear, and jumped out—no parachutes—and their gear followed. The pilot had maneuvered the bird in such a way that the back ramp had become a walking bridge just above a flat area.

"Where are we?" Andy shouted to the aircraft crew chief.

"Seventeen thousand." The crew chief's breath almost struck Andy in the face. "We'll climb and circle."

Andy knew that meant they would stay on station as long as they could without dropping below fuel minimums. The team was equipped to stay on the ground as long as it took. The helicopter rose up and was jostled again by the winds. It banked hard to the left and then seemed to climb and fly in a circle. Although Andy was a pilot and had weathered the worst of arctic weather, he felt ill.

"Not at the controls," he said to himself. Even if he had shouted it, no one in the aircraft could have heard him. It was the lack of being able to control his destiny that made it difficult. There was something about having the stick in one's hands that comforted a pilot.

The helicopter continued to circle for most of an hour. Suddenly, the crew chief turned to him and held out a big thumbs-up.

The 212th mountaineering team had worked their way up from the drop-off point to the first, best place for hope that there were survivors. The park service had a bright orange survival shelter at 17,200 feet. As the leader approached the shelter, he noticed a man standing outside.

The storm kept roaring as they approached.

"I heard your helicopter." Will pulled off his goggles for a brief moment and extended his hand.

"Wow. How did you do this?"

"We made it down last night. She's hurt, but is alive and in the shelter."

"You carried a climber with a broken leg off the football field and made it down here?" The airman didn't hide how impressed he was by this feat.

"Had to. She would never have made it otherwise." Will put his goggles back on. "Actually dragged would be a better word."

All of the men were medics with special training in arctic injures, and one went into the shelter and helped her. Frostbite had taken its toll on her hands and feet, but that happened well before Will had found her.

"You changed out everything." The medic kneeled over Robyn as he examined her from head to toe. The shelter had a small stove that brought the temperature up to something around freezing. With the winds and cold outside at well below zero, the shelter had provided some much-needed warmth. Will had taken off her gloves and boots and carefully put a dry set of extra gloves and socks on her. He then had wrapped her in a polar tech blanket. The cold helped some with the broken limb, but Will didn't have anything for pain.

"Check her pulmonary edema." Will had her on a small portable oxygen bottle. She was still a very sick woman.

"You gave her nifedipine?"

"Yes."

The medic had started a new bottle of oxygen through a facemask and given her some morphine.

"We need to get her out of here." The medic's voice was calm, but it sounded as if the patient was close to dying. He turned to the hatch on the shelter, leaned out and yelled into the wind.

The other mountaineers could barely hear the shout. A full-blown blizzard was attacking the mountain. One saw the medic and crossed over to him.

"We need to get her down stat. Not sure we can use a basket."

"OK, I will get the bird inbound for a touch on the open area over there." He pointed to what looked like no more than a white cloud, but he seemed to know what the helicopter could do. The airman stood up, signaled to the others, and headed to the landing zone.

Soon, Will saw the trace of red smoke and red flares light up the white they were immersed in.

"Can you help?"

"Sure."

"We need to bundle her up with everything we've got. The prop wash will be brutal." The airman climbed back into the shelter and started to wrap her up in the few survival blankets that were in the shelter. She was still in the survival suit and they used it as a sling to carry her.

"Wait here." The airman held her, with Will on the downwind side of the shelter as two other airmen joined them.

Another blast of air came from a different direction. Will sensed that this air was very different. It felt warm and smelled of burned kerosene.

"Our overflight says it's only going to get worse." The airman who had joined them was talking to the helicopter on a walkie-talkie on his chest. An HC-130 Hercules turboprop airplane had come on station above the rescue point. Another helper for the 212th, it provided a view well above the top of the mountain. The rescue team was trained for this and the other needs of the air force. The airmen had one of the most difficult jobs in the military. Their main mission was to find and rescue downed pilots in combat. More than one "PJ" or pararescue jumper had been awarded the Medal of Honor. When a pilot went down, the enemy swarmed like bees in a nest that had been beaten with a stick. And the PJs had to go in, find the missing pilot, and somehow get an aircraft in that could pull them both out of the firefight. When not in combat, the 212th braved just as much danger, but this time the source was Mother Nature. Alaska could be just as deadly when one was on the top of a twenty-thousand-foot mountain, known even in the middle of summer for having brutal, subzero weather and winds.

"Let's get out of here." The team leader moved to grab one side of the bundle of blankets and the screamer suit that their climber was in.

Will, the medic, and two of the airmen picked her up and made a run in the direction of the landing zone. As they approached it Will saw the other airman, who was marking the place for the pick-up. He was holding a bright red flare that was attempting to give the inbound helicopter some sense of wind and direction. As they reached the last airman, Will felt a presence above him and saw the faintest shadow cross over the snow.

The Chinook was directly above their heads, then moved into the wind just beyond where they were. Its back ramp was down and, for the briefest moment, the ramp touched the snow.

Will could see the crew chief inside the bird frantically signaling them to come on board. The medic led the way as they hopped onto the ramp with the other airmen following. Just as they got Robyn onto the bird there was a sudden shift of the winds, which caused the helicopter to suddenly rise. The only man remaining on the mountain was Will.

The crew chief waved his arms but the Chinook was quickly up in the air and well beyond any hope of setting down again.

Will signaled the chief as he stood near the ramp.

"He says go." The chief watched as they moved farther away and were consumed by the winds.

The crew intended to return, but the weather only deteriorated as they headed down. The climber needed more than field medical care. The pilot called the base camp and spoke to Andy. He told them what he knew Will would say. It was the only thing Will Parker would have said. There would be no more rescue efforts that day. The winds took over the mountain. The Chinook turned to the north, climbed up and moved as quickly as possible to Fort Wainwright and a waiting ambulance. It saved Robyn's life.

Chapter 7

Under the cover of the triple canopy of the Ula Masen forest in a knot in the mountainside not far to the south of Banda Aceh, a man came out of a hut to greet two much younger men sitting around a small campfire. The two had just arrived and their motorcycles were still warm from the journey. They didn't see the man. The two were sitting on a log, intent on a game that they were playing on their separate cell phones. They would bark at each other as one would score a win and the other would miss. Their entire attention was on the video games they were playing. They didn't see the man come from behind and didn't even know he was there until he kicked the first one, who was slightly older, in the low of his back and caused the cell phone to fly out of his hands. The other jumped and moved away from the incoming blow.

"What are you doing?" The man stood above them and the first one scrambled to grab his phone from the edge of the firepit. He was much younger than he looked. And with good reason.

"Chaniago, sorry," the first boy cried out.

Chaniago was shorter than the two boys, with skin darkened by age, a look almost of tanned hide. His face was pockmarked from a bout of chicken pox in prison. There was another noticeable feature—Chaniago's tooth was broken in his smile. He not only survived prison, he had survived Nusa Kambangan, the Ghost Island, on the island of Java, just to the south of Sumatra. Chaniago was a legend in the Jamaah Ansharut Daulah, or JAD. He was the only man known to have escaped from the maximum prison of the Ghost Island.

Nusa Kambangan held the worst of terrorists in Southeast Asia. It was also the execution island. The best ticket to being tied to a post on Ghost

Island and facing an execution squad of twelve men was to being connected to ISIS or selling drugs. Chaniago did both.

He served as an ISIS fighter in Syria after leaving Banda Aceh as a teenager. The schools of Banda Aceh were well known for raising jihadists at the youngest of ages. In Syria, Chaniago was with several fighters from Indonesia who had received the call to come and fight for Islam. Chaniago came from Sumatra, and others came from Java, the Philippines, across Indonesia, and Myanmar.

"You!" Chaniago pulled out his Czechoslovakian CZ-52 semiautomatic pistol and aimed it at the two. His anger caused them both to run behind nearby trees. He didn't fire. Chaniago was too seasoned a warrior to fire a round of the 7.62 bullets just to scare two young recruits. But Chaniago had killed men before and was known for that talent. It was said that in Syria he and his cell of men caught two American soldiers who had the misfortune of driving their truck down the wrong road in the desert. The two were mostly harmless, not seasoned warriors though serving in the US Army. He shot them both, killing one while the other watched. The man didn't have a bit of character in his soul.

Chaniago had made the mistake of coming back to Sumatra on a ship that landed in the Java port of North Jakarta City. His plan had been to land in Java and then work his way north, across a part of the island to Cilegon City and across the waters to Sumatra. Once on Sumatra, Chaniago would use a network of fellow terrorists to reach Banda Aceh on the other end of Sumatra. But upon landing in Jakarta, the authorities identified the terrorist, quickly tried him, and sent him to the Ghost Island for execution. But he had eluded death on more than one occasion in his life. Chaniago, who had the remarkable feature of black eyebrows that met above his nose in one continuous line, seemed doomed to death. He was sent to Batu prison to await transfer to the execution prison, but he used a blanket to cover the web of razor wire fence and headed into the swamp. The guards were not worried, as Nusa Kambangan island is just as much a prison as the prison itself. The island is known for its cobras, which were spread out in the surrounding jungle to punish any who might try to escape.

The jihadist had avoided death several times in his life. In Syria, on more than one occasion American airstrikes had hit close to him. And in an oddity of life, Chaniago was in Syria fighting for his jihad when the earthquake hit Sumatra and the tsunami that followed killed most of his family in Banda Aceh.

The escapes from death also hardened Chaniago. He held his own life as little value. He never married, had no children, and saw his jihad as the only reason for living. It would be in the next life that Chaniago received his reward.

"Come here!" he yelled at the two boys as he put his pistol back into its holster on a belt that wrapped around his waist. He yelled it again as the two stayed behind the tree. "Come now."

The taller of the two slowly approached.

"You have the news." Chaniago said the words calmly. He would have shot the two in a flash, except that they were warriors who were needed. The two both rode their motorcycles better than anyone else. He had sent them on missions as messengers for JAD on several occasions and knew that they could see a road block, move up in the country or on back streets in the city, and never get stopped.

"Yeah, Chaniago."

The boy was putting his cell phone in his back pocket.

"That will kill you." He pointed to the pocket where the boy had stashed the phone. It was another toy of the West that, if used the right way, would be a valuable weapon. If it was needed to set off a blast of explosives, the cell phone worked as a weapon. But with its memory, if the boy was caught, it could provide a wealth of information to them. The chip could tell all—locations, people, plans. VAT 69 was well known to Chaniago and it could be turned into a weapon very quickly against JAD.

"Yes sir." The boy agreed with the man, but the cell phone would remain. His ION cell contained a download of the game of *Mobile Legends: Bang Bang* and his character, or alternative ego, was Khaleed, the Desert Scimitar. The video game market in Sumatra, Indonesia, and all of Southeast Asia had grown as fast as quick-moving bamboo. Winners on the high end would compete in contests and make thousands of rupiah. And Khaleed seemed to be the perfect warrior, invincible in his slaying of those who stood in his way. The boy had his dreams, and being the national Indonesian champion of *Mobile Legends* was one of them.

"What news?"

The boy handed him a note. They had been trained in not using notes, but this information was too fleeting. And the messengers had been taught that they were never to read the notes and be prepared to devour them the moment there was a risk of their being stopped.

"Good." Chaniago unfolded the note.

The boy smiled at the comment. One rarely received an acknowledgment from Chaniago. The boy gladly would have carried a backpack of C-4 explosives into a police station if Chaniago had ordered him to. They were all orphans after the great flood, and their only recognition was being warriors for Jamaah Ansharut Daulah.

Chaniago read the note and tossed it into the embers of the fire pit. He picked up a stick and stirred the flame until the note was vaporized.

"I will go." He turned to the other boy, who now had joined his fellow messenger. The other one was barely old enough to sit on his motorcycle, but was just as nimble as the first. "You both are good warriors. Allah be with you both."

The two smiled and then sat back by the fire pit as Chaniago turned back to his hut. He came out and called another. They walked the trail that the motorcycles used to reach the knot in the shelter of the mountain. It carried them down to a village where a small white Daihatsu jeep was kept. The jeep followed a mountain road, full of ruts, north until it connected with a highway that continued on to the north.

"Those fools." Chaniago looked back at the two messengers who had resumed their seats around the fire pit and were back on their cell phones. "I have something special in mind for them." The boys would be convinced that this assignment would make their names known for all time to those that followed.

They were correct. If Chaniago's plan for the target on the west coast of Sumatra was a success, their names would be remembered for all time.

Chapter 8

"Any update?" The watch officer pulled up the chair next to the woman sitting at her computer with the television above sounding off on the story. CNN International Asia Pacific with its feed from Hong Kong was running through the stories of the hour. By the agreement with mainland China, the feed had to be carried through a Chinese satellite, which posed the risk of censorship or stories being blocked; however, the feed also kept the CIA office in Alaska up to date on intelligence in the Pacific that didn't affect China. It was a decent backup to the intel they received from their field officers in the area and, in particular, Southeast Asia.

"Just described as aircraft lost and no signs of survivors." She had followed the story of the downed Chevron jet from when it was first missing.

"Anyone in the field know better?"

"No, sir." The woman had worked as an officer on the Asia Pacific desk for several years now after graduating from Stanford with a degree in international relations. "Seems the private jet disappeared somewhere over the Malacca Strait or is buried in the side of a mountain somewhere in the jungles of Sumatra. The Malaysian authorities have sent out search and rescue for days with no success. Think they are about ready to call it quits."

"What about the information report?" He was referencing the Central Intelligence Agency's classified memo. "What does it say about the oil fields?"

He was speaking about one of the many information reports, some of which went back to the early 1950s.

"Just the usual stuff. Sumatra has been the gold mine of Indonesia." She wasn't suggesting gold was found on the island, but black gold was in abundance.

"Teluk Bayur has had a good year in exports."

The port of Teluk Bayur on the west coast of Sumatra had a history of changing from the export of one commodity to another over the decades. It stood near the city of Padang. Its first name was Emmahaven, as it was the only shelter for ships on the thousand-mile coast of west Sumatra. The unique name came from Emma, a member of the royal family of the Netherlands when Sumatra was under Dutch rule. Ships from all over the world came to Emmahaven to pick up rubber, coffee, and cloves. The Japanese leveled the port during the war and occupied Sumatra. And then oil was discovered.

"Any word from Langley?" The watch officer had given up cigarettes only a few weeks before and would play with his pen, constantly, like a man full of energy with no place to put it.

"Have you tried Peloton?" Her comment was well intended, but sounded like a crack at him. Especially since her boss was still fighting the urge for nicotine. She was just suggesting a way for him to burn off the excess energy.

"Yes." His answer was short. "Got a god damn gold badge. Does that make you happy?" He did end it with a smile. The gold badge meant he had ridden more than a hundred and fifty miles on the bike. It hadn't seemed to help with his anxiety.

"Very much so." She never took her eyes off her computer as they conducted the conversation. "And Langley does have something going on this. Not sure what yet."

"Really?" He pulled up his chair next to another computer and opened up an intelligence high-speed version of Google Earth. His focus was on Sumatra.

"Where did it leave from?"

"Pekanbaru city."

"The oil fields nearby?"

"And why were they there?" The watch officer continued to play with Google Earth.

"Not sure. They lose their lease next year." She had taken a special interest in the oil of Sumatra. It had the combination of every factor that should appeal to a CIA officer. The oil of Sumatra was a source of stability for much of Southeast Asia and Indonesia. The fields were at the heart of an effort by the government to terminate leases when they expired and give the fields over to the state-owned Pertamina oil company. Indonesia had decided to take the route of pulling back on foreign ownership of its oil, but at a cost. As Chevron and other Western companies lost access to the oil fields, Indonesia lost access to other markets. The world of oil was a finely balanced machine, where any change always brought a reaction that one could never predict. And the island of Sumatra was the bookend of the islands that formed the Malacca Strait. Malacca channeled virtually all of the shipping in that part of the world into a thirty-mile throat. It had all of the factors that kept CIA officers up at night. The fact that Sumatra was the breeding ground for many of the ISIS soldiers that fought in Syria only added fuel to the fire.

"What is Chevron doing about their airplane?"

"Sent out some teams, but they have come up empty-handed as well. Sounds like they are writing it off as a loss."

"Wow." He pulled his chair back from the computer station. "Sad for those families."

"Yes."

"And nothing on the satellites?"

"No."

"This has to be the most photographed part of the damn world." He was referencing the multiyear investigation into the loss of Malaysian Airlines Flight MH370. Sumatra, the Malacca Strait and the waters to the west and south of the island were covered for years, looking for the missing ship. Later, it was concluded that that airplane flew west until its fuel ran out then plummeted into the Indian Ocean. Only bits and pieces of the aircraft were found on the beaches of Madagascar near Africa years later.

"It was covered well." She still was looking at her computer while talking.

"What about Louis Maraldi?" He continued to twiddle his pencil.

"Who?"

"You work this desk and don't know that name?"

She turned away from her computer at that point.

"The stolen passport?"

"Good job. Yep."

"One of the Iranians onboard the MH370 was carrying a passport stolen in Thailand." She knew the story that Maraldi had been listed as missing. He was from Cesena, Italy, and had to call his parents to calm them down when it was first reported that he had been onboard the missing aircraft.

"Correct. No one ever cleared up what they were doing."

An airplane full of passengers disappears when flying over an island that is more than 97 percent Muslim and has sourced terrorists in Syria for years.

"Someone else was on MH370. Pull up the report on Freescale." He had served on the Alaska desk when the airplane went missing. "The semiconductor company out of Texas."

"What did they have to do with it?" This one she didn't recall.

"Freescale lost more than a dozen people on that airplane. Made the semiconductors for communications. Been bought out by NXP for nearly twelve billion and then NXP was bought out by Qualcomm for over forty billion." He had kept track of those who were involved in the missing airplane.

"Wow."

"Yeah, wow."

"Yes, sir."

"Going home to hit the Peloton!"

"Good for you." She smiled at the comment.

Just as he left her computer sounded with a message from Langley. It was a message that brought him back to the operations center.

Chapter 9

A ray of sunlight came through the thatch of the hut. It had been some time since the crash of the Gulfstream. Chuck and his engineer had been moved twice, from one encampment to another. Each move took place at night. They would be awoken with gun barrels shoved into their backs and yelling, words they didn't understand, pushed out onto trails below the canopy of the jungle. Chuck was cut up by the brush as he tried to follow the trail. It climbed up a mountain and then down into another knot.

When they crossed the top of the mountain the moonlight still illuminated their way. The moon had become a waning quarter where it was half full of light. Chuck felt a breeze coming up from the ocean and, in a quick glance, realized they were on a very large island or peninsula. To the south, the land curved inward and to the right. To the north, there was a low-lying mountain range as far as he could see, but he sensed that not far beyond that, the land ended. He look down at the beach below, but saw no sign of the crash or any debris from the airplane.

The guard struck him in the back and yelled. Chuck turned back to the trail as it descended into the darkness.

Now, the moon was in its new phase and the black jungle was so dark that he could not see his hand until he put it directly in front of his face. They had not eaten any food for several days and his engineer was getting weaker by the minute. Chuck felt a continuing fever with the sweats and aches of something he prayed was not malaria. They had all taken the medications both before and during the trip, so both he and the engineer had protection that would last some amount of time.

The sunlight seemed to wake up the sounds of the jungle. With the light, he surveyed the hut they were in. The dirt floor had a stale smell of urine and rot. The posts that held up the thatched roof were also being used as their jail. Each of the posts had a chain wrapped around it several times and then connected to his ankle. Chuck lifted himself up from the floor and sat with his back to the post.

This hut had four posts, with Chuck and his engineer locked on two posts. The guards had actually softened with time, as they had more loose links between the posts and the manacles than the first two nights. With the extra chain, Chuck could actually stand up if he tried, but just sitting up made his head spin.

The third post had no one secured to it, but did have a loop of the metal binders so it appeared that it was ready to be used. And the shackle looked like it had been used. There was a slight glisten to the metal as if it had been rubbed for some time.

Chuck didn't notice the fourth post until he saw something move. This post was in the shadows in the far back of the hut. His head was still aching with a headache that seemed to affect his vision. He rubbed his eyes and stared again at the back post. Slowly, he made out the shape of someone whose back was turned away from him and was leaning up against the post.

"Hey!" Chuck whispered. Often, a guard would be standing just outside the entrance to the hut. And without their even saying anything, Chuck knew that talking would result in a beating.

The figure didn't move. In fact, it didn't react at all.

Chuck thought for a moment that the man was dead. The smells of the hut surely didn't discount that belief. It could be a corpse left by guards too lazy to bother to unchain him or remove the body. He waited for some time, still seeing no movement.

"Bersilaj!" The guard came in swinging his automatic weapon.

Chuck stayed seated with his back to the post. The guard gave him another bottle of water and something that appeared to be fish cooked in a small clay bowl. He had one for Chuck's engineer, and as Chuck watched—as important as the food—the guard threw down the same to the figure in the back of the hut.

"So he is alive," Hedges whispered to himself. It clearly was not someone who had come from the Gulfstream. This prisoner was another soul shackled to the post. Chuck watched for movement, but there was none.

"God, I hope I didn't hear Batak." The engineer spoke up from the other post. He seemed to have regained some energy after eating the fish and drinking the water.

"What?"

"Batak." He whispered the word. "It's the language of some of the tribes of Sumatra. When Polo came through here, the Batak were cannibals. They ate the old and the ill."

"These guys aren't that." Chuck figured that the Batak's history of cannibalism ended some time ago.

"Yeah, supposedly they stopped that." The engineer pulled himself up on the post. "But there are some tribes in this part of the world that haven't caught up yet."

"That's the least of our worries." Chuck was correct that a remote tribe of cannibals didn't plan and take down a Gulfstream. "We need to get out of here."

He had trained for situations like this, trained the men and women who traveled to remote places with Chevron to deal with both capture and escape. More importantly, the training had been predicated on the idea that one would be held captive for ransom and Chevron would pay it. Chuck didn't think this was what was going on. The man in the shadows had been here for a very long time. This didn't feel like a master plan to hold someone up for ransom. The Gulfstream had been run into the ground with no guarantee that anyone would survive the crash. So it was bad odds that they would crash an airplane and then ask for money for its passengers.

"No, this has something more to it." Chuck finished the fish, emptied the water bottle and leaned back against the post. It began to rain, another squall line of showers passing through the jungle. He would try to sleep; another move would likely take place that night.

They are smart. His mind worked its way through what was going on. The constant moves were their best strategy. It would be nearly impossible for any rescuers to find them if there was a move every night. So, Chuck planned for another move once the sun went down. He would sleep on the dirt floor and try to get ahead of his captors with the hope that he would learn how they thought, what they were saying, and more importantly, where an escape could be made.

Without an escape, this ain't going to end well, he thought as his exhaustion pulled him into a deep sleep.

Chapter 10

The Kahiltna Glacier base camp was dotted with scores of the brightly colored tents of the many who hoped to climb the mountain. Only the top of the tents were visible, as the climbers had built ice walls to shelter themselves from the winds that came down the glacier. Two Otter aircraft were tied down on a marked snow runway, but would lift up and fall back down in the gusting winds. Andy's A-Star's plexiglass bubble was iced over like a thin layer of cake icing. It, too, had the blades tied up so as to be able to absorb the gusts of wind.

The food tent was one of the larger tents, which a guide service had erected, and many of the climbers were crammed in there, waiting for the weather to change. They had stacked blocks of snow in the center of the tent to serve as a makeshift table. Bottles of tabasco and soy sauces were on the ice table. The conversation continued on between the guides who had climbed the mountain dozens of times and their amateur guests. Denali was a mountain that a less experienced climber could summit with a guide. The talk was, however, the climber just brought down with the broken leg.

"She going to make it?" The climber was standing next to the table and eating some rice out of a plastic bowl. He stopped, poured some hot sauce in his rice, then started to eat it again.

"Word is yes, but lost three fingers." The ones speaking had climbed Denali before, but were not guides. This one was a returnee who had brought his son with him for the life experience.

The guides remained silent. It was not good business to discuss death or brutal injury from the mountain.

"What do you think, airman?" The man with his rice asked the question of a soldier sitting in the back next to a radio. He had his earphones around his neck with one up close to his ear to monitor the traffic. He was also a mountaineer with the 212th.

"Got to be careful on this mountain. It don't care about it being spring or summer. Up top it is one of the coldest mountains there is." The airman had pulled too many rookies off Denali to not have respect for it.

Andy listened and periodically would get up and look out the opening of the tent like a father waiting on the birth of his first child.

"What about your man?" the returnee asked Andy. "Hear he was the only thing that kept her alive."

"Yeah." Andy didn't want to engage in the conversation. As he stood there, he realized that he knew very little about the man he had recruited for the rescue. They had worked on one other job on the mountain and, once finished, Will Parker jumped out of the helicopter at his cabin and just said his goodbyes. That rescue involved a mountain as well. It was rumored that he taught mountaineering and arctic survival in the Marines. He saved a life the last time Andy had called on him for help.

"I want him here if we get into trouble." The son of the returnee spoke up.

"You don't need him. You got a good guide. Won't be a need for rescue." Andy passed on the compliment.

The guide smiled at him.

Andy opened the flap again and looked out at his A-Star.

"Need to go check my bird."

The others turned their backs to the winds as a chill ran through the food tent as he walked out.

The helicopter was well secured, but it wouldn't be good for it to go through several more nights in the bitter cold. The ceiling was still low, the snow was blowing a gale, and even if he tried, he wasn't sure that he could get above the weather.

Andy got to his A-Star and started to scrape the snow off the plexiglass. It would probably freeze over again before he could move it, but the exercise helped pass the time.

"Hey, sir!"

Andy turned to see the airman standing outside the food tent. He was shouting to him and into the winds.

"What's up?"

"Your man's coming in now."

The helicopter pilot walked over to the airman. Andy was wearing a hooded Canada Goose arctic parka and had to pull down the hood to hear what was being said.

"What do you mean?" The weather hadn't let up since the first rescue.

"Inbound now."

As he said the words, a gray Sikorsky HH-60 Pave Hawk helicopter passed overhead, turned into the wind and started to land near the A-Star. The helicopter had the H designation in its name for search and rescue and medevac. A layperson looking at it would have said "Blackhawk." This aircraft was much more. On its nose there were several extenders and bubbles that helped support its mission of going into places well behind the enemy lines and surviving. This aircraft had done much more than rescue climbers. The 212th's mission was to search and rescue, which meant the downed pilot in the Hindu Kush of Afghanistan or the victims of a tsunami in the Pacific. With its forward-looking infrared system, it had eyes in the dark. Its color radar and the anti-ice system on its engine and blades helped whack its way through the winds of Denali. But it did have one limitation that hadn't helped before. This Pave Hawk couldn't fly above fourteen thousand feet.

"How did you guys do it?"

"Had help from your man. The HC-130 had been keeping an eye out for him through the night. He moved down the mountain to Camp Three."

"Got it." Andy knew Camp Three was well below the ceiling of the Pave Hawk. At eleven thousand feet, Camp Three made the rescue possible. With the infrared system and its powerful twin turbine engines, the helicopter could see in the blizzard and hold its altitude as the PJs dropped a basket for retrieval of the climber.

But how did Will Parker descend to Camp Three in that storm?

The Pave Hawk's twin turbines blew out a hot gas that kicked up its own blizzard. Its blades continued to spin as a man stepped out on the sleds and walked toward Andy.

"You OK?" Andy studied Will. He looked like a man who had just topped Everest. Small icicles had formed on the fox fur of his arctic parka.

"Yeah. Your other equipment is still up there at Camp Three. The snow conditions made visibility tough so they took me out with a basket."

"No problem." Andy was astonished at the matter-of-fact nature of the conversation. It was as if a man was checking out of a trailer park after spending a night in his camper. "You are OK?" He asked it again.

"Yep. The guys have offered me a ride to my cabin. Will you be able to fly the A-Star?"

"Going to wait until this clears out and I can get her thawed out." Andy didn't plan on risking both the weather and an airship that had been locked down in the cold for so long. "Boy, when they say no man left behind, they meant it."

"Yeah, we were in good hands. How's Robyn doing?"

Andy hesitated, embarrassed that he had forgotten the climber's name.

"Frostbite got a couple of fingers. She was taken to Wainwright. You saved her life."

"She's tough." Will turned back to the Pave Hawk. "I'm out of here."

"Damn." Andy had never served in the military, but had tackled many a mission perhaps as dangerous as executed by those who have served. He didn't know what to do, but without thinking, gave a hand salute to the man who sat on the open door of the helicopter as it lifted off and turned back to the south.

Will returned the salute. He pulled the door shut on the military aircraft as it rose up toward the pass and back to his cabin. It wouldn't be the last time he rode in a military aircraft. In fact, the next ride was going to be much sooner than expected. And it would be at the request of someone he hadn't seen in some time.

Chapter 11

The sensitive compartmented information facility, or SCIF, was on a below-ground level at Langley. It met all of the requirements with walls, floors, and ceiling constructed of twelve inches of reinforced concrete. The specifics of this facility and the SCIF in Anchorage were detailed to the point that the steel rods reinforcing the concrete were spaced both horizontally and vertically at six inches with a vault door Group 1 combination lock and an access control lock. Only GSA-approved filing cabinets surrounded the interior of the small room and encircled a conference table where each seat had its own computer station. On the wall at the end of the conference table a large flat-screen television showed the faces of the participants on both ends. This vault had been assigned to the developing situation in Sumatra.

The time difference meant the officer assigned to the mission and stationed in Alaska had to be online with the satellite at 4:00 a.m.

"I need more coffee," she said to herself.

"What?" The IT technician on the Langley side reacted to the comment. "We have Starbucks upstairs." His morning humor didn't draw much of a reaction.

"Very funny." Lisa Kim was very happy without Starbucks at four in the morning in Anchorage if it meant staying out of Virginia. When she left Stanford, the CIA headquarters was not where she wanted to be. And with the Alaska post she covered the Pacific, which was her minor at Stanford when she graduated with a degree in international relations. She did more than graduate from IR, as they called it. She was in the honors program, and her thesis on Malaysia's economy, which she presented at the International Relations Honors conference, prompted a professor to approach her about a job. Lisa was one of only four who presented at the conference. And a job that entailed the Pacific beat the other opportunities at the time.

"Am I correct on the time?" She had a single camera on her but the flat-screen showed the room at Langley, and the only one there was the technician.

"Yep, big meeting upstairs that must have carried over. Sure he will be here shortly."

Just as he finished the words, there was movement in the back of the room. A man with gray hair and black-rimmed glasses pulled up a chair at the end of the table. He had a computer at that station, and from the perspective of the Dell computer and even sitting in his chair, she could tell that he had to be well above six feet tall. She had never met the man who controlled the Pacific desk but had heard rumors.

"Ms. Kim, good morning."

"Yes, sir. Good morning."

"You are up to speed on Malaysia."

"I believe so." She was more than up to speed. Between her junior and senior year, Lisa had traveled throughout much of Southeast Asia. She started in Manila and had leapfrogged to several other countries, ending up in Kuala Lumpur.

"Sumatra?"

"Sir?"

"I see that you didn't make it across the Malacca Strait." He knew more about her than even she remembered.

"Yes, sir. At the time, State didn't suggest Americans travel to Sumatra."

"But you got a feel for the country?"

"I think so."

"We have assets buried deep in Sumatra." He was telling her news that she didn't know nor care to know. She had learned quickly in the CIA that one needed to be very careful about what one learned, knew, or was exposed to.

"Yes, sir."

"We need to shake things up and see what the fallout is."

"OK?"

"There is someone who we worked with some time ago who has the skills to do just that." He pushed his glasses up on his nose. "And he is not too far from where you are right now."

"Sir?"

"Served in the Marines, a polyglot."

"A polyglot?" She knew the term well: as a child growing up in Los Angeles her teachers had labeled her as one. She had mastered the languages of Mandarin, Cantonese, and Hakka by the age of ten.

"You have talent, but he is a Mezzofanti."

"Sir?"

"Cardinal Mezzofanti? Never heard of him?"

"No sir." She squirmed in her chair. She had learned quickly that the CIA was a very dangerous place for someone to say they knew something that they didn't. Saying no to her boss was the reasonable and right thing to do.

"He spoke more than thirty languages fluently. An Italian who lived in the eighteen hundreds."

"Yes, sir."

"His talent for this mission is that he is not only a quick study in a language and accents, but can hear it and comprehend it instantly."

"What do I need to do?"

"We think the Chevron jet is the perfect cover story for a mission in Sumatra. Let him find out what he can about the Chevron, and more importantly, what we need to know." The officer pulled up the keyboard to his computer. "I am sending you the complete file on William Parker. You need to recruit him for this mission. Recruiting him won't be easy. If he accepts, he will come with the designated Coyote team. They're people he trusts."

"And where will I find him?"

"He's about a hundred miles by Otter from where you are right now."

Chapter 12

The small white Daihatsu jeep crossed over the bridge on the outskirts of the Sumatra village of Lho Nga. It was the farthest northern town of any size on the west side of the island and just to the west of Banda Aceh. It was also the home of a fleet of small fishing boats and trawlers. Some of the boats stood out as unusual, as they had what appeared to be a rigging of Christmas lights. These boats were hunting squid and would illuminate the waters with an array of lights as they pulled the game in.

Lho Nga had a river that traveled to the sea, and in the interior of the village and on the river, a torn, beaten, and damaged dock held the mooring of one of the squid boats. The jeep pulled down the dirt road and stopped at a shed just short of the dock. It was well before dawn, but the boat was lit up for running.

"Wait here." Chaniago told the driver. He walked over to two men who were standing at the shore end of the dock.

"Peace to you, brothers." Chaniago put his hand on his chest.

The two returned the greeting. One was the captain of the boat.

"We are ready to leave when you are." The captain had worn, leathery hands and a well-wrinkled face from his many decades on the waters off Sumatra.

"Let me speak to my brother here and then we will depart." Chaniago placed his hand on the shoulder of the other one, giving the signal that they needed to speak in private. The captain took the signal as a sign to leave and returned to his trawler.

"The other mission. We are ready for it. I have two that should do well for our target." Chaniago spoke in the headlights of the Daihatsu jeep.

"Yes, brother."

"We have the explosives?"

"Better than that. We have a boat that has several tons of the fertilizer. It was in a container stolen from Chennai." He was speaking of ammonium nitrate that had been black-marketed from the Indian port. The chemical could be used for fertilizer but was also known as the bomb material that leveled the port of Beirut. The salt made from ammonium and nitric acid served as a valuable fertilizer that increased the nitrogen in soil, but if ignited, it turned into vapor with a devastating release of energy. The Indian port on the Bay of Bengal had a backlog of containers that blocked the streets. More than seventy-five thousand containers were lined up on the sides of the roads leading to the harbor. One container went missing. It was driven to the north where its cargo was unloaded onto a small diesel fishing boat, which then crossed the Bay of Bengal.

"This is explosive grade and we have some C-4 to ignite it." Chaniago's cohort had been with him in Syria.

Chaniago looked out at the trawler while they spoke. A crewmember was sitting on the bow playing with his cell phone. He felt his anger rise.

"The two. You know who I mean?"

"Yes."

"Can you have a captain get it down the coast?"

"He is a believer and will do what we need."

"Where is it now?"

"The boat is upriver, hidden in the jungle."

"Good. Have the two prepare for their jihad. I will be back in two days." Chaniago's plan had been several years in the making. Sumatra would do what others had failed to do. It would become the true caliphate. The tsunami had delayed his efforts, but what was taking place was a rise of actions that would call the people together.

"My wife prepared something for you." The man held out a paper bag. It was stained with grease.

"Is this my favorite?"

"Yes."

Chaniago opened the bag and looked inside. It held several pieces of pempek, a fish cake fried with tapioca. The bag held some sliced cucumbers as well. It was the perfect meal for a day at sea on the trawler.

"Please thank her."

"She speaks well of you often. You are the leader we have been waiting for. You can stop the infidels."

"You are doing well, my brother. Watch out for the devils." One such devil that they both worried about was VAT 69. It kept them on edge.

"May we have blessings from our true one." The man bent his head. Although he was older, he was paying respect to his leader.

Chaniago jumped onboard the boat as it pulled out from the dock. Once it traveled down the river, past the sleeping village of Lho Nga, it reached the open sea and turned to the north. It was one of many small vessels that fished the waters off the coast of Sumatra. This one, however, did little fishing.

Chapter 13

The Pave Hawk landed on the grass between Will Parker's cabin and his runway. Will threw his mountain gear on the grass and climbed down from the helicopter. A stranger's jeep was parked in front of the cabin.

"Hello?" Will didn't think he needed to reach for the HK semiautomatic just inside the door. The room was dark, but there was a glow in the fireplace. He felt a presence. Will cautiously moved to a light switch.

"Don't need it." A voice he immediately recognized came from the couch. He was speaking about the light.

"You never sleep." Will hadn't seen Gunnery Sergeant Kevin Moncrief in several months. He hadn't known the Gunny to ever lie down in the years of combat or missions.

"Just didn't have anything else to do. No television." Kevin sat up with a sarcastic look on his face. The door had remained open and the light from outside illuminated his face. "At your farm we have television."

Will smirked at the complaint.

"And why are you here? Shouldn't you be painting a house in Atlanta?" Will put in his dig to his teammate.

"Got bored with the houses."

Will knew he wasn't kidding. A man who had been shot at more than the average combat-experienced Marine easily could get bored putting up with a housewife who wanted to change the shade of the paint in the breakfast room. The contractors in Atlanta warned their clients of two things. First, he was short-tempered, cantankerous, and could give you a look that would cause you to climb back in your Volvo and leave. But second, he was the best because he stayed on the job until he got it right. He was known for sticking with the project no matter what.

"So you came to Alaska."

"Tried the farm but no one was there."

"You were supposed to keep an eye on it." Will's farm was always open to the Gunny, his teammate Enrico, and "the Doc" as he had become used to calling Kaili Stidham. The other two rarely visited the place, but the Gunny used it often and kept the place in good shape.

"Yeah, got the grass cut in all the fields." The Gunny stood up, seemed a little unstable, put his hand on the edge of a chair, then straightened up. "You owe me."

"That I do." Will headed toward the kitchen. "Drink?"

"No, sir. You can't either."

"What's up?"

"Need you to take a ride." Moncrief's voice was sober. "I need you to meet someone."

"Must be important. Where we are, the closest place is eighty miles."

"That's why we need to take one of your airplanes." The Gunny smiled. "You have your own fleet."

"Where to? It might affect which ride." Will's little airfield had a hangar with his HondaJet, an Otter, and the Maule. Each had its own range.

"Anchorage."

The DHC-3 Otter followed the river downstream until it hit the lowlands, then Will banked it toward Anchorage. The Ted Stevens Anchorage International Airport's FBO, or fixed base operator, knew Will's Otter and was always happy to see the man who paid for his fuel with a phone call to a source that immediately wired the funds. He wasn't known for carrying plastic, and if he had a cell phone, no one saw him with it. The state required he carry a satellite phone for emergencies, but it was rarely used.

"Fuel?" The ramp worker had a microphone on his shoulder.

"Top her off." Will signaled with his thumb as well. The continuous rumble of the jumbo jets flying into the airport filled the air with noise and the smell of burned kerosene. "We need a car too."

"Crew car will be waiting for you." The ramp hand said something into his radio, which was likely confirmation that they had a car for the use of the pilots who were their customers.

"I take it we aren't going far?" Will yelled the words to the Gunny over racket.

"Not far at all." The Gunny seemed to enjoy keeping him in suspense.

The short drive left them on a side street in front of a caramel-colored Craftsman-style home, well landscaped, with pots of flowers on the porch. It was far from what Will had expected. The Gunny pulled up and parked the car.

"OK?" Will was starting to get a little irked by the mystery.

The two walked up to the door, past a small sign that said 11th Avenue Bed and Breakfast, rang the doorbell, and got no response. Moncrief knocked several times and still there was no sound.

"Let me try out back." Moncrief went to the side yard where a small path led to the rear.

"Hello?" a woman's voice called out from the back. As they circled around, she stood up from a chair on a wide expanse of a wooden deck. "Gunny, thank you."

She was petite, no taller than her frail structure could handle, with eyes that immediately captured Will's attention. The woman could attract attention in the way Audrey Hepburn did in the old films. In fact, the actor's face was the one that came to Will's mind as he stood there. It was the hidden strength of Hepburn, who served in the underground transporting and hiding messages from the Nazis as a child. But she also looked very tired. Her eyes were red, as if tragedy had grabbed hold of her and had not let go.

"Colonel, this is Margaret Hedges." Moncrief acted as if Will would immediately recognize the name. He didn't realize that Will had been in the backcountry and on a mountain for several days. "Her husband is missing in Sumatra. Marine Lieutenant Colonel Charles Hedges."

Chapter 14

The day turned into night quickly under the thick canopy of the jungle. Sounds awoke as the light faded. Chuck Hedges rubbed the chain around his ankle. His boots survived the airplane crash but the manacles were just above the top of his left one.

Meals, when they saw one, were either a small handful of rice or a fried fish of some sort. The fish came in a paper wrapper and the wrapper was soaked in grease. He had tucked the paper in the side pocket of his 5.11 cargo pants. The guards never searched their captives.

Chuck was losing weight and his fatigue was getting greater by the day.

"Got to do something." He spoke to the engineer, who had become increasingly silent. Only one guard was now posted to the hut, as if his captors had grown tired of the prisoners. Chuck took out the pieces of paper and removed his boot. He pulled down the sock and rubbed his skin with the greasy paper. The chain had a small amount of play and with the grease it started to slip over his ankle.

Like a hamster. Chuck thought of his youngest son's pet kept in its plastic cage. Inside the container there was a little cave that the child had made out of a small jewelry box his mother had given him. The boy had cut a circular hole in the side of the box and stuffed the inside with cotton. The hole seemed far too small for the animal, but he would put his head through it and with the head the body would follow. Once inside, he would stick his head out of the hole, and when the boy put out some food, the gopher's body would follow. Chuck thought of the gopher as he slowly, painfully slid the shackle over his foot. He quickly put his sock and boot back on and crawled to the back of the hut.

"How you doing?"

The engineer stared straight ahead in the dark until Chuck put his hands on the man's head. He looked up and into Chuck's eyes. They showed fear.

"Hey, Chuck." He whispered, not because he was trying to keep his voice silent, but because that was all the energy he seemed to have. His reservoir was rapidly depleting.

"I'm going to check things out. You'll be OK."

The man smiled, his face now caked with dirt. Water was not to be used for bathing. They were surrounded by an ocean of crystal clear, blue water, but none for the prisoners.

Chuck glanced over at the stranger, who stayed as fixed as a statue, bent over with his back up against the post. He crawled to the back of the hut. This hut was built on stilts in the jabu style, made of bamboo with a high peaked roof. The structure was above the run of the rains and allowed air to circulate. Slowly, he pulled the bamboo apart, and again like the hamster, wiggled his body through the opening. Extending his arms down, he slid forward until his hands struck the ground; then he pulled himself through.

Once on the ground, he stayed on his knees, taking in the surroundings. He saw the feet of the guard who was lying on the plank that led up to the hut.

Chuck stood still, waiting to see any movement or other signs of life. It became clear that the guard was doing what others had been shot for in combat—he was asleep.

The Marine moved deliberately and slid back into the jungle. The hut was at the edge of a group of several huts and next to a hill that rose quickly above the knoll. The smell of several dying campfires filled the air. Chuck climbed the hill, trying not to slide down.

God this feels good. The taste of freedom made him drunk. Chuck wanted to run as far and fast as he could. It took all his discipline as a combat veteran to hold to his plan. This was a reconnaissance mission. Once on top of the hill, he followed a trail up another rise to a point of rocks that broke through the foliage. He stood on the peak of rocks and scanned the surroundings.

"Oh, jeez." He let out his breath seeing that they were on an island surrounded by water. There was land in sight, but it was also an island. And it was dark. There was no sign of life on the other island and it looked like a long swim. His island seemed much smaller. He could see where the beach to the north ended. Chuck sat down on the rock and began to cry. It was fatigue and hunger that drove the tears, not fear. It was the memory of the two Marines in the Humvee that ran over an IED on his combat tour. They were his Marines. It was the memory of his wife and two sons who had probably already attended his funeral. Margie had been hardened by the several tours in both Iraq and Afghanistan, but this was different.

"It'll be best if they think I am gone," he mumbled, thinking that the boys shouldn't expect him to show up any minute. It would be cruel and painful, but better than they believe he was alive and endlessly hope.

Chuck slid down on the cool rock, lying on his back as he looked up into the black sky. Far above, the dim, blinking lights of a commercial airplane crossed from his far right to the left. He lay there thinking of the passengers, perhaps some in first class, drinking their champagne and eating the small steak and scallops before they watched the movie and went to sleep. It was so very far away.

There was a noise on the other side of the outcrop. Chuck crawled to the edge, making sure not to appear against the skyline. Well below on the far end of a valley he could see the lights of a boat that was stationary, as if it had been tied up to a pier. He studied it for some time.

Got to get back. This was the hardest decision of his life. He had to crawl back over the rocks, move slowly down the hill and find his way in total darkness to the small opening on the side of the hut.

In the hut, he slid over to the engineer.

"There may be a way," he whispered to the man.

"Not likely." The voice was of the other man who had remained silent until now.

"What?" Chuck crawled over to him. "What do you mean?"

"You're on an island miles away from any sea-lane. Miles away from other land."

"How do you know this?"

The man pointed to his legs. One foot was chained, like theirs, to the post. The other was a stump where a foot once was.

"God damn." Chuck rolled back on his haunches.

"They don't like escape attempts." The man's face was near black with months, years of living in dirt. He had a scraggly beard and missing teeth. His face seemed a thin skin covering of the structure of his skull.

"When did this happen?"

"About a year ago. I guess. Lost sense of time."

"What's your name?"

"I think it is Phil. Would you believe I can't remember?"

"No, I believe it." Chuck had seen a Marine who had survived a near miss of an IED. They used to call it shell-shocked. The man's history well accounted for his lapse of memory.

Chuck heard movement outside. The dull light of dawn seemed to be changing the darkness into shadows and the shadows into figures.

He crawled back to his post and pulled off his boot and sock. The chain was still tight, and he had to inch it on over the ankle.

There was movement just outside the hut. Two men were talking, and despite not knowing a word of what was being said, it was clear that the guard was being chastised for being asleep. Chuck hurriedly pulled on his sock, now stiff after days of being worn, and pulled on his boot. As he leaned back against the post, a new guard came in and surveyed the men. He went to each, tugged on the links of metal, then left.

"Water?" Chuck mumbled the word.

The guard only cursed at him. Again, the language barrier didn't stop Chuck from knowing what was being said. The man left, and as he did, Chuck leaned back to the post.

"I'll talk to him later."

That short period of freedom let his eyelids become weighted and soon he fell asleep.

Chapter 15

"I need your help." Margaret Hedges sat on the edge of the chair on the back porch of the bed and breakfast.

"I'm sorry." Will pulled up another deck chair and took a seat. Moncrief sat in another chair between the two like a referee at a boxing match. Will gave him a look that summed up the fact that he wasn't pleased with the surprise.

"My husband is alive. I know he is."

"OK. Tell me what you think is going on."

"His name is Chuck Hedges. He served in the Marines, was the CO of two units in Afghanistan and Iraq. He retired and went to work for Chevron. His airplane went down in Sumatra. No one knows anything."

"Mrs. Hedges, you said Chevron?"

"I'm Margie."

"Margie. There's a million questions." Will wanted to work the problem. "What's Chevron doing about this? What's Indonesia and the State Department doing about this?"

"It's like other airplanes that have gone down in that part of the world. They just disappear." Gunny dropped in his comment.

"It was a private airplane. Indonesia searched for several days, but has abandoned the search. The US helped as well, but this isn't a commercial airplane, Colonel." Margie added the rank without thinking. She knew his past and had the ingrained habit of calling those of senior rank to her husband by their rank.

"It's Will."

Margie opened an oversize purse that seemed weighted down with the proof she needed to persuade him. Her fingers were absent of rings, except the ring finger on her left hand had a pink silicon wedding band. Her frame was that of a runner and the ring confirmed the suspicion that in other times, when her husband wasn't missing, she might be seen passing Will in a marathon. Margie's hair was pulled back in a single ponytail. The brunette color now was mixed with several gray strands.

"These are the news reports. This is what the government is telling me. The airplane was a Gulfstream and they had four Chevron passengers onboard." She leaned over and handed him two well-organized, labeled, clear folders. Margie had to be an accountant or a teacher.

Will took the folders and thumbed through them.

"You must be an accountant." He meant it as a compliment for the well-organized documents.

"No, I'm a teacher." She said it flatly, not as a negative response to the comment, but as someone who hadn't had much sleep in some time.

"What do you teach?"

"Science. Tenth grade."

Will smiled at the comment.

One folder caught his attention. It was a detailed description in pilot's terms. The aircraft was carrying a light load, it had fuel, and the weather was fairly clear. The pilots had the hours of experienced flyers and G650s don't just crash.

"Any word on the pilots?" Will wanted to know more.

"Reports are that they knew what they were doing." Moncrief inserted his comment.

"If they were actually piloting the plane."

"What?" Margie asked the question.

"If I were going to take over an aircraft like this, I would take out the pilots. I would bet they were somewhere in the back of the wreckage." Will's scenario made sense—if it was a hijacking.

"Will, I have two sons. They don't understand." Margie couldn't hold back her emotions. "I'm sorry."

"Not much sleep?" Will tried to distract her thoughts.

"No."

"Here are my two boys. They both want to be Marines."

Will looked at the two. Their dad had made sure they had the close haircut of Marines. He thought of another boy who was a young man when he learned that his parents had been lost in an airplane crash. Those two were victims of terror on a Pan Am flight. It wasn't proven yet that this loss wasn't due to some broken valve, or stopped-up pitot tube, or some very explainable aviation tragedy.

"I'm not sure I can do much. Not sure I can do anything." Will saw her sink back into her chair as he spoke the words. "Sumatra is on the other side of the world. And I don't know what I could add."

"I understand." Margie took back the photos of her boys. She paused for a moment. "Would you keep those files and let me know if you see anything? Anything at all?"

"Yes."

The Otter took the two back north to his cabin. Moncrief was quiet in flight, and soon was slumped over, sound asleep. He mumbled, which reminded Will of another time when their ANGLICO team was well behind enemy lines. Then, Will had had to hold his hand over the Gunny's mouth until he came awake. They were between two boulders and the enemy was just above them. The sounds of the Gunny speaking would have resulted in a firefight that they would have lost.

The wheels of the Otter brought the Gunny back to life as they squealed on landing. Will taxied up to the hangar and shut down the airplane.

"I've got a steak or two in there." Will pointed to the cabin.

"Good, I could eat a horse." The Gunny stretched his arms. "Maybe some bourbon?"

Will smiled at him. The man had just dragged him to a meeting with the widow of a fallen Marine for a hopeless mission. There wasn't much, if anything, that he could do about it.

They climbed down from the aircraft.

"We could call our new friends to see if they have any ideas?" Gunny posed the question.

Chapter 16

A black Tahoe with an oversize Tuff-Bar grille guard and large Goodyear DuraTrac tires pulled up in front of Will's cabin. Will and the Gunny were finishing up cleaning their catch of rainbow trout. The fish were far larger than any in Georgia and only would fit in an oversize frying pan. They had a full stringer of their fish on the cleaning table when the noise of the tires on the gravel caused Will to pause. He laid his semiautomatic Heckler & Koch on the table. His being cautious was built into his DNA.

"Get visitors here?" The Gunny asked the question that didn't need to be answered.

"No." Will watched the vehicle pull up, stop, and the driver's door swing open. He scanned the car and the woods around the cabin and looked for any sign of movement besides the driver. Will looked for the closest cover as did Moncrief, who slid back to the side of the table and near the trunk of a tree. The men had spent too much time in combat and danger to not go on the alert.

"Hello!" The shout came from a slender woman who waved her hands. Both men noted that she waved with both hands, which was either an innocent effort or a wise ploy to show that both were empty.

"Yes?" Will shouted back.

"I'm looking for you." She headed toward the table on the side of the cabin.

"And?"

"You must be Gunnery Sergeant Kevin Moncrief."

"You are?" Moncrief replied.

"I'm Jane Smith. I'm from Langley." She was Lisa Kim, but the officers followed directions well when out in the field.

"Nice original name." Will threw the jab.

"Anyone else around?" Kim surveyed the area as well.

"No." Will hadn't abandoned the semiautomatic. He kept his hand within easy reach of the pistol.

"We have a mission for you."

Will slid his hand away from the weapon.

"Let's go to the porch." He started to head up the path to the cabin.

"Let me get my laptop." She diverted from the path and headed to the Tahoe. She brought a brown backpack to the porch.

The conversation would soon be considered serendipitous.

"An American jet disappeared after takeoff from Pekanbaru in the central part of Sumatra. It was a private aircraft owned by the Chevron corporation." Lisa Kim's laptop showed security pictures from the airport as the airplane rolled back from the ramp. Neither Will nor the Gunny made any mention of the visit they had made a few days before.

"There were four on board, one of which was retired Marine Charles Hedges."

"He was head of security for the team in Sumatra." Will preempted the conversation.

"Correct." Kim reacted with some surprise. "You know Hedges?"

"His wife," said Will.

She moved on without asking further questions.

"No sign of the aircraft. The satellites were not watching this area when this all happened. My guess is that if this is more than the crash of a flawed airplane, the fact that they moved when the sky was empty might be another clue to this being something else." Kim voiced the suspicion, which made sense. Terrorists had gotten smart over the years. Through the internet, one could track where certain satellites were in orbit and when they might pass over a territory. A well-planned attack would proceed when an area was in the dark.

"Or it could be chance," Moncrief added.

"Yes." She paused. "Chance does happen, but we all know if there are a lot of quacks you are probably talking about a duck." Her humor didn't fit the conversation, but was the truth.

"Indonesia is a mixed country. Mixed in the sense of a wide difference in the population from island to island. Sumatra is over 90 percent Muslim. Some of the other islands are Protestant, Catholic, and even some areas are Buddhist." She was giving a class in Southwest Asia. "But the Malacca

Strait is bordered by Sumatra. On its tip and near the entrance to the strait is Banda Aceh. The city had sourced more jihadists to the fight in Syria than any other in Southeast Asia." She continued her lesson with a photo of the Baiturrahman Grand Mosque in the city. "They have fundamentalist patrols in the city who whip women who are not covered."

"So what does this have to do with Chevron? If they survived, wouldn't you see the internet alive with hostages? And if a missile strike from an over-the-shoulder SAM took it down, wouldn't they be bragging about the destruction of some airplane owned by the capitalists?" Will raised the counterpoints. "So, why the silence?"

"You're right." She looked up from her computer. "And we don't know."

"OK."

"And that's why Langley wants you to try."

Will was hesitant.

"Try what?"

"See if you can find out what we can't."

"You have officers on the ground. They probably have assets buried deep." He was pushing the point. "And they don't know anything?"

"It's been silent."

"I'm not sure I can do more." Will wasn't ready to jump in.

He did, however, have one thought in mind. It was a thought that he would never share with her or the CIA. It was the picture of two boys in their Little League baseball uniforms.

"What makes you think anyone is alive?"

"Again, just don't know."

"Let me think about it."

"Would tomorrow be too soon?" Lisa Kim had been instructed to get an answer.

Chapter 17

"We must catch some squid." The captain of the boat shook Chaniago, who had fallen asleep on the bow of the boat. "You help."

He sat up and surveyed the waters. They were clear as a glass full of it, but with a slight blue tint. As he looked over the side he could see down until the crystal-clear water turned a darker shade of blue. The bottom was deep, but the light's inability to reach the depth shaded it a darker blue.

"The ICGS patrols these waters."

Chaniago reached for his AK-47, which was close by.

"We need to hide that." The captain had made this run many times since they first found Kondul. "It only would bring the Marcos."

Chaniago nodded his head.

The islands to the north of Sumatra were the pass-through islands from the Bay of Bengal to the Andaman Sea. They were owned by India and patrolled by the Indian Coast Guard, or ICGS. Shipping passed to the south of the islands, as the large container vessels would enter or exit the Malacca Strait. The ICGS was dangerous with its well-armed cruisers. But if the trawler caught the attention of the Coast Guard vessel the greater danger was the MARCOS. The letters stood for the Indian Marine Commandos. Their reputation was a fearless, brutal special operations force that took no prisoners. They were called the *dadiwala fauj* or bearded ones, as they were always bearded so as to blend in with their world. An Indian Marine was trained to be dropped into the ocean with full combat gear, swim several miles, step out of the water, kill his target, then slide back into the waves. Combat was far easier than the training they went through. If a candidate survived the selection process where one out of ten made it, he then went through weeks of hell, followed by years of training in which he could be struck from the unit by one lapse or any show of weakness. But Chaniago and his cohorts planned to avoid both the Indian marines and Indonesian military.

"The Bamars have fished these waters and they hate them." The captain was using the name he had learned as a child for the Myanmars. Both India and much of Indonesia thought poorly of them. Many of the boats stopped by ICGS were carrying illegal Muslims to Banda Aceh. "We will probably be stopped. The Chinese like to come through here as well."

He was talking about a much bigger problem. The Chinese had continued to exert their presence in many of the territorial waters of the Andaman Sea and the Gulf of Thailand.

"They all leave the squid boats alone." The captain smoked a small, short cigar that was chewed up more than smoked. He rarely lit it. The brown stump stuck out of the corner of his mouth.

Chaniago had made the trip several times as well. The island that they were heading to served its purpose well. It was beyond the suspicious eyes of Indonesia and an unlikely place to look. The Indian coast guard rarely went as far south as this one. Plus, the squid boat seemed harmless. It was an odd vessel with a rigging of rows of light bulbs on extenders that stretched out like arms for several yards when they were fishing. The boat would travel near the shorelines of the islands, especially in sandy waters, and at night would put on a show of blue, green, and white lights. The fishermen would catch the squid by jigging, in which the squid would attack a bright, shiny metal object and its tentacles would wrap around the lure. The boat seemed harmless. The MARCOS would have no reason to suspect what was below. If a shell from an ICGS cruiser hit below deck, the RPGs and explosives would spread out and vaporize anything within a hundred yards.

"Your boy, is he good?" Chaniago sat on the bow studying the man's teenage son. He was small for his age with skin already darkened by the days on the open seas. He was sitting on the deck with his back to the pilothouse intensely studying his cell phone.

"When he isn't playing with that phone."

"Yes, we need to rid our people of these games." The two men shared the disdain for the constant use of cell phones to play video games. They seemed a new drug from the West. But these weren't from the West. The games were made in Southeast Asia just as often as anywhere else in the world.

"He says he's going to win the big prize and buy me a new boat." The captain laughed at the thought.

"How much is it?"

"Over five hundred thousand!"

"That'd be a fleet," Chaniago teased the man. He knew the captain was a loyal soldier, but he was also known to like making a profit. The JAD had paid a handsome fee for each of the voyages. The captain said it was for gas, but Chaniago had done the math. The charge was for much more than the amount of gas needed. And he was allowed to keep and sell the squid. Chaniago always wondered what would happen if the Indian coast guard did cross swords with the boat. He wasn't sure that the captain wouldn't toss Chaniago to the wolves.

"Boy, let's get the lights ready!" The captain shouted the words. "Put that phone away!"

Chaniago had brought the captain's attention to his deck hand and son. It was time to put him to work. The boy slowly rose, and put the cell phone in his back pocket.

"How long?" Chaniago stood up.

"There is the first island." The captain pointed to what appeared on the distant horizon.

"We need to fish some. We need to have some catch if they stop us. So, we will fish the south side of Nicobar at sunset, make a haul, then head north." The captain's plan seemed reasonable.

Chaniago wanted to get to Kondul as quickly as possible, to see his new catch.

Chapter 18

"You have to do this." Gunnery Sergeant Kevin Moncrief had always been Parker's conscience. He already knew the answer, he just wanted to hear Will say it. They had finished their meal of trout and were sitting on the porch watching the wilderness of Alaska come alive as the sun began to set. A chill in the early summer air caused a wisp of condensation to rise from the nearby river. They watched as a moose crossed the runway heading to the water's edge.

"We'll get Langley's support or we aren't doing it." Will leaned back in the rocker. His thoughts turned to Hedges. If the man was still alive, would he be alive much longer? Was this simply a tragic airplane crash? A prisoner of a Muslim jihadist group would not be long for this world.

"I've been thinking about that." The Gunny's role over the missions had been logistics leader. "We need Enrico and the Doc."

"Why the Doc?" Will still wasn't quite ready for Shane Stidham's daughter to be pulled into a mission.

"She's a natural. She speaks the language. And I like the idea of having a doctor on board."

"Who says you are going?" Will hadn't figured out the game, but he was just making a dig at his friend. "Kidding. You got her phone number?"

"Yep. I'll call her and set up a meeting with her and Langley."

"She'll want to do it in the Anchorage SCIF and will need to set it up with Virginia." Will looked at his watch and calculated the possibilities. "We need to get to Indonesia as soon as possible."

"Tomorrow at the SCIF."

"Yeah."

A two-story block building painted in a beige-brown was on the side street of South Airport. It had a bright green and white sign over the entrance that said Green's Car Rentals and featured a logo of a clover leaf. The building had small square windows on the second floor but none on the ground floor. A parking lot was next to it, but contained only two black Tahoe's near the building. In the lower forty-eight the vehicles would have stood out, with their oversize tires and black front and rear brush guards. In Alaska, the utility vehicles didn't attract much attention.

What was missing for someone who looked closely at the car rental agency were cars. The agency didn't rent cars. A commercial-grade security camera was just above the front door. And again, if one looked carefully, the building had the same cameras on each of the four corners.

The two men, out of habit, surveyed the street before going in. Only the occasional freight truck passed by. The building was the perfect choice. It was in the industrial area of the Ted Stevens Anchorage International Airport, on a side street, and not at all likely to gather any attention. The truck drivers who passed it by were more interested in the job of the day than the car rental company that never seemed to have cars. The sound of the departing jets at the nearby airport would roar over their heads with each flight taking off. Will looked to the sky, watching a jumbo JAL Boeing climb into the blue, cloudless sky as it banked to the left and climbed out to the west.

Will and Kevin stood at the front door, waiting. There wasn't a buzzer or even an intercom system. The door was blank with no signage and its glass was black and thick.

They heard a click. The door swung open and just inside was a man dressed in all black, in combat cargo pants, a bulletproof vest, a simple black baseball hat, and an automatic rifle.

"Sir." He used the point of the barrel of his rifle to signal that they could come in. It seemed clear that they were expected.

Once inside, Will's eyes adjusted to a blue light coming from a room sanitizer. Beyond the lobby a glass partition showed another guard in a room lit with bright white fluorescent lighting.

The two stood there for only a brief moment before Lisa Kim came into the room.

"Welcome." Lisa Kim handed them each a plain white plastic pass. It had no logo on it, but did have a bar code and their picture. Will looked at the identification pass and noted that his photo had been taken some time ago. It appeared that he was registered in their system for life. It was not something he was happy about.

"Not a big building, but the system keeps track." She wasn't kidding. She led them down a hallway and as Will walked he noticed small white boxes in the corners of the ceilings. They showed a tiny green dot of light that blinked as they approached each box—blinking once for each of them. At the end of the hallway a steel door with red markings led them down a flight of stairs to another hallway. The building was silent, no sounds or people. If they were there, the employees of the Alaska office were behind other steel doors. In the hallway below ground they passed several gray doors with tumblers above the door handles like oversize safes. At the very end of the hallway, a door marked SCIF in bold red letters seemed larger than the others.

Kim stopped just short of the door and placed her hand into a reader to its side that appeared to do a full hand scan. Soon, a loud click sounded and the door opened. As he passed through the door, Will saw the thick walls. Inside, the space seemed no larger than any bank's vault. It was crowded with filing cabinets, again each having a tumbler on the drawers, and an oversize flat-screen at the far end. The screen showed another room that appeared to be much larger. Unlike the Alaska room, it had wood paneling and drapes covering the back walls.

Kim pointed to two government-issue metal chairs with green plastic seats.

"Hello, Colonel Parker." The voice on the other end was someone he had not heard from in quite some time.

"So, this was your idea?" Will asked the man on the other end of the video conference call.

"Yes."

Will Parker knew the man on the other end of the video feed very well. He was older and his well-wrinkled face showed his age. He still had that hint of a British accent and the streak of gray hair made him look more like a stateman than a well-aged spy. He and Parker went back to the very beginning. James Fordon Scott used to be tall and lanky, but even on the video he appeared to have a stoop to his body that had shortened his height. He was a bright one at Eton College in Great Britain. He wanted the challenge of the spy world and began with British intelligence before working with the Agency. He had been brought together with Will by pure fortune. A North Korean had put the world in danger with his ability to destroy America's GPS satellite system. By chance, Will Parker's world had crossed paths with the man and he had a unique ability to know and find him. The operation was tagged Northern Thunder. It went well until an admiral turned on Parker. Scott was a bystander, but in the end, helped take down the admiral.

"So, what's your plan, Scott?"

"You go to Sumatra and shake the can. Your presence should help someone raise their head over the bloody parapet." Scott was suggesting that Will be the bait that would cause those who might have been involved to show themselves.

"People who stick their heads up usually get shot," Moncrief added.

"Gunnery Sergeant Moncrief. How are you doing?" Scott threw back a reply. "Are you all right?"

"Good enough to kick your ass."

"Same old Moncrief." Scott ended the banter.

"What's the cover story?" Will asked.

"We've cleared it with State. You've got a Macbook there." Scott made the comment as Kim took the cue.

She slid a Macbook Pro across the table.

"Fully customized." Kim opened it up. "Just press here."

The computer captured, after several repeats, Will's fingerprint to access the start-up. Unlike other computers, however, this one next showed a circle with a dialogue box instructing the user to line up their eye with the circle. Again after several repeats, the computer opened up.

"This has a third security feature. It reads your passcode." She was referencing the chip that Will had in his body from a past mission. "You have triple security."

"Not sure all this process does much when I'm surrounded by bad guys." Will knew the limitations of these elaborate systems. Fingers can be cut off and eyes gouged out. An implanted passcode still was in the body even if the body had been riddled with bullets.

"Every system has its limitations." Scott didn't need to say much more. "It is another way for you to communicate with us. It has been loaded with all of the information we have on Sumatra."

"And how am I going over there?"

"It has all been set up with State. You are going over there as a concerned citizen representing the interests of the families of the passengers." Scott's pitch made sense. "You won't be connected to State or Chevron. Use your own name."

"So, I will be representing Margaret Hedges." Will thought it odd that the mission would entail doing exactly what Margie had asked him to do.

"Yes, and the others." Scott noted that more Americans had been on board. "How did you like Margaret?"

Both Will and Moncrief glanced at each other.

"Gentlemen, she's not a part of this. Don't think the CIA is behind every bush." Scott was not always able to tell the truth, but in this instance they believed him. Although Scott knew of their meeting, it didn't mean that a housewife from Virginia was in on the effort. "You will have someone from Indonesia meet you and provide assistance."

"With the agency?"

"No, not at all. Remember, you are a concerned citizen trying to get some answers for the families. Just a local helper from their government will be there helping you." Scott rubbed his chin and mouth with his hand as he finished speaking.

"He will need some support." Moncrief sounded like the perfect executive officer who had the job of protecting the commanding officer.

"Whatever you need. Your officer there has been instructed to provide everything. But this is a solo mission. No need for the artillery." Scott seemed interested in making it a low-profile action.

"Always is." Will said it, but didn't agree with Scott's conclusion.

"Good luck and Godspeed," Scott said, then the screen went dark.

"So, Mr. Scott." Gunny Moncrief spoke.

"He's the reason you are here," Kim pointed out. "They were not happy with your profile."

"What?" Moncrief wanted to know the reason for her comment.

"You've been a bit on the skyline, Mr. Parker." Kim's comment called for more explanation. "Mystery man pulls doctors out of the wilderness. Climber's life saved. Good thing is that no name was given. How did you pull that off?" She held up two newspapers.

"What else you got?" Will changed the subject. He wasn't going to regret saving the lives of some lost doctors or a climber who was clinging to life at nineteen thousand feet.

"Here's the paperwork." She slid a folder across the table. "Airplane tickets, visas, a new passport, hotels, and everything you should need."

Will flipped through the folder. It contained a driver's license and what looked like ten thousand in mixed currency. There were several black American Express credit cards. The passport had his name, his address at a place he didn't recognize, and was stamped with some international travel. It appeared he had been to Great Britain, Scotland, Ireland, France, and Germany. The trips were spread out over time and the passport was well bent, as if it had been carried in his pocket for several years. An airplane ticket for Alaska Airlines took him to San Francisco followed by a flight on JAL to Kuala Lumpur by way of Narita in Japan. The trip alone took nearly two days. The Agency had been kind. The tickets for traveling across the Pacific were first-class sky suites on a Boeing 787 Dreamliner.

"Who do I meet on the other end?"

"Her name is Retno. She will find you."

"And who is she?"

"She's with their tourist bureau. Told you are an important person with our people. She's supposed to help in any way she can."

Kim pushed a photo across the table. It appeared to be a headshot like those used in auditions. The face was of an exceptional beauty.

"What's this?"

"She won some beauty contest there several years ago. You shouldn't mind her help," Kim teased him.

"Can she be trusted?" Will asked the more important question.

"I would hope so. You are on a humanitarian mission."

"Those can be the most dangerous." Will liked missions where he was carrying his HK pistol.

Chapter 19

The yelling woke up Chuck Hedges from what little sleep he was getting. His mouth was dry as cotton. Hunger pulled at his stomach. It was still pitch-black, and well before dawn. The guards carried lamps that provided just enough light to make out the shape of the men who had burst into the hut.

"Hey up." The lead man yelled in broken English. "Hey up."

Chuck tried to stand up but his leg had been twisted under his body and fallen asleep. He fell back down onto his knees.

"Hey up!" The guard struck him on his back with the butt of the AK-47 rifle.

The guards unlocked the other two and struggled with the chain on Chuck's leg. Finally, he felt the manacle go loose. Again, a gun barrel was stuck into the middle of his back. It made him nervous, as the man had his finger on the trigger. Chuck knew that the fool had a round in the chamber of the rifle, and with only a slight squeeze, he could pull the trigger. The bullet would tear through his back. He wouldn't last a day.

"Hey go!"

Chuck slowly moved over to the other two. The engineer was up but limping. Chuck held his hands up high to make sure the guards saw him as no threat. He reached the stranger who was standing but leaning against the post.

"Put your arm around my neck."

The man's arm was thin and bony. Chuck put his hand around the stranger's waist. He felt the man's rib cage and hips through the rags he was wearing. The stranger carried a makeshift crutch in his other hand. It would have been more hindrance than help in the mud.

"Hey go!" The guard pointed to the opening of the hut and the plank walkway down to the ground.

A deluge of rain quickly soaked them. The prisoners didn't mind. It was fresh water and helped wash some of the dirt from their faces and hair. They all looked up to the sky trying to take in as much water as they could.

"Hey go!" The guard pointed toward the jungle.

"Why now?" the engineer asked as they made their way down a trail. The water washed around their ankles as they tried to walk without slipping.

"No satellites." Chuck pointed to the sky with his free hand. It was clear that the movement at night and under a cloud-covered sky would make it impossible for anyone to see the men.

They followed the trail for some time, moving from one end of the island to the other. Chuck judged from the distance that they were on a small piece of land. It couldn't have been much more than a couple of miles. But the jungle covered much of the land with a thick triple canopy.

After some time, they came to an opening that was near the shelf of an outcrop like the other campsite. The hut they were chained in was far worse than the last one. It was not on stilts so the water ran through the shelter, and with the chains binding them to the posts, the prisoners had to either stand all night or sit in the mud.

Got to do something. Chuck made up his mind that the risks needed to be taken. The hunger and pain were mounting every day. He decided that an escape had to be attempted.

Daylight came soon and with it the rain stopped.

Chuck could smell the smoke of a fire nearby. A fire meant that they would be fed soon. He heard the men talking in whatever language they were speaking. They laughed and seemed to enjoy their mission. There was the sound of grease popping as the fish was being cooked. Soon, a guard came in the hut with some paper-wrapped fish and rice. It needed flavoring, but Chuck didn't mind. He ate with his fingers and consumed every bite, including the last kernel of rice. He then put the paper in the pocket of his cargo pants.

"What do they want?" The engineer would talk after a meal. His energy level seemed to climb with the food.

"They don't know," the stranger said. "Not these men."

"Who does?" Chuck asked.

"He will come. He has come before." The stranger made the leader sound like a mystery.

Chuck waited until he heard the guards say their prayers at the end of the day. Another guard was posted on the hut, and Chuck sat in the dark looking through a small slit in the bamboo wall as the man sat against the wall, on a log, with his weapon on his lap as he played with his cell phone. The bright colors of the game he was playing mesmerized Chuck.

Eventually, the man's hand relaxed and the cell phone fell to his lap.

Chuck worked on his chain, and with the grease from the paper he soon worked his foot loose from the shackle. Again, he slowly worked his way to the wall and pulled apart the bamboo.

The jungle that surrounded this encampment was much thicker than in the campsite up the hill. He had to slide through the undergrowth for yards upon yards until he broke out onto a sandy road that cut through the jungle. Chuck followed the road, which led down to the beach. And at the beach, he put his hands in the warm water as it lapped up on his wet boots. He felt the salt water on his face again since just after the crash and realized for the first time that his face had several deep lacerations. He felt the caked blood and tasted the salt water as it covered his lips.

"I can grab a log and hope it keeps me afloat." He whispered the words. There was a long piece of driftwood nearby that would serve the purpose. "But how far would I get? And what would they do to the others?"

"I need a better plan." Chuck decided to move down the beach to see what else he could find. Not far from where the road ended in the water, he saw a pier that was aged to the point that only the posts and a few boards remained. He started to walk up to it then stopped.

Chuck dropped to the sand as two of the guards walked past him. Their sandals were so close that they kicked up sand that struck him on his face. He tried to hold his breath but realizing that wouldn't work, slowly, very slowly let out and inhaled very easy breaths.

The two were talking to each other and slowly walked back into the jungle.

Chuck pulled back from them, followed his tracks back to the road, and then headed back into the jungle. Then fear struck him.

The jungle's wall of growth gave him no hint as to where to retrace his trail back to the hut. There seemed to be no dent in the vegetation.

Can't find my way. He struggled with the undergrowth. Then another thought entered his mind. He could turn around, go to the beach, grab the floating log and make a run for it. It couldn't be any worse than his not finding his way back before the guard checked on the prisoners.

"If I am missing when he wakes up, they will kill the others." He tried to calm himself, but could feel his heart pounding in his chest.

Chuck finally decided to plunge in and began crawling on his hands and knees. He moved slowly but kept moving. He couldn't see his hands as he peeled back the undergrowth and moved slowly.

After what seemed like a long time, Chuck smelled the smoke of the campfire. He stopped and tried to get his bearings. There were voices coming from just beyond where he was. It gave him a guide to the hut, but it also meant that the guard had to have awakened.

Finally, Chuck's hand touched the wall of the hut. He slowly pulled the bamboo aside and slipped in. He reached his post just as the guard came into the hut. Chuck quickly wrapped the chain around his ankle and leaned back against the post with his eyes closed. The first rays of daylight broke through the open roof of the hut.

The guard moved from post to post. He stood directly over Chuck for what seemed an eternity.

Finally, another one of the captors called from the campfire.

The guard turned and left the hut.

Chuck didn't want to risk it further. He quickly took off his boot and sock, both drenched, slid the chain over his ankle and put them back on.

I've got to make this work.

They were in a camp closer to the water than any previous encampment. The water gave him a chance, even though a small one. With capture he risked the same fate as the stranger. The loss of a foot would end it all. The island might be miles away from a sea-lane, and even if he found his way to a ship it might not see him, but it had to happen. Hunger was growing, and he could feel a fever coming on.

"Tonight, I will try." He said the words to himself.

Chapter 20

"I have several ideas." Gunny Moncrief stood up from the rocker at the cabin. He handed the laptop back to Will. He had sat in the rocker for most of the morning studying the information provided.

"This is not going to be a simple visit from an investigator for the families." Will was stating the obvious. "Scott has another agenda."

"Yeah."

"Have you talked to the others?"

"Yes, sir."

"What about anything else you need?" Will took the laptop and studied the intelligence briefing.

"Kim's cooperating and I can avoid Scott by going through her." The Gunny had a plan. "I've got a new friend at IARPA." He sounded like a kid with a new bicycle.

"IARPA?"

"Yeah, it's DARPA on steroids. The intelligence advanced research projects activity. They take spy craft to a new level."

"How did you do that?"

"Got our local lady to send a top secret email to the director. Works wonders when you have an introduction from the CIA." Moncrief was proud of the maneuver.

"We just met yesterday."

"Had IARPA on my mind for some time." He smiled. "The director is my new best buddy."

"And how is that going to help?"

"She's let me in on some of their new stuff. One thing they have may help."

Will didn't need to know everything. He liked the idea that the Gunny would take the ball and run with it.

"They have me leaving tonight. You will follow with the team. We don't need anything that either Scott or the Agency can track. Stay independent." Will wanted the team to be a ghost nearby but not on the skyline. "You read the brief. There is only one place that makes sense for you to be located." Will was traveling on his suspicions, which had served him well in the past. If this were an airplane crash due to some malfunction, where the team was or what they did wouldn't much matter. If the airplane was hijacked, their location would matter.

"I agree."

"I have the gear on Coyote Six." Will's HondaJet had the weapons needed as well as the other combat gear they had used in the past. "She can't reach Malaysia. Can you get everything in-country?"

"Yep. Got someone who will help get the gear and us in."

"And you are bringing Kaili?"

"The Doc is coming." Moncrief had made two calls after the meeting, at the Stephens airport in Anchorage.

"You've got her." It was Will's way of saying that Moncrief was in charge of the doctor.

"Got it. And we'll use ION cell phones. Switch every day. Dr. Swan's idea."

"Dr. Swan?"

"Director of IARPA. Smart lady. PhD in physics from Stanford. Think she likes the idea of working with a real mission. Got her cranked up." The Gunny spoke of her as if she were his newfound friend.

"Don't think this is going to be so simple." Will always considered who was on his flank. A combat soldier always remembered Patton's advice that once the first shot was fired the plans went out the window. "Scott has something else on his mind."

Chapter 21

"We have a good catch!" The captain held up a handful of the fresh squid that they had pulled in by jigging. He would be paid by JAD for the run and sell the catch back at the market if they didn't stay long on the island. His supply of ice would hold the squid for a few days. In the past that had worked, as his passenger never stayed longer than a night. The light of a new day showed the beach on the nearby island that they had worked for the catch. The trawler looked somewhat like a circus train with the lights stretched out on the arms shining down on the waters. The boat's shadow glided along on the bottom as the lighting illuminated the clear blue sea below. The marine life hovered below the keel with the occasional shark passing by like an officer's patrol car surveilling his neighborhood.

"Boy, shut them off and let's pull it all in." The father barked his orders to his son. The boy jumped up at the command. They had worked the squid all night long, but the boy was used to the catnaps taken in the noonday sun as his sleep.

Chaniago was busy on his cell phone. He looked intent on the conversation as he sat on the bow of the boat. His tone made it clear he was barking at whoever was on the other end.

"We need more money." He was speaking in English. As the captain and his son didn't speak English, the conversation was safe.

The man on the other end was someone Chaniago knew well. Abd al Hamid Sulaiman al Mujil had been generous in the past to the causes of the JAD and they were getting very close now to his plan's execution. Al Mujil was called the million-dollar man for his generous donations. He ran the IIRO-IND out of its office in Jakarta. The International Islamic Relief Organization for Indonesia fed the fires of the militants throughout much of Southeast Asia. Millions were funneled from the Wahhabi movement of Saudi Arabia through the IIRO. But there were mounting disagreements. And it was mostly about oil.

"Padang will not be seriously damaged." Chaniago needed the funds but had a hard time restraining himself when talking to al Mujil. Chaniago's plan included an attack on the oil storage tanks in the harbor of Padang on the west coast of central Sumatra. It would send a signal to the world that the Muslims of Sumatra would no longer tolerate the western world robbing their assets. He had the two young followers ready for their mission of jihad, the boat ready, and it was full of the ammonium nitrate. The date was set. But Chaniago wanted the funds in place before the world saw it coming. Once an attack on this scale occurred, the international community would be following the money trail and stopping its flow. Indonesia would be moved to action. And their first act would be to try to cut off the money.

It had happened before. After the attacks on America on September 11, 2001, Washington issued executive orders under the national emergency act targeting the IIRO. Bush wanted to stop the flow of funds.

"The infrastructure will not be seriously damaged," Chaniago repeated. He was walking the line. Al Mujil had his own interests besides helping the world see a new caliphate. Sumatra would separate itself from Indonesia. Its population was as nearly homogeneous a people as anywhere on earth. The island, unlike the rest of Indonesia, was overwhelmingly Muslim. Plus, Chaniago had spent years on the front lines in combat supporting the cause in Syria and elsewhere. He had the respect of al Mujil and others.

"We will keep China out of Sumatra." This was the promise that he knew the man on the other end of the cell phone call wanted to hear. The oil would only be controlled by the Saudis. The price would be set by those in Riyadh. But there was a problem. The oil fields of Sumatra were dying off. Minas had fed the thirst of oil in Southeast Asia since the forties. The fields were getting weak. And al Mujil's interests were weakening.

Chaniago knew that al Mujil had two motivations. The oil of Sumatra was cheap. Its price was well below the Americans' even with their recent increased production of oil in the United States. It could be cheaply shipped to several growing markets in the region. Vietnam was growing on all fronts. The Philippines' economy was thriving. But with al Mujil's help, a Muslim caliphate would be formed that could spread the word of the prophet to much of Southeast Asia and the Pacific. Al Mujil would be the man who helped a new nation of Islam be formed.

"Yes, thank you. May Allah be praised." Chaniago got his funds. The money would be wired to a series of banks, eventually making it to the IIRO bank in Jakarta. From there it would move to Banda Aceh.

The fisherman never knew that a transaction on his boat would make his catch of squid seem a spit in the bucket.

Chapter 22

Where is the American? Retno Karims stood at the arrival door looking for the man whose picture had been sent some time before. She ignored the two Malaysian airline baggage handlers who continually stared at her. She had seen it all of her life. Retno's unusual perfect shape, black eyes, and dark black hair helped the Asian beauty become not only Miss Indonesia but also a finalist in the Miss World competition. She had the gift of beauty and an intellect that made her more than a passing beauty queen.

"God, what time is it?" She mumbled the words as she glanced at her Apple watch. It was just after five in the morning. Only the bright fluorescent lights of Terminal M lit up the Kuala Lumpur International Airport . It was the busiest airport in all of Southeast Asia, but at this early hour only the baggage clerks and those who worked behind the counters were moving about. Malaysia Airlines flight ME 71 had been on time, but as she watched the straggling few come out of the departure exit, it was apparent that the Boeing 787 was nearly empty. Yet there was no sign of the American. She had his photo and the description of a man over six feet tall, likely with a tanned complexion and brown-blond hair.

"Ms. Retno?"

She turned to see her guest standing just behind her.

"I'm sorry. I hope I didn't scare you." Will Parker towered over her five-foot-five frame. He was well dressed in what a British or American businessman would wear, a blue blazer cut with an inside label that said Gieves & Hawkes of Savile Row, creased slacks, and a striped sky-blue shirt. His shoes were tan Foster & Son tasseled loafers that matched the alligator belt. He seemed like an American who had just stepped out of a photo shoot for *GQ*. His face was more than tanned. It appeared windblown and rugged, as if he had just come off his sailboat after crossing the Pacific. He projected the image he wanted to.

"Oh, no, I was just in another world." Retno's English was flawless, with a mild midwestern accent that matched her year abroad as a student in Iowa City. She wanted this assignment. "How was your flight?"

"Fine. Thank you for asking."

"Welcome to Indonesia."

"And I understand you work with Kemenko Polhukam?" He pronounced the name of the Indonesian ministry perfectly.

"Yes."

"Professor Mahfud?"

"You did your homework."

Mahfud was the first civilian head of the Ministry of Political, Legal and Security Affairs. A law professor who had served as the Chief Justice of their Supreme Court, Mahfud was thought of as a law-and-order type. He made a run for the presidency, but came up short.

"So, do you work with the political, legal, or security side?"

"The legal side. And your embassy said you are an attorney?" Retno had read the extensive brief on the visitor. His visit was requested by the American State Department. They had wired that a private attorney hired by the families had asked to make an inquiry into the matter of the missing plane.

"Yes." Will didn't mention that he had abandoned his legal practice some time ago when Mr. Scott had approached him about a mission in North Korea. He was, however, an attorney. And being an attorney was the cover they needed. His history as a Marine officer was scrubbed from what State had provided, as well as who he presently worked with.

"Do you do these cases often?"

"This is my first." He smiled.

"Really?"

"Yes."

Retno didn't know how to take this man or his goals.

"I thought about law school. The University of Indonesia. I was accepted." It was the country's premier law school. It was Indonesia's Harvard. "Do you have many bags?"

"No, just one."

"Baggage claim is this way." She was walking fast. It was clear that Retno was a runner. "I have a car and I understand you have a reservation at the Four Seasons."

"I believe so. My office set all of this up." His office was in Langley, Virginia.

"Is this your first time to our country?"

"Yes." Will walked slightly behind her. She had small hands and wore her hair down. Her dress was short and showed off her shapely legs.

"You must be tired. Perhaps I drop you off at your hotel and then in the morning we can go wherever necessary?"

"I would like to meet with your team that conducted the air-sea rescue effort."

"Absolutely."

Will's room overlooked the business center of Kuala Lumpur and looked out on the Petronas Twin Towers. The two skyscrapers, at one time the tallest in the world, were connected by a skybridge on the forty-second floor. Indonesia built the buildings to show its emergence as a world capital.

The telephone rang in his room.

"Hello?"

"Sir, we have a meeting set up in Putrajaya first thing in the morning." It was Retno confirming the logistics. "We are meeting with the acting director of the Air Accident Investigation Bureau. Would eight work?"

"Yes, thank you, with one condition." He paused. "You needn't call me sir."

"Yes." She smiled to herself. "You need to go to the Menara KH building. Go to the thirty-sixth floor."

"At eight."

"Yes, eight."

He hung up and called the desk.

"I would like to take a swim and perhaps have a massage."

After coming back to his room, Will pulled out the laptop and contacted Lisa Kim to report that he had made contact. He noted that he was meeting with the acting director of MOT the next morning and requested an upload of information on the man. In less than half an hour a dossier of information arrived via email. It noted a Mr. Hussein was the most knowledgeable about the investigation. He was a pilot and had worked the investigations of two of the most horrific and notable air crashes of the decade.

Will then went downstairs and out onto the street. He walked for several miles, making sure that he changed directions and reversed course, then entered a bar at another hotel. He ordered a scotch on the rocks and drank it.

"Is it always this quiet?" He spoke to the bartender in perfect Malay.

"Ramadan starts tomorrow," the man replied.

Will spoke with the bartender for most of an hour. It was small talk of the man's family, his thoughts on the government, and his favorite football team. The man favored Persija Jakarta who had won nearly a dozen titles. But Will had a purpose. He was scrutinizing the language, experimenting with the accent and getting a feel for the rhythm.

"Good night, my friend."

Will left his tip and went back into the lobby, then took the elevator up five floors. On the fifth floor, he found the stairway and descended the stairs to the basement, where a door led to an underground garage. Will used the back ramp and walked out onto the street. He was looking for one thing in particular and found it a block away.

An ION cell phone store was nearly empty. He bought four disposable cell phones, bought several minutes of international time on each, then went back on the street. He paid cash for the phones and cards. A block away, a park with a large pool and a fountain that flowed with spurts of water was colored by soft blue and white lights. The air was warm and there was a slight breeze. Will placed a call.

"Are you ready?"

"Yes, got everything." The Gunny's voice was as clear as if he was on the other side of the fountain.

"Stand by and I'll let you know where."

"You got it."

Will knew that the Gunny had rounded up Hernandez and Stidham and they had prepared the load for what was needed. Transportation was another challenge that the Gunny and Will had discussed. The Agency wanted this to be a solo mission.

So the support team didn't exist as far as Langley and Kim knew.

Will and the Gunny needed a unique form of transportation. The cargo they were carrying was not something that one could bring on Delta or JAL. They needed a favor and an old friend did one for them. The team needed a cover. Dr. Stidham provided the plan.

Will returned to the hotel. His suite had a balcony and by cracking open the door, the cool breeze put him to sleep. He didn't need an alarm clock. He had trained himself since his first combat missions to think of a time and decide to wake up at that time. He thought 6:00, barricaded the door with a chair out of habit, and went to sleep.

At precisely 6:00 am in Kuala Lumpur Will stood up next to the bed.

Sometime later, he passed through the lobby and walked to the nearby Menara KH building. The elevator took him to the thirty-sixth floor.

He looked at his watch, which showed just before eight.

Will heard the whop-whop of the helicopter before it appeared. The black Huey seemed to approach the building with its back side. It turned, flared on its landing and set the skids down on the helipad. Retno slid the door open and waved him to come onboard. Will noted that Retno was comfortable with being on a Huey helicopter by the way she opened the door. He climbed onto the aircraft, fastened his seat belt, and the crew chief handed him a green David Clark headset. Once he had it on, he heard Retno speak.

"We are going to Putrajaya, home of the MOT."

Will knew what she meant. The Ministry of Transportation's office was in Putrajaya, which was just to the south of Kuala Lumpur. Putrajaya was a planned city to be the home of most of the government ministries. Kuala Lumpur had become a dense and crowded city of nearly eight million people. The government had anticipated the growth and created the new city.

Will looked out over the metropolitan area of Kuala Lumpur. The city glistened with the shine of new construction, as if a giant child with an unlimited supply of Lego blocks had built this new capital of Southeast Asia. He looked down on the cars stopped in traffic and watched the people, like ants, moving on the sidewalks below.

Less than five hundred miles from here religious police beat women with canes.

Sumatra was very different from this modern capital. Approval for stoning had been enacted until the governor did a most unpopular thing—he vetoed the bill.

The helicopter descended to a landing pad near a high-rise steel and glass building. Will and Retno stepped down from the aircraft and walked into the building, took the elevator, and entered a conference room on the top floor.

"Welcome, Mr. Parker. We appreciate your being here. And we are very sorry that the families you represent have suffered this loss." The man who met him at the door was the acting director of MOT's Aviation Accident Investigation Bureau. His once-black hair had changed to ash gray. The director wore a cotton short-sleeve shirt in a print of green leaves with khaki pants. His gray hair was achieved in the worst way. He held his present job in 2014 when Malaysia Air's Boeing 777 disappeared from the face of the earth. MH370 disappeared like a fog that slipped out to sea.

While they were still searching for that aircraft, another Malaysian jumbo jet was pulled out of the sky by trained Russian troops in the Ukraine. No other country- or state-supported airline in modern times had suffered the double blow of several hundred people lost in such a short period of time. And now, another aircraft had disappeared. A crash would have been horrific, but this was far worse. It had disappeared like MH370. Airplanes do not disappear, but the Chevron plane had managed it.

"We have put together what we know." The director waved his hand as an assistant handed Will a flash drive. "This is everything."

"Is your investigation still pending?" Will asked the question that would have been expected of him.

"No, we have exhausted our available manpower." The acting director was really saying that they had exhausted the funds.

"The plane departed from Sultan Syarif Kasim II?" Will spoke of the airport near Pekanbaru in the central part of Sumatra. "Near the Minas oil fields?"

"You are well informed."

"Sir, I would like to follow the path of the aircraft. I would like to go to Pekanbaru."

The director stared at Will, then looked at Retno, then looked toward his assistant. He didn't appear to be thrilled about the request. It seemed that the plan had been to meet with this American, show him the facts, then get him on the next airplane out of Kuala Lumpur.

"I guess we can."

At that moment, another younger man, an aide, entered the room, approached the acting director, and whispered in his ear.

The man's face became stone.

"Excuse me."

The man left the room.

"Wait a moment." Retno walked out and returned after several minutes. "A small bar near Puchong was attacked. They threw a hand grenade into a bar while those there were watching a football match on television."

"Football?"

"To you it was soccer."

"Anyone killed?" Will asked the question without thinking.

"A woman and her young son."

Will shook his head.

"They already posted on the internet. Terrorists with JAD saying the tourists were abusing Ramadan." Retno seemed to know more about JAD than she was saying. "Our helicopter is waiting. Are you sure you want to go to Pekanbaru?"

"Yes." Will thought it odd that she connected the two. But it seemed that they would be most pleased if he had booked a return flight to San Francisco that night. Will Parker didn't have that plan on his agenda.

The helicopter dropped Will off at the helipad on the upper floor of the Menara KH building, and he returned to the bar and his friend. This time, he visited over a cup of *teh tarik*—the sweetened black tea that most in Kuala Lumpur drank. He ordered a meal, ate it at the bar, and continued to talk with his friend the bartender. They talked of the bombing. The bartender was on edge. Kuala Lumpur had never been the target of terrorism. Police stations and the occasional unpopular embassy out in the provinces had been targets, but not a bar less than fifteen kilometers from his own bar.

Will finished the tea and meal, tossed a heavy tip on the bar and left. It was a short walk to his hotel. He stopped at a drugstore, walked in, stepped to the back, cut over to a side window that looked out to the front and saw a man in the shadows. He studied him for a few moments then walked back through the store and came out the entrance. Will stayed in the light, making sure he was easily followed. He returned to the Four Seasons and went straight to his room.

Will opened the door to the balcony, stood by the railing, and watched the streets below. The city did not seem to have been slowed down by the bombing at all.

A knock on the door brought him back from the balcony.

Will wanted to reach for his HK pistol. It hadn't arrived. His only weapon was a pen on the desk. It was crude but as effective as possible for a short-term weapon. He braced himself against the wall, put his foot within inches of the opening and slowly opened it.

A woman stood on the other side.

"No!" Will was not pleased with his guest.

Chapter 23

Another rainstorm turned the floor of the hut into a sea of mud. Chuck's low-grade temperature persisted. He was losing his appetite, and with the loss of interest in eating, he knew he was getting weaker. They continued to bring rice and fish, which he forced himself to eat.

As darkness descended on the day, again he worked the chains and removed the shackles. He crawled over to the engineer and felt his head. It was warm and sweat was pouring off his forehead.

"Did you take the Malarone?" Each of the Chevron team had been given doses of the drug to prevent malaria. It required that you took them for some time before departure, during travel, and after returning home.

"No. It tore up my stomach."

Chuck shook his head in disbelief. He had taken the drug per the instructions until the airplane crash and his capture. It gave him a window of protection. Malaria was likely not the cause of his mild temperature and loss of appetite. He was more at risk of the beginning of a case of dysentery. It was dangerous as well, but the diarrhea had not begun. He knew that dehydration could be a killer and needed to get to a water supply to supplement the bottles that his captors provided. Now the water was only once a day and no more than a sixteen-ounce bottle with an aged wrapper that had the red-and-blue bird on it. At least the bottles had caps that were still tight and unbroken.

"OK. I've got to try to get out of here. You can't make it. Our best chance is for me to get to some help."

"OK." The engineer didn't fight it. He would barely be able to walk a hundred feet let alone ride on a log for possibly days at sea.

"You going?" The stranger whispered the words.

Chuck crawled over to him as well.

"Got to."

"Get out as far as you can and try to catch the shipping traffic." He also seemed to believe that their only hope was escape.

"Do you want to try?" Chuck knew that this one had survived the captivity and had a tough resolve in fighting for his survival.

"Hell." He laughed at the thought. "Not much for swimming with a foot missing." It was a weak laugh, like one a cancer patient might make while undergoing another round of chemotherapy. "I have family."

"Yeah?"

"My memory's shot to hell. Just want to tell Sarah I love her."

"Who's Sarah?"

"I don't know."

"What's the last name?"

"I can't remember." He stared out into the dark. He was a desperate man on his last legs. "Good luck."

The guard had fallen asleep again. He still had his cell phone on and the glow of the screen cast a red, green, and yellow tint on the walls.

It was time to move.

Chuck slid back to the far end of the hut and slowly worked his way through the bamboo wall. Once he had a space no wider than his shoulders, he squeezed through, getting struck in the face by the wet ferns. The rainforest was fed by little light in the day, constant rain, humidity, and the heat. Chuck crawled slowly, pushing the growth aside as he made toward the open path. He passed a plant that smelled like something had died. Its flower had a pungent smell, as if it intended to use it to attract flies and then dissolve them in its stinking corpse lily. Chuck continued to move forward, thinking of much worse. He had trained in the jungle with the Marines and knew that there were other things more dangerous that traveled in this forest. The land of Sumatra and its islands were known for their cobras.

"Keep it straight," he whispered to himself. He was trying to steer himself in the black of the jungle. At high noon on a bright summer day the rays of the sun would not pierce the canopy.

The ferns and vines seemed endless, until finally his hand extended out into the open space of the road. Chuck was able to stand up and assess the situation. He still had the reservoir of strength from his dedicated years of working out. His clothes that were not torn in the airplane crash were now caked with mud, but he could stand without feeling the chain pull him down.

Got to keep moving. He wanted to get out to sea and far away from the island before first light. Chuck slowly moved down the path. He stopped short of the beach when he noticed a large shape to one side. He studied it for some time. It was the geometric shape of something man-made but it was nearly buried in the wrappings of vines and growth.

A Japanese bunker.

Once the thought hit, he could see the opening for the machine gun and realized the path, that once was a road, connected the bunker to some Japanese encampment from the war. He didn't linger to explore it.

"If a cobra is here, he would be in there."

Chuck moved to the beach and once he hit the sand, he felt the warm breeze coming off the water. It was a setting quarter moon, which gave him little time to get out to sea. He worked his way up the beach, away from the pier, and found a log of driftwood that might hold him.

"I wish I had some water." He considered going back into the jungle and following the path with the hope that he would find a stream. But time was running out. He removed his belt. It was a 5.11 tactical belt made of black heavy nylon with a sturdy buckle that could hold his weight. The plan was that he would extend the belt as far as it would go, loop it around the smallest part of the log, and fasten it to his cargo pants. He would crawl on top of the log and slowly paddle into the water while keeping his balance.

Chuck dragged the log into the warm water and walked out until the water was hip high.

He pulled himself up, straightened out the belt, and pulled with his hands.

"This won't be easy." He would slide sideways and have to use all his limited strength to straighten himself up again. He thought of giving up, figuring that once in deep water any wave action would turn him over and he would be easy bait for the sharks. And then, as he got farther out in the water, he saw something that changed his plans.

"What?"

Chapter 24

"Why are you here?" Will stared at the woman standing at his door.

"I thought you weren't going to help." Margie Hedges looked as tired and worn out as before.

"Come in." He opened the door farther and looked down the hallway in both directions. She stood there as he closed the door. He put his hand to his lips in a gesture for not speaking and pointed to the balcony. The breeze and city sounds filled the air.

"Drink, Mrs. Hedges?" Will stood out on the balcony. "The room bar is well stocked."

"Just vodka, ice if you've got it." The American was coming out in Margie; however, she needed the vodka more than the ice. Margie had become a desperate woman driven by her love, her fear, her determination to protect what she had left of her family and find some answers. She would have been better had they found a burned-out wreckage of an airplane with several charred bodies inside. It was the lack of closure that drove her crazy.

Will handed her a glass a third full of liquid and ice.

"How did you find me?"

"Saw you leave the drugstore."

So, it was her that he thought was following him.

"You came to Indonesia? Why?"

"What else could I do? No answers at home. No answers from Chevron. No answers from our State Department."

More than once, a widow showing up at the scene had brought the world's attention to something that had slid off the front page.

"How are your boys?" He didn't understand how she could be on the other side of the world when the rest of her family was just as desperate for answers. "Don't you need to be with them?"

She gave Will a scowl.

"His mother has them. His father is a retired Marine. A chief warrant officer." By the rank, it was clear that the parents had spent their time moving from base to base, waiting out tours of combat when nothing was heard for months. A father who was a "gunner," or warrant officer, meant that Chuck was raised tough and would have a stiff back—he could take a lot. This was good news if the man was still alive.

She took a sip from her drink. Despite the difficult time since the crash, Margie was still a beautiful woman who surprised others when she mentioned she had two boys at home. Will recognized that Charles Hedges scored a home run by winning Margie's heart.

"How did your paths cross? How did you meet?" Will leaned back in his chair on the balcony.

Margie thought about when the senior at Mary Washington College was without a date to a sorority function and let her roommate set her up. There were always one or two girls at Mary Washington who dated second lieutenants at Quantico. The Marine base was where new officers went through their introduction to the Corps. The Basic School took a green college graduate and ran him through six months of intense training. Some went from Quantico to another school in their specialty, but would be in combat within a few months of graduation.

"Blind date."

The college, in Fredericksburg, was only a few exits down Interstate 95 from the Marine Corps base. She, like many at the small college, was not keen on dating the crew-cut Marine officers that would prowl the campus for dates. He was, however, very different.

"With a Marine?"

"Yep. Crazy, huh?" She took another sip.

"What sealed the deal?"

"I was a history major. Had thoughts of teaching at the college level once."

"I'm impressed." Will resisted getting to know her. This was a person he might have to tell some very bad news to one day soon. But he had respect for someone who would go to the other end of the world to find her husband.

"I said I studied the American revolution."

"And?"

"He said he would show me something." She smiled. The vodka was taking effect. "He drove me to five-o-one Caroline Street. In Fredericksburg. Not far from the college. Do you know what that is?"

"Not up on my history." Will listened.

"The home of the William Paul family. He knew all of this." She showed her pride in her husband.

"As in John Paul?"

"You do know your history. A little wooden house that is still there. His brother was a tailor and it was his home. John Paul Jones would come to that little house between tours of duty on the high seas." Margie was proud of her knowledge of the history but also that Charles had taught her something she didn't know. "After the mutiny in which he killed a man, he fled to the colonies and took on an alias. He became known as Jones." The father of our navy was a criminal on the lam.

"And your husband taught you all of this?"

"Do you know what Jones did? He never gave up." Margie pointed the glass at Will to make the point.

"If he is alive, I will find him." Will knew what she was saying. "But it doesn't help for you to be here. He would not want you to be here."

"Get me some answers and I will leave."

Chapter 25

The log rolled on Chuck as he looked up. When he raised his head, he would turn like a carnival ride. He kicked with his feet to right himself, but the log rolled on him again. He unbuckled his belt and his boots slid down to the sea floor. He tested himself by standing up. He hadn't gone so far that the water was above his chest. Chuck stood there, holding on to the log not yet ready to abandon it.

He turned back toward the shoreline and saw something several hundred yards away.

What the hell.

There, on the dock to the south, was a boat with an odd rigging that looked like several television antennas strung, from bow to stern, with strings of light bulbs. The moon's intermittent light glistened off the glass bulbs and metal rigging as it appeared through a break in the clouds.

Chuck watched the old trawler. It seemed empty, no one on board. He studied it for some time, waiting to see if there was any movement. The boat remained still.

The log bobbed up and down as he stood there in the warm water.

Got to decide. He was now soaked from standing in the water. If he returned to the hut, the guard would see his clothes drenched and know of the attempted escape. If he committed to the log, he might make it out to deep waters but now risked a chase boat that would follow. Or drowning, or days at sea without hope of rescue. Or, there was another option.

Chuck could slide onto the boat and make his escape.

Start the engine and get it out to sea. He only needed to get it beyond the range of their gunfire. The farther out to sea, the more chance that he would be seen and rescued.

Chuck slowly walked the distance to the trawler in the water. Still, there was no movement. It was well past midnight. Adrenaline was surging through his veins. His thirst was building and the fever had not gone away.

Go for it.

The word *hesitation* was not in his vocabulary.

He slowly worked his way to the boat, still pulling the log with him. If there was any movement, he would return to the original plan. Once he reached the dock, Chuck went under the few boards that made up the walkway. He stayed there, in the dark, waiting to see any sign of life. There was none. The moonlight broke through the cloud cover then slid back under like the headlights of a car in the distance on a rough country road. The light would come on and go off.

Chuck pulled himself up on the dock and looked for the mooring lines. Two ropes held the boat in place. It was possible that he could have untied the lines and let the boat float out to sea, but the wind was blowing toward shore.

That won't work.

It wouldn't help to release the boat and have it go a few yards and be grounded on the beach. He would need to start the engine, and knew that with the first turn of the key the roar would cause them to come. He had to work quickly.

Chuck untied the lines, threw the ropes on board, and then pulled himself onto the ship. The trawler smelled of the same fried fish, and oil, and burned fuel. It also had the sharp smell of fresh fish. In this case, the smell of caught squid, but he didn't know the difference or the catch on this boat. A dim light glowed in the pilothouse. He could feel the boat start to drift and rock, slightly, in the water. He looked for a weapon of any kind. A rod like a tire iron was next to the rigging for the lights. He picked it up and worked his way to the door to the pilothouse. It was open and the cockpit was dark with the exception of the dim light that was just above the wheel. It was meant to light up the compass, which was the only instrument in the cab.

A rusty metal panel just below the wheel held a key and to its side the throttle. It was not marked so Chuck could only hope that reverse was in the standard position.

Hit the key, put it in reverse, and get the hell out of here.

He felt the metal of the key in his hand as he got ready to turn it. The key moved two clicks and then stopped. The next turn would bring it to life. The throttle needed to stay in neutral until it fired up and was running.

Chuck had worked his dad's fishing boat on the Chesapeake enough times to know that moving the throttle too quickly could choke out the engine.

Here goes.

The engine stuttered, then fired up, then stuttered, then roared to life. Even over the sound of the engine, he could hear the screams coming from the shore. Guns started to fire. The zip of bullets cracked the wood as he pulled back on the shift. It started to move slowly, backward, but the stern turned into the dock. It required a quick correction.

Chuck saw the men on the shore. One was running to the dock. He would be close at hand if the boat didn't move faster.

"Come on!" he yelled at the vessel, as if that would make a difference. More bullets popped and the splinter of wood sprayed him. The bow started to turn away from the dock and out to the water.

And then.

Chuck felt the warmth of the deck on the side of his face. A drip of blood came from his head and flowed down his cheek. He tasted, in the dull consciousness of the blow, the salt of the blood in his mouth. His ears were ringing as if a fire truck had passed by. The blow had to have been something of some weight. He opened his eyes to see two feet, wearing sandals, standing in front of his face. Words were being said; even in his best mental state he wouldn't have understood what was being said, but he did understand the tone. His arms were being pulled back and the cord cut deep into his wrists. Two of the men lifted him up and dragged him to the side of the boat, tossed him onto the dock like a bag of discarded trash. Pain surged through his body, but he couldn't move.

On the dock, he felt a bamboo pole being slid through his bound hands and feet. He was being carried like a pig ready for the pit. And then, with his head sagging, he lost consciousness. Darkness fell.

The water washed over his head. He was blinded by the blood that had flowed from the wound into his eyes and dried there. He could barely speak. It was as if the rod that struck him came across his temple and fractured his jaw. He gagged from the blood that had flowed into this mouth and tried to spit it out. With the spit came several fractured teeth.

"Hello." The man was squatting as if he had often sat like that before.

Chuck focused his eyes to see he was in the corner of the hut with the other two prisoners. He could only mumble a reply. The man spoke in English with a heavy accent. Chuck could only nod his head.

"Our boy slept in the pilothouse. Lucky for us that he did." The man smiled and Chuck could see a broken tooth directly in the front. Chuck understood that the boy had been curled up in the shadow of the cab until he was awoken by the stranger starting the engine.

"You the Marine." Chaniago smiled with that same broken smile, his skin as dark as well-tanned hide, with a black monobrow that met just above his oversize crooked nose. "Marine are worthy soldiers. You need water? Of course you do." He held a plastic bottle up to Chuck's lips.

Despite the pain, Chuck inhaled the water. The man yelled something and one of the soldiers brought another bottle, which was also quickly consumed. The ringing in his ears hadn't subsided.

"I'm Chaniago."

Chuck focused on the man's face. He wasn't farther than the spit Chuck could muster if he had any and if he wanted to do so.

"You Marines. I remember you well." He smiled like a fellow warrior reminiscing over past battles. "Were you in Al-Tanf?" He was speaking of the outpost just inside the Syrian border near the M2 highway Iraqi al-Waleed border crossing. The highway had been the main connector between Damascus and Baghdad. It was a lonely post, surrounded by barren desert and held, at different times, by different militaries, including the Marines.

"You fought without hesitation. You should have been followers of the great one." He looked around as he said it, being cautious around his men that he didn't mention Muhammad even when meant to be a compliment to his enemy.

"They wanted to cut off your head, my friend." He smiled. "Or one of your feet."

Chuck heard the words over the ringing.

"I would not let them do it. Not to a worthy warrior." He smiled again. "But try that again and I may not be around."

A man approached the two. He spoke in his language and Chaniago stood up. Chaniago nodded his head in the affirmative.

"I must go." Chaniago responded to the message from the man. "Not again, my friend, not again." His warning was clear.

Chapter 26

The Indonesian helicopter's trip from the thirty-sixth floor helipad to Sempang Airport on the outskirts of Kuala Lumpur took Retno and Will less time to fly than the time it took for the aircraft to be cleared by air traffic. Once cleared, the helicopter lifted off and flew just over the tops of the skyscrapers. It only flew as high as the midlevel floors of the gigantic Petronas Twin Towers. Will could see people in the upper levels of Petronas looking out their windows and down on the helicopter. But even at low altitude, the skies over Kuala Lumpur were as busy as if they were traveling across Manhattan.

The helicopter banked over an airfield on the outskirts of the city and just above a line of American made C-130s. The Royal Malaysian Air Force base was a single strip runway. The tarmac also had a cross section of aircraft from virtually all the arms providers in the world—a line of Soviet Sukhoi Su-30s, American Boeing F/A-18 Hornets, and British BAE Hawk combat fighter jets were parked in several rows.

They give everyone some business.

Will twisted the headphones as he stared down at the aircraft on the field.

Must be a maintenance nightmare.

Keeping up a line of aircraft from different manufacturers would usually mean a lot of aircraft waiting to be repaired. The field looked like an airshow with American Sikorskys, French Eurocopters, and a German Airbus A319. One other aircraft was on the apron with its engines running. A Spanish CASA CN-235 twin-engine transport airplane painted bright white with bloodred stripes stood parked at one end near the markings on the asphalt of a yellow circle with a large white *H* in the center. The helicopter set down in the middle of the circle, Retno slid the door open,

Will grabbed his bag and they ran out under the wash of the turning blades to the waiting airplane.

Nothing was said as they crossed to the transport airplane. One would not have been able to hear even if words were said. The hot breeze of the twin engines washed over them with the pungent smell of burned kerosene. The tail of the aircraft was down and an airman helped Will with his bag. He noticed that Retno refused help with her bag. They entered the dark hole of the cargo airplane and sat down in the web seats. Before Will even had his seat belt tightened, the cargo ramp came up and the aircraft started to taxi.

The airplane was cleared for takeoff and its nose was soon pointed up in a steep climb out of the airbase. In a short while, the aircraft leveled off and turned to the west.

Will looked out the rectangular window just behind his head and soon saw the blue waters of the Malacca Strait. As they left Malaysia, the aircraft passed over a massive container port with containers lined up, stacked on top of each other like bricks in a wall. Nearby, on the water and at the wharf, container ships were lined up in a straight row with a variety of colors of containers on their decks.

The water crossing was little more than seventy miles until they were back over the land of Sumatra. The journey to Pekanbaru's Sultan Syarif Kasim II Airport took less than an hour. The aircraft circled to the north of the airport and as it did Retno stood up and signaled Will to come to the crew chief's open hatch. She and he both had on the headsets with microphones.

"Look to the north." She pointed to a valley north of the city where the ground gave the appearance of a child's game of connecting the dots— dozens of sandy-looking spots connected by lines, many of which went to a central line like the arteries in a body.

"The oil fields." She pointed directly down as well. "And the Siak."

The Siak River curved and twisted as it headed down from the upper plain to the Malacca Strait. He watched it pass through the heart of the city of Pekanbaru.

The crew chief tapped them on the shoulder. They sat down and soon were on the ground.

Will walked out onto the asphalt with his bag to a waiting white sport utility vehicle. He stopped just short of the vehicle as the transport airplane raised its ramp, cycled up its engines and soon was back in the blue sky. He noticed something else parked on the tarmac.

"Was that theirs?" Will pointed to a white Sikorsky S-92 executive helicopter with the markings of Chevron Pacific.

"Yes."

"Can we speak to the pilot?"

"It is set up for tomorrow morning." Retno was staying one step ahead of him. "Let's go to the hotel."

The two met in the lobby of the Grand Central Hotel after checking into their rooms. Retno had suggested they eat at a place she knew well and they took a short taxi ride to a building that straddled the bank of the Siak River. It was near the base of a modern, cable-stayed bridge.

"You must try the fried baung fish." Retno seemed to be taking on the Indonesian tour guide role with relish. She wore her head covered, with slacks and sandals. She placed her small black backpack, which she had started carrying after their arrival in Sumatra, near her feet. "Pondok Tanah Longsor. I always eat here when I come to Pekanbaru."

The restaurant seemed more like a barge that had gotten washed ashore on the bank of the Siak during a monsoon or earthquake. It was a simple affair with plastic dishes, plastic cups, and metal bowls of rice. Mostly men sat at the tables, some eating and some smoking their cigarettes. Four women sat at one table with their heads covered by their hijabs.

"The Siak is a deep river. It cuts through the heart of Sumatra." She sat across from Will, staring at him with her deep, dark eyes. "The Japanese occupied this city during the war. They tried to build a railroad from here to the Strait. Most of their workers were British prisoners of war and Javanese. Over fifty thousand died."

"This climate can be deadly." Will thought of Chuck Hedges's chances of survival.

"Is this what you expected?" She moved closer to him.

"Of Indonesia?" Will drew out the conversation.

"Yes, of us."

"I didn't expect this much beauty."

She turned her eyes down, looking at the table and her tea.

"You must see the mosque." She was acting the tour guide again. "An-Nur has been called the Taj Mahal of Indonesia."

"I would prefer to see the helicopter pilot that last flew the Chevron team."

She looked up at him with a quick serious glance. It was as if a light switch had been turned off.

"That is set up for tomorrow morning."

"Can he take us to where they were last before leaving?"

"I assume so. The man from Chevron will be there as well."

Will looked out at the river.

"The earthquake was an eight point eight." She stared at the river as well. "The banks in several places caved in and dammed the river in the highlands until the waters built up and broke through. A magnitude eight earthquake has the same destructive force as more than fifty million tons of TNT."

"What did they see here?"

"It became still, then the water fell several feet." She paused. "You know that they call this the black river. It's choking itself to death. The peat soil upstream robs it of oxygen."

"And this history is what caused oil to be found."

"Yes. The highlands are rich in oil."

"What do you do?" Will struck hard and fast with his pointed question.

"I don't understand."

"You carry a semiautomatic. You are not a tour guide." Will pressed the point. She moved the small backpack like a child who had been discovered stealing candy.

"I'm here to help you learn what you can for your people." She shied away from the question.

Retno drove their Yukon through the gate at the airport and pulled up near a hangar with a large CP logo above the open doors. She had become very quiet since Will had confronted her. Just in front of the hangar was the white helicopter and, inside and in sight, was a Gulfstream G280 passenger jet. This was also white with the striping and colors of the helicopter. It was much smaller than the missing aircraft. A man was standing next to the nose of the Gulfstream with another who was dressed in a blue flight suit. The one in the flight suit was dark skinned, with jet black hair and a mustache, while the other was white, perhaps in his thirties, with short brown hair, dark shorts, socks over the calves of his legs, white shoes, and wore a white shirt with epaulet on the shoulders like a professional pilot.

"Hello!" Retno opened her door, as did Will on the other side, and left the Yukon parked in front of both the helicopter and hangar.

"Ms. Karims?" The one wearing shorts walked over to meet her halfway. In the two words spoken, Will picked up on what was clearly a British accent.

"Yes, this is Mr. Parker from the States."

"Welcome to Pekanbaru. I'm Michael Hancock. Head of flight operations for Chevron Pacific in Sumatra." He turned to the man next to him who had joined the group. "This is Iskandar Muda. Our helicopter pilot."

"William Parker." Will studied the helicopter pilot, who was much shorter.

"Young Alexander?"

"You know the meaning of my name?" The helicopter pilot smiled.

Both Hancock and Karims were puzzled.

"Are you a descendant of the sultan?" The pilot's name was the equivalent of a child in the United States being named George Washington or Abraham Lincoln. But in the United States the name would have a surname, such as George Washington Carver. Muda didn't mention a surname.

"I am told so. One of many."

The Sultan Iskandar Muda ruled Sumatra in the 1600s. His galleys sailed from Aceh, conquering all armies within hundreds of miles, including the Portuguese who had their own army on the nearby island of Malaysia.

"Where are you from, Iskandar? Where were you raised?"

"Banda Aceh."

"You had losses?" Will didn't need to preface the question. Like New Orleans after Katrina, the city knew of only one hurricane. The 2004 earthquake was similar. All with connections to the city at the top of the island of Sumatra were touched by the destruction.

"Yes, my parents."

"Sorry." Will paused before making the next inquiry.

"So, what happened, Iskandar?"

"Would you like to go into our office in the hangar for some tea?" Hancock interrupted and pointed the way.

The hangar office was like so many Will was familiar with. The desk was metal, a small table sat in front of it surrounded by four metal chairs. Hancock had laid out several white plastic coffee cups with a teapot and the milk and sugar. The wall of the office had an oversize map of the Indonesian islands, a scheduling board marked with aircraft maintenance dates and several clipboards hung out for use.

"I picked them up near the northern field and brought them here." Iskandar held the tea with both hands. He didn't wear any rings or jewelry. He never took a sip from the tea. He was using the cup to hold his hands in place. He didn't look at Will, but stared at the map on the wall. He paused before speaking again. "Just brought them here."

Will noticed the slightest quiver in his hands.

"Lloyds of London and Gulfstream have been here. MOT was just the starting point," Hancock added. "You lose a $65 million aircraft and everyone wants some answers."

"But they haven't gotten any." Will's comment was both a statement and a question.

"Only that it dropped from the sky." Again, Hancock spoke.

Retno sat there, quiet, taking it all in.

"Where did it drop off radar?" Will continued to ask the questions that had been asked and answered many times before.

Hancock stood up and walked around his desk to the map.

"Here." He pointed to a small circle just off the coast of Sumatra on the Malacca Strait side of the island. It had been drawn with a black magic marker as a reference point for the many inquiries.

Will walked over to the map and studied it.

"Its last direction?"

"South-southeast."

Will continued looking at the map.

"No sign on the bottom. They ran soundings for a hundred-mile arc." Hancock waved his hand over the Strait.

"How many islands in Indonesia?" Will knew the answer.

"Over eighteen thousand." Hancock pointed along the Sumatra coast. "But not that many in the Strait. Plenty of jungle though."

"What do you think happened?" Will looked at both men.

"The pilots were good. Well trained. Each had over ten thousand hours flying, and many hours in that aircraft." Hancock was speaking like he was defending his program. And he was. The loss of one of Chevron's mainline aircraft with one of its primary engineers did not fare well back in the States.

"And?"

"Pressure problem. Like what killed Payne Stewart." Hancock floated his theory. The golfer's Learjet lost its oxygen supply, causing the pilots and passenger to fall into a deep sleep. The aircraft flew for several more hours until it ran out of gas and crashed in a South Dakota field, killing all onboard.

"No." Will dismissed the theory. "Last altitude wasn't high enough and probably not on autopilot." The airplane was climbing out of Pekanbaru and just crossing over the water when it disappeared.

"What did you see, Iskandar?"

"We came in and the jet was ready for takeoff. Its engines were running. The ground crew had pulled off. A steward was standing at the door. My passengers wanted to leave quickly so they hopped off my helicopter, got onboard the jet, and were gone."

"Did you talk directly to the jet?" Will's days as a district attorney had his mind working the facts.

"No, I don't think so."

The man continued to grip the cup like a vise.

"So how about flying the route?" Will put his cup down.

"Happy to. Chevron is ready to help the families any way they can." Hancock stood up from the table. "First thing in the morning?"

"Yes."

"Wheels up at eight?" Hancock looked at Iskandar as well to confirm the trip.

Once the two returned to the Grand Hotel, Will went straight to his room. He pulled out the computer and opened it up. The Agency's laptop had a special feature. It confirmed what he had thought. Russian hackers would have tried for a month to break into it and not succeed. But this computer did something else. It videoed the person attempting to open it.

A young man with a military haircut fumbled with the computer. Will watched him and studied his actions. It was the same man who had followed him out of the drugstore in Kuala Lumpur. Margie was not the only one following Will. The man made a call on his cell phone. The computer recorded the voices. He was speaking in Malay.

"It's a small computer." He studied it as he took a stab at opening it.

"No markings."

In short order, he gave up. He did make another call. It was to a woman. She seemed to be his superior. He then closed the case and the video went dark.

Will booted up, using the password sequence and coding in his body, which quickly yielded a screenshot of Kim in Anchorage. The time difference covered several time zones, but it seemed clear that she was on station and available during this entire mission.

"I need you to find out what you can on Iskandar Muda. The helicopter pilot for Chevron. From Banda Aceh."

"What's going on?"

"Did you ever learn the five signs?"

"Of a liar?"

"He had four of the five."

"Our intel says there are signs that Sumatra is getting hot." Kim was vague in her comments.

"What do you mean?" Will's temper was rising. He was on the front lines for the Agency and it was still holding back on what they knew.

"Some grumblings underground."

"Grumblings."

"Close to time for you to get out of there." Kim pushed him to abandon the mission.

"They may be out there." Will wasn't ready to abandon the passengers of the Gulfstream. "If I leave the only guarantee is that they will be dead."

"If they aren't already?" Kim didn't seem worried about the men on the flight.

Will went out on the balcony to make another call. He used one of the cell phones he had bought in Kuala Lumpur and called the international number.

"Banda Aceh." He kept it short.

"Yes, sir."

Everything was pointing to the city on the northern tip of the island of Sumatra.

Chapter 27

The squid trawler entered the river passing the village of Lho Nga on Sumatra's western coast. Its engine chugged the boat up to the dock and the young boy jumped off with the lines. The older white Daihatsu Rugger was waiting at the dock, with the driver standing outside the car's open door.

"Get those squid to market." Chaniago slapped the captain on his shoulder as he climbed over the rail and onto the dock. "As-Salaam-Alaikum!"

The captain returned the greeting as he carried a white Styrofoam container up to the railing and handed it to his son on the dock.

Chaniago walked quickly to the waiting vehicle with its engine running.

"Are they together?" He spoke to his senior lieutenant, who stored his AK-47 between the seats and climbed in behind the steering wheel.

"Yes, waiting at the camp."

They drove several miles by highway and several connecting dirt roads. Once they reached the village deep in the Ula Masen forest to the south of Banda Aceh, they began the walk up the trail, going deeper into the forest. Each was carrying his rifle as they walked the muddy path. Once they reached the encampment, several men turned away from the firepit that was located just below an overhanging rock and greeted their leader.

"As-Salaam-Alaikum!"

Chaniago didn't wait long to get down to business.

"We need to pick up the container tomorrow."

"The truck is at Kuala Tanjung and awaiting orders." The man held up his cell phone. "If there is any trouble, they are ready."

"Good, the shipment from Cipacing must be distributed as fast as possible. We have discussed who gets what." Chaniago knew the Java city of Cipacing well. On the island to the south, the merchants of Cipacing had manufactured guns for over a century. Its claim to fame was the manufacturing of some of the best air rifles in the world, and on that basis the government had tried to let them continue to manufacture arms. But it didn't take much to change their process from air rifles to automatic rifles. The AK-47 was an easy weapon to make. The automatic Kalashnikov of 1947 dominated the world as it was easy to make, durable, and reliable. Its thirty-round magazine put out rounds at a rate of 600 per minute if one could reload that fast. It could be buried in the bottom of a swamp, pulled out, loaded, and fired. Even then, it would fire its bullets at 600 rounds a minute without jamming.

"We have three containers. The first goes north, the second to Padang, and the third to the south. Each container has twenty thousand rifles and half a million rounds." Chaniago pointed to each man responsible for the distribution of the automatics. "With that, we need to capture the weapons from the military and police we overrun."

The army would descend out of the jungle and from the mountains. It would raise the holy flag and overcome any resistance. It would cover the land like the tsunami did in 2004.

"And the boys?" Chaniago looked for the two that he had left several days before. "They will be the first strike. It will take the eyes of our enemies off what we are doing."

"The boat is ready and will leave Lho Nga when you give the word." Chaniago's senior lieutenant again held up his cell phone.

It was like the squid trawler, but much older, worn and barely seaworthy. It didn't need to be very watertight. It would stay near the shore for its journey.

"The captain will be with them until they reach Pariaman. From there, they will take it in." Pariaman was south of Lho Nga on the western coast of Sumatra. It was another small fishing port. The boat would grab little attention as it sailed down the coast intermingling with the others that worked the waters off the western shore.

"Good, send them." With those words, the young followers would begin the war.

Chapter 28

"You Marine?"

The guard on the hut spoke the words in very broken English. He was a kid, at best fifteen, skinny with bony knees showing below dirty shorts, wearing some well-worn flip-flops. He used a piece of rope as the rifle sling for his AK-47. Chuck could have strangled the kid with one hand, but it would have done little good. More would converge on the hut, as if he stomped a fire-ant hill with his boot. Plus, the boy didn't understand mercy. He was likely an orphan whose belief that the Koran and Chaniago would tell him how to live was the only thing that kept him going. The food he saw, the cars, the Western living on what television he got a glimpse of in Banda Aceh, were a dream world he would never know. If he shot Chuck or the engineer or the stranger it would matter little. There would be no remorse.

"Yeah."

"A US Marine?" The boy acted like he was meeting a superman.

"Yeah."

"First to fight!" He held up his cell phone. It was some type of video game.

"On your phone?" Chuck pointed to the cell.

"No, no." The kid knew of the game but didn't seem to have the money to own it.

Chuck wanted to grab the phone and dial the numbers to anyone and anywhere. He knew that the kid would spray the hut with gunfire if he tried. Chuck gritted his teeth while the cell was so close.

"Tolago, Khaleed!" The boy was communicating in his broken English. Chuck realized that the other guard, an older boy, had another video game.

It must be that guard who stood the night watch.

He recalled the teenager who would fall asleep sitting at the opening to the hut with the glow of the game shining in. Khaleed made sense; when he glanced at the phone, an Arab with a large scimitar waved it at his enemies. Khaleed was the hero of the video game.

"Water?" he asked the boy.

The young guard hesitated. It was clear that the attempted escape had made them more on edge. If Chuck succeeded in another attempt, several others would pay the price.

"OK." He was nervous, looking out of the opening then turning back to those inside. He held up his hand with a gesture like "wait right here." Chuck wasn't going anywhere. They had supplemented the chain around his ankle with one around his neck.

The boy dashed out, and in less than a minute returned with several plastic bottles of water. Some still had their Malaysia Airlines labels. He handed two to Chuck and one to each of the other men.

The water was warm, but his head still screamed from the blow he had received. His jaw ached and some blood still oozed from the wound to his mouth. As he drank Chuck tasted the salt of the blood he was swallowing.

"Name?" Chuck pointed to the boy. It was like out of a scene from a black-and-white Tarzan movie of the thirties. "My name is Chuck. Yours?" It was important for Chuck to try to connect with his guards. Once hired by Chevron and assigned to overseas duty, he was sent to FASTC for hostage training. FASTC, or the Foreign Affairs Security Training Center, provided classes at its facility on a thousand acres at Fort Pickett, Virginia. He would cooperate with his captors as much as possible and try to get to know them. It would be harder for a captor to kill someone they had gotten to know. Or at least, that was his plan.

"Tobo." He smiled at the fact that this Marine would want to know his name.

The kid was somewhat older than Chuck's oldest son. He felt the pain of being with someone who reminded him of home.

"Tobo, water, thank you." He extended his hand from his chest in a small gesture to make the captor understand his appreciation.

"Where are you from?" There were too many words strung together for Tobo to understand.

A weak voice came from the back of the hut.

"Where are you from" was repeated by the stranger in the language of Acehnese.

"Banda Aceh!" the boy immediately answered.

Chuck smiled. The boy heard a call and left the hut.

"So, you speak the language."

"I tried to be friendly as well. My employer sent me to hostage training. It didn't work. They change them out all the time. As soon as you get friendly with one guard, he is gone."

"Phil?"

"Yeah."

"Who was your employer?"

"Funny, I remember that. IBM."

Chapter 29

The trawler sailed with a list like the damaged goods that it was. If rough seas had come up, the waves would have crashed over the bow and sent it to the bottom. The metal on board was rusted and what paint covered the wheelhouse was bleached to a dusty red. It stayed close to the shore as it sailed south along the coast of Sumatra. The two in the wheelhouse could be seen, if one looked closely, by the glint of a dim light, but the boat carried no lights that marked it. If another boat had been cruising in the opposite direction, it could easily have slammed into the nearly invisible trawler.

"Bandar Udara." The boy pointed to the lights of a jet that was climbing out from its takeoff at the airport on the shore of western Sumatra. A rain was falling, but it was light and came from a layer of nimbostratus clouds that stretched out into the Indian Ocean. Several islands stood off the shoreline as they headed south and some had lights, but most of the lights came from the shoreline of the mainland of Sumatra. "The captain said we would see the airplanes."

The seaman had left them a few hours to the north. He pulled the boat near shore, where the waters were shallow, and slid off into them. It came up to his chest. They watched him wade ashore as they turned the boat back out to deeper waters. He had wished them well. He said he was proud of them. And that Chaniago would be proud as well. This was something that they had never heard. They were like men in the desert with a desperate thirst who had been given cool water. They would do anything asked of them.

"I see it." The other boy held the wheel tightly. The waters were deadly with small outcrops of rocks that jutted up from the seabed. They had to slide out from the shoreline every so often to avoid the rocks. He was guided by his cell phone, which provided a Google Earth picture of the waters as they headed south. If the vessel was intended to fish or carry cargo, it would never have been captained by so inexperienced a crew.

The boat was traveling above a massive subduction zone that followed the Great Sumatra fault just inland from the shoreline. If the two had any rational fear of death, they would have realized that they were sailing on top of one of the most volatile powder kegs of earth's structure. It had proven itself in the years before when the fault slipped and devastation raked the island.

"What's that?" The boy felt the vibration.

"Nothing." The one at the wheel dismissed it.

"There is the last point." The boy pointed at a dark spot off the bow with the barrel of his AK-47. The geologic fault hundreds of feet below was the least of their worries. A patrol boat could be just as deadly. "Not long now."

The boat continued to chug along.

Just to the side of the wheel, screwed into the woodwork, was a small box with what looked like a light switch. It had a piece of electric tape over it.

"We won't win." Khaleed the Scimitar was their hero. A figment of 1s and 0s gave them inspiration to fight the infidels.

"No." The boy at the wheel never looked up. His hands were white as he squeezed the wood, holding the trawler on course. His friend was speaking of the video game that they had played every day until Chaniago had asked them to take on this mission. It was an honor that their parents would have been proud of if they had lived. The two were orphans left to survive on their own after the earthquake leveled their village to the north. Chaniago had taken them in, with the other orphans, provided them food and taught them the ways of their faith in his *madrasa*. The school taught them that there was much more than this life.

The boat began to round the point. The lights of Padang lit up the cloud cover above, providing a yellow-green glowing tint. The moon came out for a brief moment and its light reflected over the water. The bay was still. The only sound was the chug-chug of the engine.

"There!" The boy at the wheel pointed to the large shapes on the docks that were illuminated by security lights. A large tanker was moored to a dock just short of the holding tanks.

Their boat continued to move quietly across the bay, past the jetty and into the harbor.

A brilliant light suddenly blinded them. The search light was aimed directly at the pilothouse. A loudspeaker shouted out warnings followed by a screaming siren.

"We need to move!" the boy screamed. The throttle was pushed open and the boat lurched forward. The two were standing next to each other when the first rounds of machine gun fire tore through the cabin. The one on guard was lifted up by the spray of bullets as they sliced through his chest. He lay on the deck, moaning until he became quiet.

"Allah help me!" He turned the boat toward a farm of large tanks just beyond a wharf and on the bank of the harbor. The bullets continued to splinter the wood around him. Then a horrific noise rose from the shore.

A much larger-caliber machine gun was firing at the craft. The fifty caliber bullets ripped the roof off the pilothouse. It sprayed the boat like a water hose from front to back, from the bow to the stern.

The boy got on his knees, holding the wheel as straight as possible toward the last sighting. He held the wooden helm with both hands, trying not to let go, as if by holding on to it he would be saved. Another wave of the large bullets started to make its way up the craft. This time the bullets were moving from stern to bow like a scythe cutting the boat down layer by layer.

The engine kept running and the boat kept moving forward. The boy pulled the tape off the switch. The splintering of the wood came closer. In another second, it would shred the wheel, the pedestal it was on, and the switch.

"Allah be praised!"

He flipped the switch.

For a split second, nothing happened. The boat moved forward, then the several tons of ammonium nitrate released its energy. A core of plastic explosives ignited, releasing heat, which instantly caused the fertilizer to violently decompose into nitrogen oxide. This instantaneous decomposition released an explosive force that vaporized the small boat.

The wave of energy of the explosion tore through the oil and gas storage tanks, causing an eruption that broke the windows in nearby Padang. The fire raged on and extended to the other storage tanks nearby. A mushroom cloud rose up from the refinery.

"Do we want to send out a message?" Chaniago's lieutenant held up his cell phone. The confirmation of the explosion came from one of their men on a mountaintop near Padang. "He can see the flames."

Chaniago smiled.

"Where are the containers?"

"I'm not sure."

Chaniago's smile turned to a torrent of screaming.

The guard at Kuala Tanjung looked at the paperwork again. It was poor quality, with the name of a shipping company he had not heard of before. The three trucks stood waiting at the gate with a container on each. The container port had only been open a short time. Its paint was fresh, its infrastructure was clean and new, and its guardhouse was well built.

The lead driver smiled at the guard. He pulled the AK-47, hidden under the towel next to his leg, closer. The machine gun had a round in the chamber and the safety was off.

The trucks were old, however, and they were only able to move slowly through the gears. If he made a run for it, the last truck had little chance of making it through the gate. His cell phone rang. He answered it and the screams on the other end broadcast without it even being on speaker.

The driver pointed to his phone as if to say "my boss is not happy."

The guard smiled back with an acknowledgment that they both had bosses who could be unreasonable. He waved his hand to signal the trucks to move forward.

The driver smiled, lifted his hand from the towel and waved. He moved his hand to the stick shift and put the truck in gear. Its gears crunched as he forced the truck from neutral into first.

The truck stuttered and then shut off.

Frantically, he shifted back into neutral and turned the key. It fired up again and he shifted it back into first. The truck jumped forward as he lifted his foot off the clutch too quickly; however, it didn't shut off this time.

The gate had several floodlights that lit up the scene. The driver was nearly blinded by the lights that were trained directly on him in the cab and the other two trucks following. He pulled down the visor, trying to see as he began to move forward. The guard had started to cross in front of the truck and the driver didn't initially see the man.

Again, he hit the brakes and the truck lurched to a stop as the guard nearly was struck by the front bumper. He signaled a sign of apology and the guard didn't seem to mind. It appeared that this wasn't the first time that a near miss had occurred at night with the bright, blinding lights. The guard moved on to the cement pillbox-like structure that served as the guardhouse. Inside and behind the thick, green bulletproof glass the driver could see movement of the several other guards on the shift.

The truck started to move forward and passed over the strips used to slow down the vehicles. He moved out, past the gate and onto the paved highway. He was to turn right and to the north while the other two trucks were to turn left.

The driver looked at his phone. With the guard's attention, he hadn't answered the call and started to redial Chaniago.

The siren screamed as he began to dial. In his rearview mirror, he saw the area around the gate come alive as if a nest of hornets had been struck with a stick. The pang-pang sound of bullets as they passed through his container filled the air. The driver shifted up a gear and pressed the gas. The truck picked up speed. When he was separated by some distance, he looked into his rearview mirror.

The second truck had made it through the gate, turned to the south, and was moving away into the darkness. The spark of bullets ricocheting off that container lit up the scene like fireworks thrown up into the air.

The third truck was still, stopped just outside the gate. Its cab was dark. He could see the bright metal where the bullets had passed through the door's paint and left little circles. The glass of the truck was shattered.

The driver's eyes welled up with tears as he cussed the men at the gate. He wanted to stop, grab his weapon, and run back to the gate firing as he ran. His younger brother was the driver of the last truck. He had told him to take the last truck as it stood the best chance of being safe. The blood, if shed, would be of the first driver, not the last. But his cargo was too important.

The truck moved to the north to the meeting place. He followed the paved two-lane highway as it turned to the west and parallel to a railroad line. The driver looked for a man with a motorcycle stopped at the Ji Access Road. He was standing there in the dark with his light on. As the driver's truck approached, the man hopped on his scooter and waved for the truck to follow him. They turned onto the access road, crossed the railroad tracks and headed north into groves of palm trees.

The man led the way through several back roads, always heading north, and climbing several hills. The truck strained as it climbed the dirt road, but the road was dry. They had the good fortune of the lack of rain for a few days before the pick-up. After moving along the back roads for hours the sun started to light up the sky.

The driver was tired, scared, and the memory of the blacked-out cab of his brother's truck piled up in his mind. Finally, they came across several smaller trucks parked in a circle in an opening at a crossroads. He pulled up the truck and climbed down. The sun now had lit up the day and he walked around his truck to survey the damage. The other men all were walking past the container and cab. Several bullets had struck the cab on the passenger's side. The men slapped him on the back as if he had just scored the winning goal for the soccer team.

"Yeah, they tried," he told the others. He wasn't in the mood to brag.

The motorcycle driver seemed the senior man of rank. He broke the seal on the container. The men acted like it was Christmas morning as they pulled the new, polished weapons out of the crates. Boxes of 7.62 rounds were thrown into their trucks along with the rifles.

"These will go to our squads across the north!"

"Yes." No one asked him about his brother. That truck was meant to head in the other direction so it was not missed. At least, not missed by these men.

Chapter 30

"We should get him out of there." Kim rarely was this assertive in her conversations with Langley. The video conference had several parties on the line. Besides Langley, and Kim in Anchorage, the CIA officer in Kuala Lumpur seemed strained by lack of sleep. The attack on Padang had changed the circumstances. "He's there under his own name, no cover, and if the JAD were to capture him it would be deadly."

The chairman of the meeting was the deputy director.

"How important is his mission?" The director weighed the risks.

"Very." Another man Kim did not recognize spoke up. At Langley, a number of people were at the conference table.

"Why?"

"Sir, we need to go offline on that. Need to know." The other man used the spy agency trump card. The meeting was top secret but the information could be restricted even further by letting only those who needed to know participate.

"What do we know of Chaniago and the JAD?"

"He is a battle-hardened terrorist who fought us in Syria." The same man spoke to the meeting. "He and JAD want to establish a caliphate in Sumatra."

"Is that possible?"

"The island is over 97 percent Muslim. The terrorists in the region come from Banda Aceh. Yes sir, it is possible."

"Will the Indonesian Army permit it?"

"They will fight it, but you are talking about a long, well-waged guerilla war that will put a choke hold on the Malacca Strait."

"Damn." The deputy turned back to the question. "So, do we pull him?"

"Not sure if he would come out anyway." The other voice Kim did recognize. It was James Scott.

"What do you mean?" The deputy director acknowledged the comment.

"He doesn't care about orders. If he thinks what he is doing is right, he'll stay." Scott's tone was very matter of fact, as if he was a chemist stating the formula for some chemical mixture.

"And what is right, Mr. Scott?"

"He's had a visitor out there. The widow of the Marine who was lost on the Gulfstream." Scott seemed to know more than Kim.

So, they are keeping an eye on my man, my mission.

She understood the need for secrecy and the multiple layers of a mission, but still was perturbed that there were things happening that she was not in the loop on.

Kim graduated with highest honors and was selected to present her paper on the region. She didn't land that achievement by accepting being one in the crowd. But she did have enough sense to keep her mouth shut.

"So, what do we do, Mr. Scott? This is your man." The deputy waited for an answer.

"Leave him alone." Scott paused a second. "Better yet, order him to come out."

"What?"

"Yes. Order him out."

Kim knew what Scott was getting at.

Chapter 31

"How does it handle?" Will watched as Iskandar moved the stick on the Sikorsky after their takeoff from Pekanbaru. The man's hand still had a noticeable tremble despite being on the controls of the helicopter. It was odd. Will knew that a pilot who was experienced was calm when at the controls, never rattled.

"Good."

"Mind if I try it?" Will put his hand on the stick.

"You fly?"

"Yep."

"Helicopter time?"

"Yep."

"OK."

Will felt the energy of the aircraft pass through the stick into his hand. One was on the stick and the other was on the collective pitch control. He banked the bird to the left and right to gain the feel of the response. The machine had more power than it ever needed for the few passengers it carried. Retno was in the back with Hancock. Will glanced to the rear and saw Retno's hands tightly clenched on the arms of her seat. He smiled at her.

"Heading should be three-two-o." Iskandar's voice came through the headset.

"Three hundred twenty degrees. Check." Will looked at the compass. They were heading north. He glanced out the side window, seeing the oil derrick pumps pass below. They were no more than five hundred feet off the ground. The sucker rod pumps dotted the landscape in no particular pattern that made sense. They moved up and down, pulling the crude oil out of the wells and up to the surface. The derricks covered the landscape as far to the right and left as Will could see. The pool of oil must have been the size of an underground sea with its dimensions roughly measured by the parameters of the derricks on the surface. It seemed to go for miles both up and down the valley.

A series of small hills were on their starboard side as they continued to head north. The foothills were covered with palm plantations. Smoke rose from the other side of the hills.

"Burning?" Will spoke.

"Palm plantations. Clearing the land. Palm oil is the other gold from Sumatra." Retno's voice came through the headset. "It is used in everything. Infant formula, shampoo, toothpaste, you name it."

"We go just above that next rise." Iskandar pointed to a series of hills just beyond the nose of the helicopter.

Will pulled up on the control and the aircraft rose. The sound of the turbines was to the rear. As an executive helicopter, it was well insulated. Between the insulation and the headsets only a hum could be heard. A forest of palm trees covered the hill that they passed over. Will saw several workers below and watched as they reacted to the noise of the visitor. They glanced up and turned back to their work. It was as if they had seen the helicopter pass over many times.

The other side of the hills led to a small valley that was longer than it was wide. It stretched to the north beyond their sight.

"Here?" Will pointed to a grassy field just below.

"Yeah."

Will circled the field, got a sense of the wind as it moved the grass below, turned into the wind and gently let the helicopter down. The Sikorsky's wheels touched the ground. The engines wound down as Will stepped out onto the knee-high grass. The others joined him at the nose.

"So, they came from here?"

"Yes, sir."

"How long from when you dropped them off to when you picked them up?"

"Several days."

"OK." Will knelt down and felt the grass. "Let's go."

The Sikorsky lifted off under Iskandar's control. He tilted the aircraft to the south and they followed a path farther to the west. The helicopter passed over the ridge of the hills that outlined the valley on the other side of the Minas oil fields.

The journey would be short.

"What's that?" Will pointed to something he saw on the western side of the valley.

"Just smoke, more burning." Iskandar spoke through the headset.

"No, that's not smoke." Will put his hand on the controls. "Mind if we take a look?"

Iskandar looked back at Hancock as he released the control. Will saw from the corner of his eye that Hancock had nodded his head in the affirmative.

The Sikorsky banked to the west and descended. It flew for some time until it reached the billowing smoke.

"That's not smoke." Will circled it as it rose up into the sky. The smell of rotten eggs filled the cabin as they passed through the cloud. "Steam."

"The fault is always alive." Retno spoke from behind.

The Great Sumatra fault was where the Indo-Australian plate collided with the Eurasian plate just west of the valley.

"All that energy." Will watched the cloud as it climbed up and dissipated into the sky.

"We can get our transport here in an hour and you can be taken directly to the airport." Retno meant the commercial airport and a flight back to the United States.

"I would like to go to Banda Aceh." Will was standing next to the Yukon.

"Why?" Retno asked.

"Always wanted to see the city that Marco Polo passed through." He had his history correct. Eight hundred years ago the explorer visited the port on his way to the east.

"But," Retno hesitated. "There has been an attack in Padang."

"I know." Will's laptop had kept him updated on the situation. He was also aware of the intercepted arms shipment.

"We don't feel comfortable with a visitor at these times."

He wasn't clear as to who the "we" was.

"You don't need to escort me."

"We could ask you to leave," Retno asserted. "For your own safety."

He didn't think his safety was the greatest concern of her or her bosses.

"Not good press." Will played the media card. The representative of the victims of a downed aircraft being sent home would not play well with many of the companies that sold Indonesia the aircraft on the airfield in Kuala Lumpur. Likewise, that decision would make Chevron look bad, and it still had a relationship with the government that meant billions in revenue.

"OK, we will get you there, but it is dangerous."

"I understand."

The CASA CN-235 twin transport flew north over Sumatra. It followed the eastern edge of the island and Will stood at the window looking out over the Malacca Strait. The shipping lanes were having a busy day. The waters looked like a child infected with measles. The dots covered the waterway from shore to shore.

The aircraft reached the northwestern tip of Sumatra and headed out to sea north of the city. It circled over the waters of the Andaman Sea, then headed back toward the land and the airport.

"Over a hundred thousand killed." Retno joined him at the window as he looked out at the destruction. "A wave over a hundred feet high and traveling faster than a jet came out of the sea. It was morning. The day after Christmas. The few Christians were getting ready for church."

"The '64 Alaskan earthquake happened on Good Friday." Will interjected a history lesson on the irony that both earthquakes occurred on religious holidays.

"Sorry?"

"It was nine point two." Will held on to the rigging of the aircraft as the airplane banked again. "The ground was raised thirty feet in some places."

"Some say this one was nine point two as well. Some registered it as being in the eights, but it was equal to more than a thousand of the atomic bombs dropped on Hiroshima." Retno pointed to something on the outskirts of the city. "That's a ship that was pushed inland. They call it the generator ship."

A large boxy vessel stood in the middle of rows of houses, many of which had gaping holes in their roofs.

"Do you know what the name means?"

"Banda Aceh?" Will asked. "Yes, the porch of Mecca."

"All the true believers from the east came through here on their *hajj* pilgrimages to the Holy Land. Millions from Southeast Asia stopped here before heading west over the centuries." Retno spoke like a humble follower of her faith.

"And now who comes?"

"We are still bringing the systems online." Retno started to sit down in preparation for the landing. The aircraft banked sharply as it dropped in altitude. With the turn of the airplane they looked out the windows to see a closer view of the injured city. "The cell phones are back up but the service has not been reliable. More towers are needed. The water is still a danger."

"Yes." Will sat down next to her. On the other side a Malaysian airman with a bulletproof jacket and a more modern AKM automatic rifle sat in silence. His AKM was the next version of the AK-47, with a collapsible stock, several rust-colored Bakelite fiberglass and resin magazines taped together in such a way that an exhausted one could be instantly loaded into the weapon, and a simple iron sight. The rifle had a larger 7.62 or .30 Russian short round with the bright brass showing in the clips taped as backup to the loaded one. The man's jungle utilities didn't show a unit, which made Will think that he was probably not an airman.

"VAT 69?" Will asked Retno as he nodded with his head toward the guard.

"Sorry?"

He knew that she understood the question. And in her answer, she gave him the answer.

The tires squealed as the airplane struck the landing strip.

"The airport is named for our friend." Will stood up as they came to a stop on the military side of the airfield. He stopped at the ramp and looked out over the new apron and runway. "Sultan Iskandar Muda airport."

"Yes, it is," she acknowledged. The airport, rebuilt and modernized after the earthquake, carried the same name as their Chevron helicopter pilot.

Like in Pekanbaru, a black Yukon was waiting for them on the ramp. This one was accompanied by another Yukon with several armed guards standing by the open doors.

"Let's not linger." Retno pointed to the lead vehicle and they both climbed in. The vehicle took off with the chase car following. They traveled through the city, passing the ruins of destroyed neighborhoods one after another. Workers patched up many of the structures, trying to bring the city back to life.

The Yukon pulled to a gate with several armed guards behind a bunker-like pillbox. They stopped until the driver was cleared. The hotel's canopy was below the large letters of the Grand Arabia Hotel. A valet, dressed in red, met them and grabbed their bags.

"We'll meet at the rooftop. Perhaps this evening?" Retno stopped at the hotel desk.

"Yes."

Will checked into his suite. The Grand Arabia had been refurbished and rebuilt since the tsunami. The building had the appearance of a federal courthouse in America with a façade of marble, columns, and stone. The structure had a glass entrance that led into a lobby of marble, wood, and chandeliers. Will handed the valet a tip, waited for him to leave the room, opened one of his cell phones and then dialed the number. The voice on the other end was one that he had expected.

"The address?"

He opened up the laptop and studied the map of the city. A river ran through its heart. They were only a block or two away from the Park of Kings and just beyond that, the river.

"Got it." He put on a black baseball hat and sunglasses and went down the stairs to a side exit. The door took him to an alley. He passed the guards with a wave of his hand and crossed the side streets, passing the Park of Kings. On the other side of the gardens, he flagged down a Pidie taxi which took him across the river and then followed Jl Politeknik road along the river. Short of the address, he got out of the taxi. He kept moving, trying to not engage anyone or look directly at them. Scooters zipped past as he stayed to the side of the road. In less than a mile he came upon the brick-and-wood building with a tall peaked shingled roof. A mahogany door with an arched roof stood as the entrance.

A sign was posted next to the door. It had the commercial lettering of Indosat Ooredoo Cellular Project. Will knocked on the door.

"Hello," Kaili Stidham greeted him. She wore a hijab that covered much of her face.

"Yes."

"Come in."

Inside the door, the entranceway opened up to the interior of a villa with a swimming pool surrounded by two stories of rooms that looked into the inner court.

"Hey, Will." Enrico Hernandez was standing just inside with a HK semiautomatic rifle.

"So, cell tower repair crew?" Will liked the cover story.

"They are very happy we are here. Everyone likes their cell service, so no one asks questions." Kaili pulled her hijab down. "Not used to this yet."

"Watch out. They have the Wi-Ha Sharia police," Will warned. The greatest danger of their being in Banda Aceh was the risk of being detected as westerners. The city was covered by the religious police. A woman who violated the law, nay one of many, risked flogging. One woman received a hundred lashes for showing affection in public.

"The Gunny has schooled me on this. I'll behave!"

"That's the least of our worries."

A slam of a door turned Will's attention to just beyond the small interior swimming pool.

"You found us!" Gunny Moncrief had on a shirt brightly colored with flowers of red and yellow. The shirt was pulled out over a pair of cargo style khaki-colored pants.

"No problem getting here?" Will walked through the interior courtyard and inspected the place.

"None whatsoever. Our friend made it happen." Gunny pointed to several FedEx boxes stacked up. A friend from the past had helped the team get into Sumatra. The FedEx pilot's son had been saved by Will from a cartel in the Baja. He had offered to help whenever he could. The FedEx system carried the team and its equipment into Modea, Sumatra. No one knew they were there, including Langley.

"Do you have something for me?" Will had felt naked without a gun for the past several days.

"Here." The Gunny pulled an HK VP40 semiautomatic pistol from behind his shirt.

"Thanks."

"Got some extra clips upstairs in our op room."

They headed up a flight of mahogany stairs to a second-floor walkway that connected the rooms like a motel. The third door down had a yellow sign that said in bold black letters Keep Out.

"I want you to meet someone." The Gunny knocked on the door twice in a fashion that alerted the one inside that a friend was coming in. A man in his early twenties with glasses, short brown hair, and a pasty white complexion turned around from his chair at a panel of computer screens. He had a pistol on the desk in front of him and put it down when the Gunny appeared.

"Ben, here's who we are helping."

"Yes, sir." He had a boyish smile. Ben jumped up and stuck out his hand. "I have heard a lot about you."

"So?" Will was taken aback by the new member of the team.

"Ben's a loaner." The Gunny had a smile on his face like someone who had completed a crime and made off with the loot. "He's with IARPA. Got some new toys for us to try out."

"And?" Will stood there waiting for more information.

"Well, with our new best friends, some of the agencies have been more apt to help." Seemingly, the Gunny had parlayed the fact that this was an approved mission with the CIA to access resources not available before. One was IARPA, the spy world's version of DARPA. The Intelligence Advanced Research Projects Activity owned several projects that were beyond cutting edge. Both agencies worked on the development of support for the missions of the agencies they worked with. In the case of IARPA, its missions were all about spies.

"I know IARPA, but how did you get him here?"

"Seems they have something new they wanted to try and I told them I had the perfect field test environment." Moncrief stood behind the computer screens as Ben sat back down at the table. "Ben, show him what's going on."

"This is something we pulled up yesterday." He displayed a dark but visible image of a kid looking into a cell phone. The kid had an intense look on his face as if he was studying the phone with all his energy.

"So, what's this?"

"We mined the video game that is so popular here." Ben pulled up another screen and another one, each showing a player studying his cell phone. "They made it simple. They all like the same video game."

"You are saying that you have reversed their cell phones so that when they are playing the game you see them and everything they are doing?" Will realized the implications.

"Yes, sir." Ben pulled up several video screens, some in daylight and some at night, that showed players, of which nearly all were teenagers. "But the problem is that we have tons of these."

"So, you need to narrow it down?"

"Exactly." Ben looked up from his desk.

"Can you go back to a certain date?" Will asked. "A certain person?"

"No. It's not like a time machine." Ben stopped what he was doing. "But there is something that can help. There's a program we are working on called DIVA."

"What's that?"

"Deep Intermodal Video Analytics. It uses artificial intelligence to analyze video feeds for behavior."

"So, it can pick out a terrorist in a crowd?"

"That's the idea." Ben kept talking. "It looks for primitive activity like someone carrying a backpack."

"Or an automatic rifle?"

"Of course." Ben pulled up another screen. "I've got it tied into our security cameras as well. Anyone coming close to us is picked up and it identifies whether they are a threat."

"I see." Will watched as the camera somewhere on the road out front picked up a motorcyclist. It showed an analysis of his face, his clothing and his backpack as he flew by. "Back to the calls."

"Yes, sir."

"Would it help to have a starting point? A lead?" Will had an idea.

"Absolutely." Ben had a cup of coffee that he would occasionally sip from. The aroma filled the room with the sweet smell of caffeine.

"Like the coffee?"

"It's the best."

"You are in the mecca of Sumatra coffee." Will knew that a caffeine lover was within miles of some of the best coffee plantations in the world.

"Yep, worth the trip."

"I have a name. Can you get his cell from that?"

"If you narrow it down to where he might be using it."

"Sure."

Will took a piece of notebook paper, wrote down the name and handed it to the tech.

"Find this guy and I'll buy you a lifetime supply of your Sumatra special." Ben smiled.

"Right on it."

Chapter 32

The Gunny had a small Toyota four-wheel-drive truck in the alley behind the villa they were using. It was white and had a logo in black, yellow, red, and white on the doors that said Indosat Ooredoo. The cell provider covered much of northern Indonesia.

"Hop in. I'll take you back."

Will got in the truck and moved several bulletproof vests to the floor.

"Not too close." Will didn't want the truck anywhere near the Arabia.

"Got it." The Gunny had an Apple cell phone on the dashboard with a Google map pulled up.

They pulled out of the alleyway and followed the road next to the river, crossed over, and the Gunny pulled up next to a green tree-lined park. A sign said Park of Kings in Arabic script.

"You got a backup rally point?" Will always went back to Patton's comment on war—once the shooting begins all plans go to hell.

"FedEx has a station at the airport. I'll send you the coordinates."

"Good." Will trusted his life to the Gunny. He always had. "Coffee shop on the other side. Not too far from the hotel."

"Yep."

Will hopped out of the truck and crossed over into the park. Children were playing on the grass as their mothers looked on. They were born after the great earthquake and only knew the Banda Aceh of the present day with buildings still under repair. None of the ones he saw were exempt from the death of that storm.

And none are exempt from the future.

Will knew that the ground underneath their feet was just as much a risk now as the day before the earthquake. They lived on the edge. The city was within miles of forces that could eliminate every child within his sight.

Will bought a coffee like the tech from the coffee shop. He used it as an opportunity to practice his Acehnese.

"Similar to Vietnam," he said to himself after he left the shop and headed through the back streets to the hotel. He was speaking of the similarity of the languages. It made sense that either the past people of Sumatra went north to Vietnam or the Vietnamese came south in the hundreds of years before.

He stopped on the corner across from the hotel and watched, standing behind the entrance to an abandoned building. The guards were at the front. They seemed bored and not too alert. What he saw at the entrance did bother him. Retno was in front of the glass doors, walking back and forth as if her child was not on the bus coming back from school. She continued to pace.

Will waited and watched.

Finally, after some time, she headed in.

He crossed the road, waved to the guard and walked past the guardhouse.

"Hai rakan lon!" He smiled as he walked past. His walking in so matter-of-factly caused them to believe that nothing was unusual.

"Peue haba?"

"Haba get," the guard responded.

Will took the elevator to his room, checked his computer, and saw the same thing he had seen in Pekanbaru. The man had entered the room, opened the computer, went through his bag and closet, played with the computer, then gave up. He spoke to another on his cell and then left.

Will locked the room and went upstairs to the deck patio.

"Where have you been?" Retno was sweating.

"Went to try some coffee."

"They have coffee here."

"But not native. I wanted to try the local."

"There have been several attacks. You need to leave the country now." Retno didn't sit down.

"Attacks?"

"Our refinery on the coast was hit by a suicide bombing." She told him what was on CNN but didn't mention the stolen containers. Will had been given an update on all this by his team back at the villa.

"Do you think it's related to our airplane?"

"No. Your airplane just crashed. Somewhere in the sea." Retno sounded like she wanted this to end. "We can have an airplane here first thing in the morning."

"OK." Will wasn't ready to fight her. At least, not now.

"What about dinner?" She changed the subject. "There is a place just on the other side of the river."

"Sounds good."

"In an hour?"

Chapter 33

"Where?" Chaniago's cell phone was glued to his ear. He was standing outside his Daihatsu parked under a tin roofed carport. "We need to move now."

Chaniago had relocated to a cinder block and thatched roof cabin near Lhoknga Beach and close to the ocean on the west side of the city. The cabin was built on stilts with wooden walkways that led into a series of rooms. It served as his headquarters when he needed to be near the city. Palm trees had been allowed to grow up through the boarded floors and the breeze of the water helped keep it cool. Thatched bamboo walls separated the rooms. The most important thing, however, was that it was tucked away, in the edge of the jungle not far from the Trans-Sumatra highway that followed the coastline on the western side of the island. The highway also connected him with Lho Nga. It provided a place that allowed a quick getaway to the south and then into the mountains or out to sea.

A girl, barely a teenager, stood nearby and held a metal cup of chai for the leader. Her face was covered by her niqab, except for the deep chocolate-brown eyes. The scarf was a drab gray that matched the burqa that covered most of her body. Her bare feet stuck out from underneath the dress. She dressed so as to not tempt men.

"You need go back and get the others." His order caused her to scurry away with the cup of tea.

The men soon joined him.

"A VAT 69 agent is in the city." He sat on the wooden floor looking at his telephone. "The Grand Arabia."

The others nodded their heads anticipating the next orders.

"They are going out to eat at this restaurant." He held up his phone. It was clear that they had a source within the hotel.

Chaniago wanted an agent of VAT 69 as much as they wanted him. The Very Able Troopers, which the initials stood for, were the special forces unit that conducted counterterrorism operations. Those who wore the sand-colored berets were well trained, hardened military men who had killed more of Chaniago's soldiers than any other force in Indonesia.

"I want the VAT alive."

Two black Daihatsu trucks pulled out of the road behind his headquarters heading north. Each truck carried three men armed with machine guns and several RPGs.

"You will like this place." Retno sat in the front seat of the Yukon with Will behind the driver. They had the driver, and one other in the back. The men were dressed in all black, with shoulder holsters for their pistols; the other VAT passenger in the back had his AKM with the butt against his leg and a brown Bakelite magazine in the weapon.

"What is it?" Will watched the driver weave through the traffic and cross over the Aceh River bridge. One would not know the city had survived a tsunami by the traffic. Motor scooters weaved back and forth across the lanes causing the driver to brake and speed up.

"Karibia. Best seafood in town."

"Sounds like you know the food here." Will held on to the handle of the door as the Yukon shifted lanes. He sat up, adjusting the HK semiautomatic pistol tucked in its holster behind his back and below his flowered shirt.

"Your last meal in Indonesia should be a good one."

"One to remember."

"Yes, so you can come back." She paused. "In better times."

There was an air of unrest in the city. Will looked out on the street and noticed two men walking the sidewalk carrying short bamboo canes tucked under their arms.

"The religious police walk the streets. I understand if a woman is caught with a married man, she can receive a hundred lashes?" Will watched the streets and saw some young women, their shapes undetectable in the covers they wore, move out into the street when the men with canes passed.

"Yes, both were punished. They were beaten and then dumped into sewage." Retno kept looking forward as she spoke. "It is here." She pointed to a side street that was several blocks to the east of the river.

"You approve?" Will asked.

"No, but Banda Aceh is its own world."

"And Sumatra?" Will asked. The remainder of the island was heavily Muslim. It wasn't clear if all of the island was as extreme as the northern tip.

"Here we are." Retno didn't answer the question.

The Yukon pulled up to an outdoor restaurant that had a line of tables under a thatched roof. On the far inside, the counter had a display of the dishes one could order. The posted menu was a brightly colored array of photographs of the different meals. Only a few sat at the tables, and one woman stood at the counter apparently ordering her meal.

Retno told the driver to park nearby.

"You can stay with the truck," she told the armed man sitting next to Will.

"Let's go, Colonel." Retno opened the door and stepped out.

Will heard her slip of the tongue. It was clear that she knew more than she had said—and that she was more than she had said.

Will stepped out into the small side street and started to walk around the Yukon as it pulled away. Retno was waiting for him on the sidewalk.

A boom of thunder lifted the two off the ground.

Shards of glass and a whistle of wooden splinters ripped through the air. The heat singed Will as he lay, shaken, on the cement. His ears were ringing. Will pulled himself up on his knees and looked to where the Yukon had last been. Only a fragment of metal stood in the road and was engulfed in flames. Two shapes were visible in the flames. The crack of bullets igniting in the fire caused the zip of rounds flying in all directions. Will dropped down again and tried to crawl over to Retno.

She lay in a heap only a few feet away.

He saw two shapes come out of the smoke. She struggled, but the men lifted her up like a bag of lump coal and dragged her away.

Instantly, Will tried to reach for his pistol. He pulled the slide back to chamber a bullet. He looked up to aim. They were gone. They were gone in the fog of smoke and the sharp smell of gunpowder.

She was now a prisoner. They took the wrong one.

Chapter 34

"Hey, hey." The older guard prodded the stranger with the barrel of his rifle. He and two others had surrounded the man, who was slumped over with the small of his back against the post he was chained to. The hut still had some light even though it was the end of the day. The sun's rays barely made it through the cover of the jungle.

"Huh?"

Chuck watched the three as they undid the chain that held him.

"What are you doing with him?" Chuck shouted. The man was barely holding on to life, weighing no more than eighty or so pounds.

The guard came over and took a swing at Chuck's head with the butt of his rifle. Chuck dodged the blow. The stock bounced off the post as it made a loud thump and shook the roof. A square hit would have been a killing blow.

"Ma-eine!" It was clear that the order was for him to shut up. It was clear on his face that taking a swing at Chuck had been a mistake. Killing the Marine would have led to the guard's death as well. He lost his temper, but Chaniago would have made him pay.

Chuck sank back down, watching them as they dragged the man out of the hut. The stranger no longer had the energy to complain.

Both Chuck and his engineer listened as the men carried Phil off. Soon, it became quiet. A guard had been posted at the entrance.

The two sat there in the darkness.

In the distance, Chuck could hear the sound of an engine. The boat had returned and had come for the prisoner.

"They are taking him to the mainland." The engineer started to laugh. "This has to be good news. They are going to trade him, then trade us."

Chuck didn't respond. A trade would mean that they would have to acknowledge that the Gulfstream didn't crash because of a mechanical failure. It meant that any acknowledgment of them being alive would launch a resumed search. There was another reason to be taking the man to the mainland.

"We need to consider an escape." He whispered the words.

"Are you crazy!" The engineer barely held his voice down. "You heard what they said. Next time it will be both you and I."

"I don't like the feel of this." Chuck had a different sense of what was going on.

"Maybe they are going to release him." The engineer's optimism was his only hope.

"Don't think so." Chuck knew them better. They were stone-cold killers. A person who was going to be released wasn't dragged away. "We need to get out of here."

"Can't make it. And you can't leave me here if you go. If they don't capture you, they will take it out on me. And if they do grab you, they will kill us both."

"OK." The chain around Chuck's neck was tight and it rubbed. When he would fall asleep, the chain would jerk him wake as it squeezed his neck. He followed the chain with his hand to the post, then followed the post up. The pole was loose and barely fastened at the top. The guard's blow had loosened the post and pulled it away from the beam in the ceiling.

What if we got out? What if we hid in the jungle? Or made it to the other island?

The Japanese had a garrison on the island from the war. It might provide shelter. They might find water. And the few guards that they had as captors wouldn't find two escapees hidden in the jungle for some time. The undergrowth could hide a man for days.

Better than being led to the slaughter.

"Maybe we can get out of here and hide in the mountains." Chuck shared his thoughts with his cellmate.

"They will kill us." The engineer spit out the words.

"They may do that anyway."

Chapter 35

"So, you wanted to find Chaniago?" The man leaned over Retno as she lay hog-tied on her stomach on the wooden floor. The ropes cut into her wrists and ankles and were bound tightly around her neck. "I'm Chaniago, and you found me."

She let out a muffled scream against the gag in her mouth.

"So beautiful. I heard of you from your raid on Kuala Berang." Chaniago knew of the attack on the Myanmar Embassy and the following pursuit of the terrorist cell to the village of Kuala Berang. "My brothers of the Arakan Rohingya. You know how many of our brothers and sisters are murdered every day in Myanmar? Killed them all. The man never made it to prison."

She looked at him with a tilt of her neck. The rope would choke her so she had to lift up her head to relieve the pressure.

"You took him on a helicopter ride. Dropped him out over the Strait." Chaniago had his facts correct. The man who designed the attack on the Embassy and had been captured and injured, and when barely alive had been taken out over the waters and dropped from several thousand feet.

"You will want to do the same to me?" Chaniago laughed. "But not you. Maybe your friends after several more are killed by me." He had little to lose. He knew that they had him marked. She and VAT 69 were in Sumatra for one reason. They wanted to find Chaniago. The weapons shipment only made matters more immediate.

"Now, we are armed." He looked to his two men in the room. They stood there with their automatic weapons, dressed in black shirts and black shorts. The two would follow Chaniago to their death if necessary.

"We will overrun your police stations and then your military outposts." He spit out the words. "And the people will follow us. Soon, your precious

Strait will be shut off. Only those who pay will be allowed to pass." He would impose a toll that would affect half of the world's economies.

She twisted around, flipped over, then fell back again.

"I want you to witness something. You will see what we can do. The people are with us." He repeated himself. "Guard her well." He pointed to two men who lifted her by the ropes and dragged her into another room. "No harm to her yet."

"When the boat arrives." He looked at his cell. It didn't seem that the boat would take too long. "Then they will see and know who we are and what we do!"

Chapter 36

"Mr. Scott, this is Kim. Have you seen the report?"

Scott looked at his watch. He was just finishing up reading the *Washington Post*, which he had retrieved from his porch a short while before. In Washington, the sun was starting to come up.

"Anchorage?"

"Yes, sir."

He looked again at his watch and calculated the time. The officer seemed to care little about rest.

"Is this your first mission?"

"Yes, sir. Why do you ask?"

"Nothing. What do you have?"

"One of the VAT 69 people were kidnapped. And Parker was there at the time."

"Let me get to my computer." Several thoughts passed through his head as he headed upstairs to his laptop. Foremost, it must have been a well-planned raid for Will not to be able to stop it. And second, no matter the value of the VAT officer, they missed the gold. "I'll call you back."

He didn't really plan on returning the call.

Once on his computer, Scott studied the intelligence reports that had just come off the wire from Kuala Lumpur. Sumatra was going to hell. Its oil refinery had been attacked, but the boat carrying the bomb had been far enough off shore that the damage was able to be contained. A tanker had been sunk at the dock, which would delay shipments, and a farm of tanks had been destroyed, but the heart of the refinery was still intact. He was worried more about the second report of the arms shipment.

God, one container had over ten thousand guns and half a million rounds. And there were two!

"I could start a revolution with half that." And he had in South America years ago. What worried him the most, however, was that the population was overwhelmingly of the same religion.

"They'll start slaughtering the nonbelievers next." The minority Christians and Buddhists would be the targets. Islam was the only religion based upon a military mindset. The leader was a general of armies and had suffered his own injuries in the battles he fought. In the Battle of Uhud, Muhammad suffered a nearly fatal blow to his head. Violence was a part of the DNA of the religion.

"He hasn't gotten what we need yet." Scott opened up the email traffic between Parker and Anchorage. It was a tough game, but Will Parker was the best in one characteristic—survival.

"Let's see how this plays out." He closed his laptop. Scott wasn't going to call her back. In a few days, she would try again and he would ignore the call again.

Chapter 37

The banging on the door happened at well past midnight. Enrico grabbed his HK416 automatic rifle and checked the magazine. He pulled back on the bolt and saw the brass in the chamber. Enrico pulled on his bulletproof jacket over his olive tee shirt and went downstairs. Kaili and the technician had also heard the noise and were on the balcony looking down over the courtyard.

"What is it?" Kaili had on a 5.11 shirt, cargo pants, and boots. They all slept dressed and ready to go.

The Gunny was missing.

"Where is he?" Enrico whispered to Kaili from below.

"He's out."

This isn't the Gunny I know.

"OK, stay up there. Grab him and get out the back if you hear anything." One of two four-wheel-drive trucks were parked in the alley for just such a contingency. The other was parked in an alley a few blocks away. It was the backup to get out after an attack in case there was a firefight.

"Remember the rally point. Destroy the computers." As a Marine Enrico had been trained to step in when other leaders had fallen. More than one Medal of Honor was given out to the young corporal who stepped in when his commander and senior enlisted had been taken down in battle. "You got the phosphorus?"

"Yes, sir." The technician had to sleep with the gray grenade. Its scorching heat would cause a fire that would melt all the computers and take the entire villa down with it. He held it up for Enrico to see.

"Everyone stay still."

The walls on both sides of the door were made of cement blocks. If they were filled, bullets would be stopped, but if the cylinders were empty and the bullets of large enough calibers, they would tear through it like a knife through cheese. Nevertheless, he stood on the side of the door with the barrel aimed center of the door. If the person on the other side was foolish enough, several bursts from his automatic would cut them down.

"Hai rakan lon!" Enrico spoke in a calm voice, as if a homeowner had been awakened from his sleep by some pedestrian.

"It's me." The voice was Will Parker.

Enrico put his weapon safety back on and opened the door.

"Holy shit!" Will was covered in dust and his shirt had been torn on the sleeve. "OK?"

"Yeah. Where's the tech?"

"Upstairs. What happened?"

"You didn't hear the blast?"

Enrico hesitated. "I did! I thought it was another thunderstorm."

"Where's the Gunny?"

"I'm here." Gunny Moncrief stood at the bottom of the stairs.

"You look like you've been run over by an Amtrak." Will stood at the entrance while Enrico closed the door and locked it.

"Hard time sleeping. Sorry."

"The VAT 69 with me has been kidnapped. Can Ben bring up the videos?"

"A VAT officer? She's not going to make it with these bastards." The Gunny knew the lay of the land. It was said that if one of the JAD had been captured by VAT 69, he stood no better a chance than if one of VAT 69 had been captured by the JAD.

"Let's find her." Will leaped up the stairs to the tech's room. He stood over Ben as the technician pulled up several screens.

"I'll try with DIVA."

"Your program that can connect all of the available video?"

"Yep. What's the address?"

"It's called Karibia."

"OK, quick search. Got it." Ben pulled up several sources of video and a feed from a satellite on the CIA system. One of the other benefits of the operation and working with the Agency was access to the satellite that had been parked over Sumatra ever since the operation had started.

Ben pulled the video down and DIVA ran its analytical program. The two trucks came in view.

"Damn, what accuracy." The Gunny looked over the shoulder of Ben. The picture was as clear as a noonday photo even in the dark. The men with their AKs pulled the shape of a woman into a truck.

"They'll take her to the first stop before they move her again." Will knew that time was of the essence. "We need to get to her at the first stop." They all knew that the second move would make her disappear into Sumatra.

The video feed followed the trucks west to the beach area. The trucks stopped at a villa that was barely visible under the canopy of palm trees and vegetation.

Will watched as Ben switched over to the heat sensor projection. Several men were bent over a shape on the floor.

"OK, two trucks. Convoy there. Leave the tech here. Kaili, are you ready?" Will ran through the plan.

"What about VAT 69?" The Gunny asked the question.

"They'll get here fast, but it will be too late." The VAT team would be on aircraft as soon as the word hit the street and would come full force, but time would not be on their side. "Plus, no one knows we are here." The element of surprise would be in their favor.

"Let's go."

Both the Gunny and Enrico went out the back door and returned with the two Toyota trucks. Kaili climbed aboard the truck with the Gunny and Will got in with Enrico. They had loaded the trucks with HK416s with suppressors and dot sights, as well as their HK semiautomatic pistols. Will screwed a suppressor on his pistol, pulled back the slide, and let a bullet go into the chamber.

"OK, Ben, can you hear me?" Will had a cell phone in a holder on the dashboard with a Google Earth map. "We need the feed of information."

"No problem." There was some static on the line as the signal faded out and then returned, as if they had switched cell towers. "Got some movement."

"What?"

"Looks like some are leaving."

"Oh, shit." Will didn't like the odds.

"The shape on the floor is still there."

Chapter 38

The squid boat from the island to the north pulled into the river at Lho Nga. It moored at the same dock up stream near the shack on land. The two guards and Chaniago's lieutenant pulled the man over the boat's rail and onto the shore. With his foot missing, the two had to carry him.

"He stinks!" one of the guards, a younger one, complained.

"Next time, no foot cut off!" the other said in laughter. "He needs to walk."

"Shut up." The lieutenant barked at the two. "In here."

The hut's door was on an angle. Inside, the fishermen had stored several nets, ropes, and supplies.

"Chaniago? Chaniago?" The lieutenant spoke into his cell phone. There was static but a response came. "We are here."

The lieutenant had been one of the earliest followers of their leader. They had fought with ISIS in Syria and took pride in saying that they had killed many infidels.

"I'm on my way." Chaniago's voice could be heard through the phone.

The boys sat their prisoner down on the floor and went outside. The three were standing at the hut with their AK-47s, waiting for orders.

"What was Syria like?" the younger one asked. "What was Chaniago like in combat?"

"Not much to be said." The lieutenant didn't dwell on their time in the war. He would talk if it was dragged out of him.

"How long were you there?"

"I was there for a year. He has fought there for more than five."

The two acted as if they were talking about a celebrity. A holy warrior was, to them, a celebrity.

"Where were you?" The younger one stayed on the subject.

"Ar Raqqa. On the Euphrates. A beautiful city. We fought with the Jabhat Fatah al-Sham. Brave men." The lieutenant described a different city than the real one. "It followed the true teachings of Abu Bahr." The religious police, like the ones in Banda Aceh, enforced the followings to the full extent of the law. The only difference was that in Banda Aceh, the violators were caned until they bled through their white robes. In Raqqa some were crucified. The violators were nailed to crosses until they pled for their death. Executions occurred daily in the center of the city.

The first caliph and father-in-law of Muhammad took over the religion upon the death of the leader of Islam. Over the decades that followed, the Salafi movement grew stronger and more restrictive in their beliefs. They were united by their hatred for the oil sheiks of the Arabian Peninsula. But in the twists and turns of religion, it was some of the rebel oil Muslims that provided the money that kept the movement alive.

"We were a band. We fought for our fellow warriors. We would die for our fellow warriors." The lieutenant smiled with a distant look, as if remembering past glory days.

"But Raqqa is no more." The younger one regretted his comment as soon as it came out of his mouth. Raqqa had been pummeled by air strikes and the city was lost.

"You went on the Hajj?" The boy tried to change the subject.

"How did you know about that?" the lieutenant asked.

"Everyone knows the stories. You left the battlefield and went on the Hajj."

He was right. Both Chaniago and his lieutenant had left the war in Syria and traveled to Mecca for their pilgrimage.

"It was a blessing. They gave us the time off. We had to sneak through several borders and countries. They know of Chaniago and even the keepers of the holy Mecca would kill him if given the chance."

"How was it?"

"Thousands walk the path. Once done, you are blessed for eternity." He paused. "As long as you do not betray the path."

It meant that the lieutenant was more than a dedicated soldier. His place in eternity meant that he had to wage the war against the infidels. He would fight even if it meant the lives of him and these two boys.

"We are close to our own world. Chaniago will lead the way. We will have a caliphate here in our country that will be at the crossroads to Asia.

And you will be a part of it!" He slapped the younger one on the back. "If in this life, or the next, you will have an honored spot!"

"Yes, we will!" the boy cried out in jubilation.

The three cared no more about the man in the hut than if they had captured a dog with rabies.

Chapter 39

"Here. On the right." Will directed the lead truck to a cutoff near Lhoknga Beach on the mainland of Sumatra just south of Banda Aceh. The second truck followed as they went on a dirt road that led down to the water's edge. Several mountains surrounded the area, and to the north they went down to the beach. Palm trees that had been sheared off like pencils twisted until they broke surrounded both sides of the road. They passed a shack that had been flattened and only the roof remained on the ground. It was followed by another and then another. The huts near the water had been vaporized by the tsunami. It was a clear morning when the wave struck, Boxing Day, which followed Christmas. It was meant to be the day that those with good fortune would share with others. The wave didn't have such mercy. A quake had ruptured a nine-hundred-mile fault more than thirty miles below the surface of the water. It lasted for more than ten minutes.

"Tsunami. Took down everything." Will surveyed the land. "Bodies were thrown around like corks floating on a pool."

The destruction of the hundred-foot wave on Boxing Day had reduced the village from seven thousand to the few that had returned. Lhoknga Beach was a mecca of surfing for those few who traveled the world looking for the right waves in the most remote places they could find.

The jungle was returning. In the hills surrounding the beach, the rainforest had survived the wave. And the palm trees in the lowlands and scrub vegetation were turning the sand back into a green landscape.

"They are up in that mountain. Stop here." Will turned off the lights of the Toyota and the one behind followed suit. He closed the door quietly as the others did the same.

A few minutes later the lights of a truck came out of a notch between two hills. It followed the base of one hill to the east then disappeared around another one. Its lights reflected off the palm trees as it bounced up and down on the road. The lights moved frantically, as if the truck was speeding over the bumps in its hurry to run away.

"Don't think we missed them?" Enrico whispered the question to the others at the rear of the lead truck. He was watching the movement with a night vision light with his elbows braced on the side of the truck bed.

"One way to find out." Will twisted the suppressor on the end of his HK416 and chambered a bullet. "I'll lead."

The team crossed over the open area at a fast pace in single file. They followed the center of an old road that was rapidly being covered by new growth. At the end of the road, they came to another that had been used by the fleeing truck. The vehicle's wheels had scored the sand where it had run through the potholes.

Will stopped them as they crossed a highway. The lights of a small village were several hundred yards to the north and west of the highway. Lights illuminated the sky to the south and just beyond the range of hills.

"Cement factory." Will whispered to the others as he looked at his cell phone and the map of the area. It lay off the main western highway just beyond the valley of Lhoknga.

The hills to the east were dark. There was no sign of life in the knoll where the truck's lights had come from.

The team proceeded east for more than half a mile, and as they did the rainforest became thick with undergrowth. They found the rutted road that the truck had followed when coming out of the hills and moved slowly up it. At a bend in the road, Will held up his hand.

They stopped and spread out. The Gunny had the rear and turned back down the road. If another vehicle approached from that end, he would either signal the group or level it with his suppressed automatic.

Will moved silently up the road and slid off to one side. He used the night vision light with Enrico as they studied the small hut tucked into the forest. Two men stood near an open window looking down at something. A girl covered in her niqab left the room and crossed over to another small hut that had smoke coming from it.

"She's in there cooking." Will whispered to Enrico. He signaled him to pull back to the road. There, they gathered together.

"Here's the plan. Two are with Retno. If we hit them with a raid, they will finish her off." Will drew on the ground. The white sand of the road reflected the low light, so they could see as if a candle had been lit nearby.

"Kaili, you and I will go to the cooking shed. A girl is inside. We need to get her out and get her niqab. You will go into the room with this and be ready to put down the guards." He held out his HK pistol with its extended suppressor. "Can you do this?"

The time had come for the test. Kaili had asked for the chance to be a part of the team. She was a physician, and perhaps thought that her role would be only tending to the injured. Now, it was much more.

"They will not only kill this woman; they will cut off her head on video so that the world can see." Will didn't hesitate to describe what the stakes were. "Only you can get close enough that we can stop them before they kill her."

Gunny Moncrief knelt nearby. He had vouched for her and pressed for her being added to the team. He stayed silent.

She took the pistol and pulled back on the slide, inspecting whether the bullet had been chambered. She then flipped off the safety.

Will and Kaili moved silently up to the cooking shed as the other two moved to the base of two palm trees within a football's throw of the windows.

"I'll get the girl." Will led the way to the opening to the cooking shed. He watched as the girl knelt over the firepit. A pot was on a grate over the fire and steam was rising. He moved quietly to just behind her and grabbed her with his hand over her mouth. Will held pressure on her carotid artery until she fell limp. He released the pressure on her neck. She would wake up a few minutes after they were gone.

Kaili and Will pulled off her niqab and burqa and Kaili quickly donned the gray head covering and dress. There was a mattress in the corner, and Will laid the girl down on it.

"Hope they are as kind." Kaili whispered to Will as the girl lay there unconscious. They were not likely to be so. She would need to flee, for no matter what her excuse Chaniago would not offer mercy.

"I'll follow you." Will put his HK416 on single fire and put his hand on the center of her back. When they got to the entrance, he would fall to the side so as to have a clear shot.

Kaili put the pistol under her borrowed clothes.

The two moved up the wooden plank walkway. The hut was on stilts and the only noise was the two men talking to each other. Will understood their Acehnese as they spoke of the slow and painful ways they would kill their prey.

"*Houm meujak?*" the one guard said as he looked up at the girl.

"*Ja keu deh.*" She was asked where she was going and Kaili had spoken back in near perfect Acehnese. It didn't matter what she said. It caused them to take their fingers off their triggers for a split second. At the same moment, the guard's eyes shifted to look at Kaili's feet. Her boots stood out below the dress. He reacted in the wrong way. He stood up and aimed the weapon at her. As he rose, the thump-thump of two suppressed rounds came from Will's rifle. The one standing was lifted up and thrown back through the bamboo wall and out of the stilted hut. The other took a shot to the back of his neck that sliced through his spinal cord, causing instant death. If he had wished to pull the trigger on his AK with the barrel aimed at Retno's mouth, his finger would not have reacted to the command from his brain.

"Good job." Will grabbed Kaili at her shoulders from the rear.

She pulled the pistol out from underneath the burqa. Will took it and put the safety on.

"But I never fired it."

"You were ready to. Sometimes, that's all that counts."

The others joined them in the hut and the Gunny pulled out a knife, cutting the ropes on Retno.

"Thank you, thank you." Retno sat up, shaking as she rubbed her wrists.

"We need to get out of here." The Gunny headed out the opening. "Best to burn this place."

The fire might buy them some time by creating confusion about what had happened. The girl would remember nothing and saw no one. She would think that she fell asleep, which would be a good defense. The number of bodies would take some time to count.

"Let's go." Will grabbed Retno by the arm to lead her out. She was still shaking and unstable on her feet.

Enrico went back to the cooking shed, used some tongs to lift up some hot coals and tossed them into the hut. Smoke started to rise from the fire, and before they made it back to the truck the glow of the flames reached up into the sky.

"Hell, we forgot to get their cell phones." The Gunny had taken out the magazine from his rifle and was unchambering a round. The 5.56 brass bullet bounced off the bed of the truck.

"So, who are you?" Retno stood at the back of the truck.

"Here, some water." Will handed her a bottle. "These are some of my friends."

"That was Chaniago. We have been looking for him for some time." Retno leaned against the side of the truck. They were parked on the other side of the highway and down near the beach so the chances of others discovering them was remote.

"Who is Chaniago?" the Gunny asked.

"Hard-core jihadist. Fought in Syria with ISIS." Retno would speak, stop, drink some water, then speak again. "Killer."

"And someone who would capture some Americans if given the chance?" The Gunny spoke as Kaili and Enrico stood nearby.

"So, you weren't here to help this American find other Americans?" Will asked the question.

"We think the airplane crashed. Nothing more. No survivors." Retno answered the question, but she had just been saved by these people. "But, yes, you were warned to leave Sumatra. When you refused, we thought that you might bring him out of hiding."

"I was the bait, but you were the caught fish." Will held the semiautomatic pistol in his hand as he unscrewed the suppressor.

"So to speak." Retno was humbled. "What can I do to help you see if there are any Americans left alive?"

Chapter 40

The military outpost Kodim 0211 stood on the edge of the coastal village near Sibolga on the west coast. It was a distance south of Lhoknga. The village looked more like a continuous strip mall of buildings that fronted the highway. The buildings were a hodgepodge of small market stores and counter restaurants. The small block building on the other side of the road was a lime-green structure with red and white banners along the roofline. A green metal roof matched the roofs in the compound. A small, low, dark green railing about knee height was the only fencing between the outpost and the busy roadway it faced. Inside the railing, a small parking lot held a row of motor scooters. A red and white barrier gate pole stood upright. It seemed to never have been lowered and only served to announce that the building was something official. It provided no further protection for what was to come. A dark-skinned man wearing only a loose white shirt and shorts sat on a bench outside, waiting for his ride. He was smoking a cigarette when the two black Daihatsu trucks sped up and suddenly turned through the gate.

The man ran across the street looking for cover. He got behind the edge of a building and watched as several men jumped out of their vehicles. A man in a uniform came out of the door of the outpost, apparently looking for the source of the noise.

Automatic gunfire rang out and the soldier fell back into the building.

The man watched as several men ran into the entrance. The sound of gunfire peppered the air. He watched as flashes of light reflected off the windows in the outpost. Soon the gunfire stopped.

The men dressed in black came out of the building carrying what looked like more weapons. They brought out load after load, throwing them in the backs of their vehicles. Soon, sirens could be heard off in the distance.

One man, his face covered by a wrap of black cloth, seemed the last one to come out of the building. He stopped, looked across the street, and spotted the man behind the wall. He lifted his rifle and pointed it at the witness, but the man ducked farther into the alley on the side of the building.

He waited at the far end of the alley until he heard the squeal of tires then walked out onto the street. The two trucks were gone. Soon, several police cars surrounded the outpost with dozens of armed men in the blue uniforms of the police.

Chaniago's army had obtained more weapons. At the same time, raids occurred on posts in Padang City and near Mount Sinabung.

Chapter 41

The sun was just rising in the east when the two Toyota trucks came back into Banda Aceh. The lead truck headed to the Arabia Hotel while the one following passed it by and turned east across the bridge of the Aceh River. The lead truck with Will and Retno stopped a block away from the hotel near the Park of Kings.

"Needless to say, we go back alone." Will helped her out of the rear door. He had saved her life. It was a simple request, that no one know that Will was here with a team.

Retno didn't say anything as they started the walk toward the hotel.

The guards seemed to have doubled since earlier. They were on edge and had added sandbags to the guardhouses. Several military jeeps were parked at the entrance to the lobby. Men in uniform, many with sand-colored berets, stood at the vehicles with their AKM automatic rifles.

Retno waved as the two walked toward the gate. The first reaction was from the two guards, who pointed their weapons in that direction. Both Retno and Will held up their hands, open, and faced the guards. Being shot by an overly anxious guard at this point was not what they needed. As they approached, several of the men with the sand-colored berets saw the two moving in and ran to the gate.

They also had their automatics pointed toward the pair.

Slowly, Retno and Will continued to walk until they reached the gate. A colonel in the VAT 69 stood just inside with his pistol in his hand.

"Lieutenant, are you all right?" He was addressing Retno.

"Yes, sir."

"The American is with you?"

"Yes, sir."

He waved his hand forward to signal they could come in.

Retno walked up to the colonel.

"So happy you are safe." He almost took her hand off her arm shaking it so hard. "So happy!"

"He saved me."

"The American? Just him?"

She paused.

"Yes, sir, just him."

The colonel stuck out his hand to Will as well.

"Thank you, Colonel!" It seemed that everyone in VAT 69 knew of Colonel William Parker.

"It was Chaniago."

"Is he still there?"

"No, sir."

"Any idea?"

"He took a cell phone call and ran out."

"There have been attacks on several outposts and police stations over the last several hours." The colonel pointed them toward the entrance. "We have set up an operations center at the airfield."

"Yes, sir."

"I guess you are now ready to get back to the States?"

"Perhaps in a couple of days." Will stopped. "Maybe we can get something to eat." He changed the conversation. The bombing had derailed their plans for supper, and with the adrenaline wearing off, he realized they hadn't eaten in nearly twenty-four hours.

"Of course. Lieutenant, go eat with our guest. It sounds like we owe him our gratitude."

"Yes, sir, I do." Retno smiled at Will. It was the first time that she noticed more than an American and more than a Marine.

Will looked at her eyes. They were bloodshot and welling up but the smile showed more than just gratitude.

"I'll change and meet you on the terrace."

In Will's room, everything had been moved slightly from its place from the night before. He didn't expect anything less. Chevron Pacific was missing an American and an officer. He opened the laptop and pulled up Anchorage.

"Chaniago." He gave the name to Kim.

"Served with ISIS in Syria. Bounty on his head with the reward program." The Rewards for Justice program was the same one that had rewarded Will in the past for the elimination of a target identified by the United States. Those on the list were identified for death. A reward was put out for twenty men who had killed innocents. The first eight names carried bounties of ten million dollars. Chaniago was number fifteen with a bounty of five million. Or at least, it was five million when the Department of State last issued the list. It was likely that his name and number would move up. The Presidential Authorization had been cleared several years ago. Like Bond, anyone who found Chaniago had a license to kill. "We thought he was back in Sumatra but hadn't confirmed it."

"He is."

"There is something else." Kim seemed hesitant to say it. "The hard drives mention him."

"Hard drives?"

"The computers captured in Abbottabad."

"Bin Laden's compound?"

"Yes. This is well beyond top secret." She seemed to be saying that she had just told him something he should not have heard. "I don't believe it has ever gotten out."

"I can see why." If his followers knew Chaniago was blessed by the king of terrorism, it would only increase the call to arms. It meant that he was far more dangerous to the world than the hundreds of other terrorists who only hoped for attention.

"Our incoming reports are that several police stations and military outposts have been raided." Kim flashed up on the screen a satellite picture of a building on fire with smoke blurring some of the picture. Several bodies were on the ground.

"He is the key to the Gulfstream." Will studied the picture.

"It may be best for you to return home." Kim pressed him.

"Is that what Scott wants?"

She hesitated. She knew enough of Will that any lie would be a waste of time.

"No. He thinks you can handle it."

"He's right."

A knock came on the door. He closed the computer, grabbed his HK pistol out of habit, and put his foot behind the door just enough that it would swing open only several inches. Retno was standing there. Her hair had been washed and combed, she had on a red-and-yellow flowered shirt, shorts, and was barefoot.

"I'm still shaking."

"Come in."

Chapter 42

The Daihatsu pulled up next to the hut on the river at Lho Nga as the light of the morning sun reflected off the river. The boat was moored at the dock and the waters were still. A current in the center of the river was carrying some palms toward the sea. A man smoking a cigarette was standing at the door to the hut. The other, a teenager at most, was sitting on the dock with his cell phone in his hand.

"Where is he?" Chaniago stepped out of the truck holding his rifle.

"Here." His lieutenant swung open the door to the hut.

Chaniago's cell phone began to ring.

"What does she want?" He looked at the phone and the caller. "Yes?"

The voice on the other end could be heard by all of the bystanders. The person was wailing, speaking the words in long lines of slurred speech.

She would stop for gasps of air, then resume.

Chaniago got a sense of what was being said.

"Was she in it?"

The answer was blurred with a resumption of long rants. He knew the chance of a random fire that killed two of his guards was beyond remote. Her body would not be found in the burned-out cinders of the hut. They had been attacked.

"Yes, yes." He hung up the cell phone and made another call.

"Are you there?" This call was to his man on the roof of a building across from the Arabia. "What do you see?"

The report was that the hotel was covered by men in uniforms and sand-colored berets. It had been turned into a fortress.

"Watch for her."

The caller stopped talking for a moment. The voice then resumed.

"You see two?"

Chaniago listened as the man reported that his former prisoner was with another.

"Does he have on a uniform and beret?" Chaniago shook his head and walked in circles as he held the cell phone in a tight grip.

"Take his picture. Send it." He hung up the call.

"So, someone else is helping them." Chaniago had two questions running through his mind. Who was the man? And how did they get to her so fast? The plan had been to take the captive American to the hut in Lho Nga and send his message from there. Now, they would never return to the hut. The girl would have to find her own way.

"We must do it here. Now." He signaled his lieutenant to pull the American out of the hut. The man called for the younger one at the boat to come help. "You need to record me."

Chaniago handed his cell phone to the man as they pulled their captive out of the hut.

"Under that palm tree." He pointed to one up the sandy road. The background needed to show nothing that would allow them to be traced. They carried the prisoner to the base of the tree and put him on his knees. He barely whimpered. The inevitable was about to occur.

"My friend, it has been a long time from when we first met. Do you remember that night?"

Chaniago moved to his side.

"Are you ready?" There would be only one take. The lieutenant nodded his head. The red light appeared on the cell phone.

"This is the last infidel from the Malaysia flight. The last prisoner. An American." He was recording the answer to one of the most-asked questions of the past several decades. The cell focused in on the face of the man. He looked tired. He would not scream or talk. The many agencies of the world would look at his face and reconstruct who he was. They would use computer graphics to eliminate the wrinkles, the beard, the dirt and the mud to determine his identity.

"He is an infidel who came to our land. Sumatra is a Muslim holy land and any infidel who comes here will meet the same fate." Chaniago held him by his hair.

The knife cut through the flesh and dark blood gurgled out and onto the prisoner's chest. The blade kept cutting, just as he had done in Syria. He kept pulling until the head was completely severed. And then he held it up so the video could fully capture the death.

"Jamaah Ansharut Daulah has spoken."

Chaniago didn't even try to disguise his face. He was making a statement. He was saying "come get me if you dare" to the sand-colored berets. Chaniago would win or would become a martyr. He would be spoken of long after the hanging or firing squad if that was Allah's will. And with victory, he would live a long and happy life well respected by his people.

Chaniago walked away from the shot.

"Toss him in the river." He went down to the dock as well, bent over and washed the blade and his hands.

Now, who is this other one? Chaniago thought of the stranger who was in the photograph with Retno. He also appeared to be an American.

Chapter 43

"Look at your computer." The call from the Gunny caused Will to cross over from his bed to the table near the window. He opened it and saw the feed from Ben back at the villa. It showed the execution.

"An American?" Will looked at the victim. It was clear that the man had been a prisoner for some time. Will studied the background. It gave no clues.

"It's a call for jihad. The word will go out to every Muslim terrorist in Southeast Asia," said the Gunny.

Will studied the video. The vegetation seemed similar to that near the hut they raided to save Retno.

"How about the surrounding sound?" Will asked. "Can Ben get anything out of the background noise?"

"He's working on it. He says they have another program that can compare vegetation on Sumatra and possibly narrow it down."

Will sat at the table and looked out his window from the fourth floor. Men in uniforms with their sand-colored berets were moving around like an ant hill, setting up barricades with machine guns. He looked at the surrounding buildings. All was quiet.

A curtain in a window moved ever so slightly.

A hunter always knows game is caught by movement.

The curtain moved again.

Will took his cell phone and snapped a picture. He then enlarged it several times. The Apple's clarity was amazing. A figure was in the shadows of the window. Will continued to watch. The man was looking out, across the street at the hotel, and would move slightly every so often.

"Look at this."

Retno came across to the table and stood behind him.

"Don't move too fast," Will advised her. The man would disappear if given the chance or, worse, a gunfight and then an explosion might end the trail.

"Yes." She quickly left the room, quietly closing the door.

Will continued to watch. He knew that she would go to her colonel, tell him of the spy, and they would map out a plan. Another team from the airport would be dispatched. The VAT 69 team at the hotel would take another picture identifying the window and the building. It would be relayed to the attack team.

Will watched as nothing moved. For nearly half an hour the street remained quiet. He then saw several uniformed men on the roof of the building.

"Not good." He spoke the words to himself. The spy might have another team watching as well, who would also be keeping an eye on behalf of the man behind the window. He guessed right.

The street remained quiet until he heard the staccato of gunfire. A flash of light came from the window. There was more gunfire, then silence. He watched as the men in uniform came out onto the street, dragging a body behind them. One man in uniform carrying his automatic walked across to the hotel and was met by the colonel at the front gate. They spoke and headed to the entrance to the hotel.

Will watched as the two were joined by Retno just to the side of the portico. She looked at an object, then looked up toward Will's room. It was clear what was being said. The cell phone had a picture of the two of them.

"You must leave." Retno was more emphatic than ever before. "They have your picture."

Will listened as he sat at the table.

"I can't."

"Why?"

"The man they executed." He sat without moving his hands.

"Yes."

"They made the point that he was an American." Will worked his way through his logic. "It is proof that Charles Hedges is alive."

"I don't understand." She stood there across from the table. His logic began to sink in. She then changed course. "You are right."

"Their captive was a survivor of another airplane disappearance. They kept him alive all this time. They made the point on the broadcast that they were killing an American." Will worked his way through the facts.

"So, the Gulfstream was hijacked." She nodded her head in agreement.

"But why wait so long? And why now?"

"We may have had a hand in it." Will looked at his hands.

"What?"

"As to why now, two reasons. Foremost, he is ready to wage his war. He must think that everything is in place now." It made sense. The prisoner was a deposit in an account that was ready to be withdrawn. The execution would put the movement on the front page of the world's media. Others from the Philippines, Indonesia, Myanmar, and Vietnam would come to the holy war in Sumatra.

"And the second?"

"He knows we got you back."

She now had a vested interest in helping Will. Her escape may have meant the death of the American. A life for a life had been the trade. Neither could regret it, but a price had been paid.

"They won't let you leave." She looked out the window.

"I need to get to my team."

Retno pondered a plan.

"Take as little as you need. Nothing more." They now had two enemies. VAT 69 would not want to harm Will, but they also wouldn't want him to disappear. And when Retno disappeared, they would be furious.

Will picked up the laptop and put it in his satchel. He tucked the HK pistol under the back of his shirt.

"Let's go."

The pair's only chance was to walk out the way they came in and hope that none of the officers were there. They went side by side out the front door and past the guards at the gate. She smiled at them. It was clear that the others of the VAT 69 unit knew of the young lieutenant who had once been Miss Indonesia. They smiled back, yelled out something and waved. Once beyond the gate, Will and Retno turned east toward the Park of Kings, crossed through the gardens, and stopped at the street on the other side. It was an act of incredible courage on her part. She had been a prisoner of men who would, in what they considered a gentle form of death, bury her in a hole up to her neck and then throw rocks at her until the blood blinded her eyes and death came. If there was another lookout he would have been on his cell as soon as they crossed out the gate. This time fortune was on their side.

The taxi took them across the river and stopped a block away from the villa.

They passed through the back alleys until they arrived at the rear. The white Toyota was parked near the door. Will knocked. Kaili's voice came from the other side. She said the greeting again in Acehnese. He replied.

"Welcome back."

Retno followed Will into the villa.

"Where's the Gunny?"

"He crashed."

Will gave Kaili a look of "are you telling me everything?"

"He'll be up in a second." She was right about that. Once the sound of their arrival passed through the villa, the Gunny and team would be in the computer room.

"OK, the Marine is still alive." Will spoke to the crew as Ben studied his computer. "We need to find him."

"I've got something," Ben spoke up. "The name you gave me. Iskandar."

"Yeah."

"I couldn't trace his cell back as far as the missing airplane, but I did follow it on the day you were there." Ben pushed up his glasses as he switched from screen to screen. "He made several calls, but they were to burner phones."

"So, dead end?"

"Thought so, but pulled up cells in the same area. Got two boys playing the video game. This is what showed up."

The pictures were of two boys, one with an AK-47 on his lap, playing the game. They were in a jungle.

"Location?"

Ben switched to another screen and put in the coordinates. It was in the Ula Masen jungle just south of Banda Aceh.

"We need more than that."

"The younger boy's phone moved."

"What do you mean?" Will watched Ben coordinate the screens to show another location. This time, the cell phone was moving. "Where's that?"

"Looks like he is playing the game on a boat on the western waters of Sumatra."

The game was not constantly on, so the video came in bits and pieces.

"We need more and need it quickly."

"I need to call in about Iskandar Muda." Retno wanted to move fast on the man who was obviously a traitor.

"No." Will looked up at her from the computer table. "He may be the only one we can be assured of following." He needed Iskandar right where he was. The man was not using a burner phone and he would call again.

"OK."

"Right now, we need to find out where the prisoner was killed."

Chapter 44

"We must stop this." The Commander of the National Armed Forces was on a video conference call with his major components. The Air Chief Marshall led the meeting with the Chiefs of Staff of his Army, Navy and Air Force. "What is the force on the ground in Sumatra?"

The Chief of the Army pulled up a slide.

"The MRC is fully equipped and all have been mobilized. The Raider Infantry Brigade is moving units to the north." He flipped through several slides showing the force on the ground.

"You have several units that have been attacked. Four of the Kodim—0104, 0106 and 0108." He was describing several outposts of the military.

"Also, 0211."

"What of the Navy?"

"The attacks have all been on the ground except for the bombing of the refinery in Padang." The admiral seemed ready to minimize the Navy's role.

"If I were Chaniago, the sea would be the last place that I would ignore. As soon as he consolidates his forces, you will see the attacks spread to the Strait."

The commander was correct.

"What of VAT?" The Army Chief of Staff didn't want the police to get in their way. The Army had a reputation of taking the law into its own hands. A rebel group had taken the life of one of the US Army in a café in Java. The Army's special forces unit wreaked its revenge by raiding the jail where the suspected killers were being kept. The prisoners' bodies had been riddled with bullets from the Army's AK-47s. It wasn't the first time that the Army's justice came swift and deadly. After a soldier's wife was kidnapped and murdered in the Samalanga district of Aceh, men were beaten and shot. A village was burned to the ground. Muslim prisoners associated with the Free Aceh Movement received electric shocks and cigarette burns. The Army did not play and didn't want anyone or anything to get in their way.

Several outposts had been raided, leaving behind the blood of the soldiers manning their posts. The Aceh Province command would not stand by while their fellow soldiers were being killed. No one would get in the way of the Army's response to the violence and that included the officers of VAT 69.

Chapter 45

Chaniago moved his headquarters a third time. This time, he went farther into the mountains of Aceh. The jungle to the southwest provided several valleys that cloaked his efforts.

"How did they know of the hut?" He sat on a rock deep within the canopy of the jungle. It was at the base of a cliff that provided shelter from any satellite passing over. The hike to the new headquarters was more than two miles through the thickest jungle.

"A spy?" his lieutenant answered.

"No, the only ones that knew of her were you, me, and the two in the ashes."

"What of the girl?"

"No, she wouldn't know who to tell or what to say. Her brother was on the raid in Padang." Chaniago had confidence in his ability to judge people. He never failed in picking out the traitor, even when he was in Syria.

"Then who?"

Chaniago looked across the encampment and saw two boys at the base of a rock. They both were focused on their cell phones.

"Or what?" He stood up. "Tell the men to communicate only by couriers from now on. As we did in Afghanistan and Syria. Only couriers."

"It will slow us down."

"It will make it impossible for them to track us." Chaniago poked the ground with a stick. "Especially with our next move."

"Lhokseumawe?"

The city was on the far northeastern shore of Sumatra. Of more importance, it was within eighty miles of the center of the Strait.

"Yes. They need to be ready. We need an American container ship. Our man, can he find one?"

The lieutenant knew what he was talking about. The cell in Lhokseumawe had a computer technician who tracked all of the potential targets coming in and out of the Strait.

"Yes."

"Send a courier to tell him. We need a boat. We have several more tons of the ammonium nitrate at our outpost. Have it moved it to Lhokseumawe and load it on a fast boat." Chaniago's plan would bring more attention to their war. It would put pressure on the Indonesian government. The small seaport of Lhokseumawe on the coast was less than fifty miles from the southern lane of the Strait. Nearly a hundred thousand ships passed through Malacca every year. The traffic was so dense that they had to follow a specific sea-lane. The southern sea-lane was on the side of the Strait closest to the seaport village. If the shipping stopped, the world's attention would turn to Aceh. Even Bin Laden didn't control a chokepoint as valuable as the Strait.

"Day after tomorrow. Have them pull up a ship heading south in the lane. One that is American. A container ship. You conduct the raid. Do it."

"Do you want to give the command?"

"It is given. Do it. May Allah bless your efforts." Chaniago didn't need to give any further instructions. Like Bin Laden, once the plan to attack the towers was set in place, he learned of its success when they fell.

"Yes, a container. Good video."

The loss of life would be small, but the video would be played around the world. A three-hundred-gross-ton behemoth would clog up the Strait for days. Shipping would be backed up to India.

"It will bring every warrior within ten thousand miles." Chaniago stopped. His gaze went to another world. He was away fighting in Syria when his family disappeared on Boxing Day. It was a sign from God that he was to return to his homeland and covert it to a holy nation. He had no other purpose in life.

"I'll need the other two—" Chaniago stopped midsentence. "We need to send a courier to tell the boat to be ready. I will join them shortly."

Chapter 46

The rain moved across the island and with it the winds shook the hut where the two men crouched next to their poles, trying to stay as dry as possible. Chuck used the paper from the fried fish to rub around his ankle but it would be of no help with the chain around his neck. Darkness closed in as he worked on the chain. With the rain, there was no guard. They were huddled together in another hut several yards away.

The food had diminished over the last several days and the plastic bottles of water had stopped coming. They were getting weaker by the day.

Chuck freed his foot from the chain and was able to stand up. He slid the chain around his neck up the post as high as he could get it.

"What are you doing?" The engineer's voice was getting weaker all the time.

"If we get out of here, we can make it into the jungle. We can get some coconuts and find some fresh water." Chuck was using the best psychology he could think of to muster his fellow captive's cooperation.

"Coconuts?"

"Yeah, some food."

"I don't know."

"If you stay here, you will die. Either they will come for you or you will die in this hut."

The engineer was silent as he seemed to absorb what was being said.

"Coconuts?"

"I promise I will get you a coconut." Even Chuck could taste the sweet milk and meat as he mentioned the word. He didn't say that on his last adventure he didn't find any, but he had headed away from the jungle and not into it.

"OK."

Chuck grabbed the pole and moved it with his shoulder. It was not buried very deeply in the mud and the blow from the rifle before had loosened it from the roof. He eased it back and forth like a child's loose tooth. It rocked several times until it suddenly fell into his arms. He stood there, watching to see if the thatched roof would fall in. It held in place.

The chain around his neck was held on with a small brass lock. He gathered it up and tucked it into his shirt and down into his pants so as to move freely until he could get it unlocked.

The chain on the engineer's ankle was easy. He had lost so much weight that it only covered the bone of the ankle and slipped off even without the use of the greasy paper.

"OK, follow me." Chuck led the way as the two crawled on their hands and knees to the bamboo wall in the rear. He pulled the wall apart and stuck his head out into the rain. The warm water pelted his face and washed away some of the mud and grime that had built up. Chuck used his hands to pull the wall away and make a hole for himself and his fellow prisoner.

"Stay close." Chuck wiggled out into the jungle, turned and waited for the engineer to follow. The man was weak and barely made it through the hole. Chuck grabbed the rag of a shirt and the back of his pants as they both fell into the jungle.

The two worked their way through the undergrowth slowly, the engineer managing to stay within reach of Chuck. The rain poured down in torrents. *This will give us some time.* The rain came in sheets. He knew that the guards were lazy and would stay in the shelter of their huts as long as possible. Perhaps in a day or two they'd feel guilty enough to bring food to the prisoners and would discover the empty hut. It was the time that Chuck needed, and the rain would cover whatever ferns or plants were bent by the two crawling away. And unless they put their hands in the wrong hole by mistake, the vipers and spiders would stay out of the rain as well.

Once Chuck felt the sand of the road he stood up and lifted the engineer to his feet.

"How does freedom feel?" he whispered to his fellow prisoner.

"OK."

"We need to work our way into the jungle." They headed up the trail, which climbed into a notch between two hills. A grove of benzoin trees waved back and forth in the wind. Chuck felt the bark as he leaned against it. His hand smelled of vanilla as the sap oozed out.

"We need to find some shelter." Chuck surveyed the lay of the land. The trail led to an opening. Daylight was making its way through the clouds.

"Coconuts?" The engineer tried to smile.

"Yep, promised you that. Almost there." Chuck led him to what appeared to be a path in the rocks that led to the top of an outcrop. He would put the engineer in a protected place then search out food, water, and protection. At the top of the rocks Chuck's hand felt something smooth.

"Here you go."

Luck was finally on their side.

The structure of a bunker was built into the outcrop of rocks. The Japanese Army had built a lookout on the small atoll. They would have to risk any other occupants as Chuck pulled the vines away from a small entrance.

"We can hold out in here for some time." He pulled himself into the dark, cold hole and helped the engineer follow. "With daylight I can find some coconuts and water."

The engineer smiled in the low light inside the bunker.

I'll also see where we are. The bunker would give him a lookout on the waters on both sides of the island. From this vantage point, he would see where the other nearby islands were and plan a further escape. And he would be able to see if the boat had returned.

"Get some sleep." They hadn't had the sleep of free men for some time. The lack of food, exhaustion, and the constant fear of death had weighed heavily. As he fell asleep, Chuck thought of the jet he had seen crossing the clear night sky and the passengers sitting in their seats, free, sipping drinks with ice. He could imagine the sweet taste of cold Coca-Cola. His stomach ached as his mind wandered through the memory of the taste of steak. Chuck leaned against the cement wall and held his fellow prisoner against his shoulder as if the man was a child. The warm rain blew across the island.

He was not going back to the chains no matter what.

Chapter 47

"I've got something." Ben was out of breath after running down the stairs to the Gunny. He looked like someone who hadn't been to bed for several days and had lived on a diet of Red Bull. In this case, it was Sumatra coffee.

"OK, what you got?" The Gunny followed the tech upstairs to the computer room.

"Followed Iskandar Muda's cell traffic. You know his name is famous around here. To the Aceh people, it's like naming an American George Washington." Ben pulled up two screens. "He spoke to a cell phone near a cluster of phones. I followed the cluster until I found a boy playing the game." The face of a young man was focused intently on a screen. His brown eyes didn't move. The cell phone would shake as if he was pressing down on the keys too tightly. "He's on a boat."

"How do you know that?"

"See the rigging in the background?" Above the boy's head was what appeared to be a network of wires and aluminum poles. It was as if he were in a metal cage. Beyond, the sky was dark. He appeared to be under the shelter of the lip of the pilothouse.

"Odd."

"It's a squid boat." Ben's degree from the Massachusetts Institute of Technology meant he was much smarter than being just a computer whiz. He fit well with IARPA. Besides technical sense, he was endowed with common sense—particularly when it came to world knowledge. And his father was a lobsterman from Kittery, Maine.

"You know your boats."

"Had to. Spent my childhood on a boat out of Portsmouth." Ben smiled. "Never going back."

"But squid isn't a New England thing?"

"Can be in the spring. Most squid fishermen fish around lights like bridges or docks."

"And this boat's got lights."

"Yeah. Lots of them."

"Where?"

"The west coast has boats that head north to the islands to catch squid. They fish for them by running a rigging of lights that they shine at night. They run close to the shore of the islands." Ben was giving the Gunny a lesson in Southeast Asian fishing.

"So, what's that got to do with us?"

"There, on the edge of the picture, watch when he moves the phone."

The cell would jiggle in his hands as he switched it from one hand to the other. The barrel of an AK-47 appeared in the corner of the shot.

Then a man appeared, grabbed the cell, and it went blank. For a split second, his face appeared on the screen.

"Can you hold that shot?" The Gunny pointed to the computer.

"Got it recorded."

"Great. Pull it up. I want to show Will."

"No more cells. No more cells." Chaniago tossed the cell phone into the sea as the squid boat pulled out of the channel, turned north and went into the waters of the Nicobar-Simeulue Basin off the western coast of Sumatra. To get the point across, Chaniago struck the boy on the side of his head.

The waters were rough as the winds pushed in weather from the west. Chaniago stood on the side of the pilothouse opposite the winds and looked over the railing. The water was clear and deep. He studied the rocks and sand, thinking of the monster that lay below. They were now well over the fault line. If it suddenly opened, they would be pulled into the chasm or tossed over like a cork bobbing in a sink until the sink was unplugged. The earthquake in 2004 was a divine warning that God would not tolerate the people's failure to follow his laws. Chaniago preached that it was like the bible's story of Noah. He took it one step further. If God were to be disobeyed, another scourge would come that would end the world for all people. At least, it would be the end of the world for Indonesia, and with damage to the Strait, do great harm to the capitalists whose ships passed.

"You didn't need to come." The captain hollered at him from behind the wheel. He was right. If the trip was to retrieve the last two prisoners and the guards, their leader was not required.

"Yes. But if Allah is willing, and we need to move them somewhere else, I want to be there."

The movement was building. CNN International had reported the attacks on the Indonesian military outposts and the mobilization of the Army. With an attack on a ship in the Strait, it would quickly become a world crisis. He wanted the execution of two of Chevron's people to send a message to the rest of the world.

Chaniago had destroyed his own cell phone. He had become convinced that the phone was the key. But it made communications more difficult. As he left on the boat, he sent a young courier on his motorcycle to the cell in Banda Aceh. They had sent him the photo of Retno walking with an American. He wanted that man very badly. The mission now was to find the man and capture or kill him.

They would use the many Wi-Ha in the city to look for the man. The Wilayatul Hisbah Islamic Police covered every corner of the city looking for violators of Islamic law. Women who were uncovered or wore clothes too tight would be arrested and sentenced to a lashing. The network knew every alleyway. They would soon find the man and his accomplices and report.

"We will find him and the woman again. This time they will not escape the dull edge of the knife." Chaniago spoke to the waters under the boat as they headed north. Then he asked, "How long?"

"The wind is slowing us down. We may not make it until daylight tomorrow." The captain looked at the compass behind the wheel. "Yeah, daylight. At least the weather helps."

"Why?"

"They won't stop us and ask why we are not fishing. They will expect us to make it to the north and pull into the shelter of one of the islands. We won't stand out."

"Good."

"If it becomes too rough, we may need to do just that."

Chapter 48

"It must be near here." Will had taken one of the trucks back to the coast near where the hut and the two men had been. Retno sat next to him on the front seat. Both were armed; they would not be prisoners, Retno not again.

"I have an idea." Retno pointed down the highway back to the north and Lho Nga. "On the other side of the beach is a river. There is a bridge on the Trans highway. Just short of it is a café on the water."

Will's cell phone began to ring.

"Yeah."

The Gunny gave them the news that connected the dots.

"Squid boat. I'll call you back." Will looked at Retno. "Did you say a café on a river?"

"Just off the highway."

They rode back to the highway and followed it back toward the village of Lhoknga, heading north. Just after crossing the bridge, Will pulled off on a side road to another sandy path that led to a blue-roofed restaurant perched on the river bank. They took a table on the water's edge. Retno looked at the menu.

"Are you thinking what I am thinking?" She smiled at the American.

"The squid?"

"Cumi Masak Hitam." She laughed at the name. "Not like your quarter pounder with cheese."

"Did I hear it right?" Will gave her his best grin. "Squid in ink sauce?"

"It tastes better than it looks." She bowed her head, covered with the hijab, as the waiter approached. Will spoke to him in perfect Acehnese. Nevertheless, the waiter stared as if wondering why an American was here with an Asian. When the waiter returned later with the food, Will asked, "Is the squid from here?"

"Yeah, some of the boats come up this river."

The rain continued as they sat under the cover of the restaurant and watched the drops fall on the surface of the river. A breeze came in from the sea to the west.

After a while, a boat rigged with lights and two metal structures like wings stowed up in the air passed by.

"This is it." Will felt that this was the river and this was where the video was made of the execution.

They finished their meal and started to walk out of the cafe. As they did, a black truck tore in from the main road. The driver made the mistake of not blocking the road or setting the truck up as a shield. Two men in the back were carrying their AK-47s and as the driver slammed on the brakes, one of the shooters in the back fell over the cab. The other raised his automatic.

"Get down," Will yelled at Retno. They were still at the entrance and she fell to the floor behind the counter. He went down on one knee, making himself as small a target as possible.

The automatic sprayed bullets above their heads. The gunman didn't take the time to aim. He reacted to his targets and failed to realize that an aimed shot always killed better than thirty rounds in a magazine. None of his bullets struck anything but the walls of the café. The wood and plastic were splintered and small pieces flew up in the air. The smell of spent gun powder quickly filled the air.

The other gunman, who had fallen when the truck stopped, struggled to get up as the driver climbed out of the cab.

Will's HK VP40 pistol rang out.

The first gunman fell back from the impact of the bullet to his forehead. His gun flew up in the air. As it did, it kept firing for a brief moment. The dead man's finger must have kept pressure on the trigger as he fell back into the bed of the truck.

The other man turned to see the gunman fall. His head turned away from his targets. It was a mistake. He took his attention off the immediate danger to himself.

Another shot rang out.

Will's semiautomatic put a slug into the side of the man's throat. The gunman grabbed it and fell to his knees gasping for air.

Will stood up.

Another shot rang out. It was a blast like a small stick of dynamite.

It wasn't Will.

The driver had an automatic and was aiming it when he fell back against the side of the truck.

Retno stood up with her pistol in her hand. She had a short-barrel Colt Python in her hand. She fired only one shot from the .357. It had caved in the chest of the driver.

"I said I would never be without again." Retno slipped the pistol back under her clothes.

"We best get out of here." Will ran to the truck and they pulled back on the highway. They headed north, and in several miles came to a roadblock on the coastal highway. It was a unit of the Army just to the north of Lho Nga. Several Humvees blocked the road with soldiers on top with M-60 machine guns, helmets, and bulletproof vests.

Retno showed her credentials and spoke to the commander of the unit. He called on the radio and was soon joined by several other armored vehicles. The Army vehicles headed south to the café.

"We can go." Retno climbed back into the truck.

"Need to go back to the café?" Will didn't know if the Army needed any help in describing the incident. Several men had been killed. It was all justified, but blood was shed.

"No, be best not to." Retno looked directly ahead. The response sounded like there would be more bloodshed committed indiscriminately.

The café owner likely fled as soon as the gunfire stopped. His café would not be there when he returned.

Chapter 49

The winds grew stronger in the night as the storm worked its way over from the Bay of Bengal. There was only open water between the island and Sri Lanka on the east coast of India. The storm's strength grew in size as it passed to the east. Daylight tried to peek through the clouds but it only created a miserable dull light. But the murky light meant that Chuck could move and have a better chance of not being seen. Hunger and thirst were winning out. He needed to try.

"I'll be back." He lifted the engineer's head up from his shoulder and pulled him up to the wall.

"OK." He didn't protest. Death was making its way toward both of them.

Chuck slowly pulled his way out of the bunker and into the torrent of rain. He studied the tree line carefully, looking for any movement. The rain kept coming. The only sound was from the waves of rain as they continued to fall.

"Still hunkered down," he said to himself, imagining the guards huddled up in their hut and caring little for their prisoners. It had been some time since the escape and there was no noise from that side of the island. If they had made an effort to feed the men, they would have seen the empty hut.

Chuck worked his way down a rocky wall heading toward a small beach. As he got closer, he saw a line of coconut trees. Several of the nuts had fallen to the ground. He took a few back to the rocky trail and looked for a sharp-edged rock. Soon he had bored down to the nut of several coconuts. With the rock, he broke one open and drank the sweet milk.

"God, this is something." The warm milk spilled over his chin as he cracked open another one. The meat hurt his teeth as he bit out white chunks. Chuck wanted to bring the coconuts back up to the engineer, but the animal in him couldn't stop. He drank another and ate more of the sweet meat. Finally, well before his appetite was satisfied, Chuck gathered up and tore through the hard husk of several until he held an armful of the nuts.

"One more thing." He took the sharp rock and looked for a boulder that jutted out from the hillside. He laid his head down on the flat surface. Fortunately, the chain had some slack in it. Their guards didn't think that the chain needed to be too tight as it would never be pulled over his head. They did him a favor, which he imagined would never be repeated. Chuck pulled the slack out of the chain and was able to put the small brass lock on the flat of the boulder. He swung the sharp edge down on the lock. It was a cheap one, probably bought in the market in Banda Aceh. With two swings it popped open, like striking a combination lock with a hammer. He pulled the chain out from his clothing and left it on the rock.

The rain had continued nonstop as he worked his way up the rocky path. Near the top, Chuck stopped in the tree line and waited across from the opening. He waited as the rain continued to soak him. It was warm and he tasted it on his lips. But still he waited, making sure that no one had found the bunker and that he hadn't led anyone to the opening. Finally, he crossed over and tossed the coconuts in through the opening. He followed them into the dark and wiggled through the small space. The bunker was as black as a coal mine after the lights went out. He felt around and touched a leg. The man didn't react.

"Come on," Chuck whispered. "Got you something."

Still the man didn't move.

Chuck took one of the coconuts, put the sharp rock between his legs and slammed it down on the sharp edge. It broke open, and some of the milk spilled on his hands. It was sticky and he licked it off. With the half left, Chuck worked his way up to the engineer's face, lifted his head, and put the makeshift cup to the man's lips.

"Drink, drink this." He wet the engineer's lips.

At first, there was no movement, then the man gagged, coughed, and lifted his head.

"There you go."

Just then, the sound of automatic gunfire rang out.

"They found out we're gone," Chuck whispered. They would be as desperate as a pack of wild dogs, and if they found their prey, would not hesitate to kill them.

The gunfire continued. It sounded like they were randomly shooting into the rain forest and the air. The cloud cover, wind, and storm dampened the sounds. The shooting seemed random and came from far to the right and left. But one shooter seemed close.

"He's going to follow the path." Chuck spoke to himself. It was natural that the man would proceed uphill. The human species would head uphill. And on top, if he found their hole, he would fire into it. The bullets would ricochet inside the bunker and chew them up like a swimmer who fell under a ski boat's prop.

"We can't stay here." Chuck broke up some of the coconut meat and put it to the engineer's lips. At first he resisted, then took a small bite. Like a child trying some new vegetable, once it made it to his taste buds, the man started to eat more and more. He winced as the hard meat tested his teeth.

The gunfire stopped.

They had been given a reprieve for now. The rain had won out. The shooters had become soaked and returned to cover. They would regroup, reload, and start all over again. Despite his eyes having been adjusted to the darkness, the bunker was rapidly becoming darker as somewhere well above the clouds the sun was setting.

"I'll be back." Chuck needed to risk leaving the bunker one more time before the light disappeared. He hoped that the lack of gunfire meant that no one was around. If a guard randomly crossed his path, he would have no chance. But if they stayed in the bunker, it was only a matter of time. The island they were on seemed no larger or longer than a mile or two and no wider than a quarter mile.

The guards could work their way from one end to another, and if more came with the next boat, they would be found. Chuck broke open the remainder of the coconuts. "Eat this. Eat all of this."

He climbed out the opening and worked his way down the path to the beach. From there, he made his way around the east end. There would be a small cove of beach and sand, then rocks that jutted out into the ocean, followed by another beach. He stopped at the third outcrop of rocks and saw something through the waning light.

"Another island."

The wind continued to come out of the west. He sat there, on a rock, studying the distant island as the light continued to fade. It was dark with no sign of life or hope. There were no ships or boats. It was as if they had gone beyond the ends of the earth.

Just then a sound came from behind.

Chuck didn't move. His instinct was to drop behind a rock or try to make it to the water, but instead, he used every ounce of control in his body to stay perfectly still. One of the guards passed along a nearby trail heading to the beach beyond.

Chuck held his breath. The man had his automatic rifle slung over his shoulder. Chuck continued to watch him knowing that the first reaction would be for the man to point his weapon. He held his breath. The man continued to walk.

It's the boy.

The young guard that had seemed excited to know the Marine continued to walk. And then he stopped as if he heard something. Chuck's heart stopped. He used his combat training to control his brain and his breath.

Then the boy began singing. He was only a child. He seemed so harmless. He reminded Chuck of his youngest son. Still Chuck didn't move. He wanted to scream and grab the boy. He wanted to shake the boy until some sense was made of it all. The boy was singing, then started walking again into the rain.

Chuck waited until everything was still then waited some more. Finally, he moved slowly, as slow as a deer stepping through a grass field, until he was well beyond the path where the boy had come from. He climbed back up the path to the top, which had become slippery with the rain and with water flowing down it like a waterfall. The storm had saved their lives. At least for now, the torrent of rain had issued a pardon. But the pardon would not last. He made it back to the bunker, finding the opening only by the feel of the man-made sharp edge. He climbed in.

"You OK?"

"God, yes."

"I've got a plan. And it needs to happen soon."

Chapter 50

"What do we know?" Will looked at the computer monitors in their operations room back at the villa.

"I know it's getting hot around here." The Gunny wasn't talking about the weather. The rain was pelting the metal roof, but Army patrols were on the streets. One of the computer monitors was flashing with DIVA system as jeeps well-armed with men and machine guns drove past the villa. The city of Banda Aceh was becoming a war zone. Roadblocks covered the city. Retno had become an asset; with her identification, they made it through the roadblocks with ease. She stood in the operations room with the others. Retno had become a part of the team.

"The last cell I captured was of the boy on a boat heading out to sea from Lhoknga." Ben pulled up the file.

"With our guy in the last shot." Moncrief pointed to the face of Chaniago as he took the phone away and tossed it into the sea.

"So he hasn't kept his prisoners on Sumatra. He likes to keep them somewhere safe. Pull up Google Earth." Will watched as one of the monitors showed the north end of Sumatra. "Makes sense. Not everyone can be trusted. One slipup and the Army would be on top of them."

"What does the satellite show?" Moncrief asked.

"Before the weather came in, it showed this." Ben focused in on a trawler that matched the location of the last tag of the cell phone. The boat was heading north.

"The American was killed when?" Will wanted the time and date.

Ben pulled up the video. Kaili turned from the screen as it showed the execution.

"Can the satellite zoom in on the boat that matches the cell tag?"

"Yes, sir." Ben focused in on the trawler. There were at least four men with AK-47s on the boat as well as the captain in the pilothouse. The view was obscured by the metal rigging of the lights, but the image was as clear as if they were standing next to the terrorists.

"Its heading?" Will studied the map.

"North." Moncrief spoke.

"But north where?" Retno leaned over their shoulders. "We have over eighteen thousand islands."

"Damn." Moncrief swore his complaint.

"How accurately can you plot his course?" Will asked Ben.

"If he doesn't vary, pretty close."

"Where then?"

Ben extended the graph on the screen using the ruler function. It pointed north to a group of islands.

"Best guess is here." Ben pulled out the focus of the Google map. It landed on a large island well north of Sumatra.

"Nicobar?" The word was over the larger of two islands. "Great Nicobar Island?" Will studied the land mass, which was the closest one in a chain of islands that extended from near Myanmar south to Sumatra. The islands appeared to be the peaks of an underwater mountain range that separated the deeper waters of the Bay of Bengal from the Andaman Sea. One could follow the range even farther south as it extended to the group of islands that paralleled the larger island of Sumatra. The chain formed a large crescent shape that extended for over a thousand miles, reaching almost to Papua New Guinea. The formation also marked the boundary of two tectonic plates of the earth's crust.

"Brilliant!" Retno spoke.

"Why?" Ben's curiosity took over.

"It's not Indonesia. It's India."

"You mean those islands are not part of Indonesia?" Moncrief listened to the lesson in geography.

"Few people live there. And they are owned by India."

"So, he's beyond the eyes of India. And they are remote enough that he could have an outpost there that no one sees."

"Including the CIA." Moncrief said the three famous letters.

"What do they have to do with it?" The room got quiet when Retno asked the question.

"Just a comment." Moncrief tried to blow it off.

"We need to get to that island." Will reached for the mouse and zeroed in on the large one. "Here, this spot." He pointed to a small runway near several buildings and turned to Retno. "We need a small airplane and a boat."

"Why not just get the military involved?" Retno knew that the Indian Army wouldn't hesitate to go after a wanted terrorist.

"Maybe later, but our Americans would be the first to go if helicopters show up." They had no idea of the number of survivors from the Gulfstream, but few, if any, would make it if Chaniago was forewarned.

They had that one benefit—the element of surprise. Will had made a promise to a woman sitting in a hotel in Kuala Lumpur. He was not willing to bring a body home if they were this close to having a real chance.

"I'm on it." Moncrief had a new source of friends and money.

"Just three. Retno and Kaili and me. You guys need to stay here and provide us with the best information you can get." Will was letting the doctor play in the game. Retno would keep the Indonesian Army off their backs and Kaili's medical training would come in handy if the men were as bad off as the executed man looked.

"Here. Here is where we will go." Will pointed to a name that sounded neither Indonesian nor Indian. "Campbell Bay."

Chapter 51

The trawler rode low in the water as it headed out from the bay of Lhokseumawe on the eastern side of Sumatra. The storm had made the nights on the water as dark as the inside of a buried coffin. On another night, the lights of ships in the sea-lane of the Strait would twinkle off in the distance. On this one, a boat could nearly run up on a ship before seeing its outline. The ammonium nitrate bags were stacked in the hole of the trawler as high as a man standing. In the center, a case of plastic explosives was tucked in among the bags. The Semtex 10 explosive had come from Czechoslovakia on a freighter from Iran. It was paid for by Chaniago with the funds from the friend in Saudi Arabia. The source of the explosive, the source of the freighter that transported it to Sumatra, and the source of the payment were all kept separate from each other, as they all didn't share the same purposes. Some did it for money, and some did it out of anger. The weight of the cargo caused the boat to list to port.

"Where is it?" The boy with his hands on the wheel was another recruit who had lost everything in the great tsunami. He lived on the other coast. His father was a fisherman, and if the boy had been older when the wave came, he would have been on his father's boat that morning. The father probably heard the rumble of the ocean and saw the water receding just before the wall came out of the blue horizon. The boy didn't know. He was only a child then and was with his mother and the others at their hut, which by the grace of Allah, had been up the side of a hill. What the boy did know was that his father was never seen again. His boat disappeared off the face of the earth. The boy's mother said it was Allah's voice that spoke that December morning. And the boy believed his mother.

The boy was raised in a madrassah outside Banda Aceh. It was Chaniago's school. He believed the words of his teacher, that few would be honored to become martyrs, and those few whose names would never be forgotten. When Chaniago came to him, he felt like a child chosen from the crowd of children to wear the special hat, or receive the jealous slaps on his back from the others who were not chosen.

"Where is it?" he asked again of the boy standing next to him.

"He said hold this heading. We couldn't miss it." The compass pointed to an east-northeast heading. The boat rocked, as the winds were coming out of the northwest and the wheel pulled.

"The button, you have it?" His shipmate had the job of flipping the button at the exact moment. It made the boy at the wheel less anxious to know that the last second would not be his to worry about. All he had to do was keep the boat heading out into the shipping lane.

"Yeah, man, got it. We can't miss. So many ships out here." He would be right. He was from the fishing village of Lhokseumawe and had been raised seeing the horizon dotted with the lights of ships coming down the Strait. But the storm had made this night different.

The boat cruised for what seemed like several hours. The smell of diesel filled the pilothouse as the chug of the engine kept its same rhythm. Occasionally, the wind would push the waters against the port side causing the old trawler to lift out of the water, and when it did, the prop would spin up like a horse being let out of the corral.

"You know the world will hear of us." The boy at the wheel was right about that. "It must be a big ship."

"He said this one is an American container ship. Have you ever seen one?"

"No."

"It will be a wall of containers, fat and full of containers. Probably full of guns and ammunition for the Americans."

"Maybe boxes of bikinis?" The boys laughed at the thought. "They will float to Singapore!"

The boat continued to move.

"I feel something." The boy at the wheel grabbed it tightly.

"What do you mean?"

"Something."

Whether he felt something or not, they were getting closer. The boy pulled the throttle down to neutral and the two stuck their heads out of the cabin.

"Can you hear something?"

"No."

"Yes, you can!"

A deep, low, bass sound came from in front of them. The water on the surface seemed to change direction.

The ship would have radar, but their boat was so small and insignificant that those on the bridge would think it nothing more than some debris floating on the water. They would think that the storm might have raised some logs or an abandoned fisherman's boat.

BOOMMMM...

The horn sounded. Suddenly, out of the darkness, the lights of a ship crossed their bow. The vessel's containers seemed to go far into the sky.

"Oh, praise Allah!" The boy at the wheel held fast and laid on the throttle. Their boat needed speed to keep its course or the displacement of the water by the larger object would turn it around and point it in the wrong direction.

The other boy held on.

"Not yet!" he yelled to the other.

The boat corrected its course again.

"We are on it now!" They had built up speed and were heading at a ninety-degree angle to the center of the wall of steel.

A ribbon of red crossed the bow like a car that had lost a wheel, sparks flying everywhere. The two stared at it as if they were watching a fireworks show when the ribbon of fire turned toward them. The tracer rounds were every fifth bullet from the heavy machine gun on the patrol boat. The boy at the wheel saw it appear from their starboard side on a path that cut them off from the container ship.

"Faster!" the one holding the fuse device yelled.

They could now see the sailors onboard the patrol boat running around in a panic. It kept on its course of intersect. The firing increased and as it did, the boys ducked as low as they could.

Suddenly, the bow of the trawler struck the patrol boat midship. It pushed the patrol boat into the container ship and the two collapsed into the wall.

"Allah be praised!" The boy flipped the switch.

The explosion vaporized the small trawler and the patrol boat of the Indonesian Navy. The PC-40 patrol boat KAL Mamu disappeared in the blinding flash of light. The container ship was raised up by the explosion and the containers on the tops of the stacks fell into the water. They bobbed like corks for a while until they slowly sank into the sea. The ship's horn screamed as its hull was fractured by the blast. As water poured in it listed several degrees, but it was not going to sink.

CNN International reported the attack.

The oddity was that the ship was under the Iranian flag. It was not an American container ship. It limped along until it was able to reach the port near Singapore and be off-loaded. Some on the vessel were injured by the force of the explosion, lifted off their feet and thrown against the bulkheads.

The Indonesian Navy lost twenty-two good men.

The US Navy dispatched the USS *Gabrielle Giffords* from the South China Sea to the Strait. The littoral combat ship, or LCS 10, was ordered to assist the Indonesian Navy in patrolling the Strait and protecting US ships. CNN reported the USS *America* with the 31st Marine Expeditionary Unit, or MEU, would follow, ready to assist should it be needed.

Chaniago was far to the north and never knew that the attack missed its intended target. But the war had risen to a new level. The insurance companies of the world put a hold on shipping through the Strait. Some turned to another, longer route and some waited in the Bay of Bengal until more was learned.

Chapter 52

The squid trawler pulled out of the shelter of the harbor on the south side of Great Nicobar Island. Once it hit the open waters of the Bay of Bengal, the small vessel rocked violently from waves coming over the bow. The men were sheltered in place in the pilothouse as the captain held his course to the north.

"This is not wise," the captain said quietly to his main passenger.

The others were soaked and huddled in the back of the cabin. Their eyes were wide and staring down at the deck. The fear was palpable. Some did not know how to swim. The boat's sinking would be the end for most of them.

"We need to get there." Chaniago stood next to the captain. "No more delays." They had spent most of the night in the shelter of the bay waiting for the storm to pass. It only seemed to get stronger.

The trawler's metal towers swung back and forth to the limits of the ropes that tied them down. They would swing together until there would be a loud clap and swing away. Several light bulbs would break and be washed away in the wind.

"My boat is my living," the captain protested. The loss of the lights meant the loss of the ability to fish for squid. He could fish the other way for tuna, dogtooth, wahoo, and Spanish mackerel, but the money was in a good catch of squid.

"You will be well paid."

"Not enough if we are on the bottom."

The boat had made the run many times and he was aware of what to avoid as they moved north.

"Wish we could have gone on the eastern side."

"It would take twice as long." Chaniago needed to get the prisoners and get them back to Sumatra. He could have had one of his lieutenants bring them back, but events were moving fast. He was out of communication with the others. There were no carriers on the sea. And this was personal.

By early morning, the next island in the chain came into view. They headed directly to the tattered dock and pulled in to meet the men waiting on shore. The boat had been sighted as it passed the point of the more southern island and they were waiting.

Chaniago saw them standing under the protection of several coconut trees. All four of them were there. He immediately knew that something was wrong.

"Why are they all there?" he asked himself while standing next to the captain as he worked the wheel and brought the boat to the dock. The boat hand opened the door and ran into the rain to grab the lines.

"Tie it up loose. Not too tight," the captain shouted.

The others stood up on rocky legs and moved quickly to the hatch, onto the main deck, and slipped over the side to the dock. The water washed over the dock as they hopped from one plank to another until they were on solid ground. They ran up to the cover of the coconut trees with their automatics slung over their shoulders. Chaniago followed them.

"Why are all of you here?"

The oldest knew he had to speak.

"They are on this island."

Chaniago knew what that meant.

"You let them escape." He slapped the man with the back of his hand. He reached for the man's AK-47 and aimed it at him. The weapon didn't have a bullet chambered. The click of the trigger could be heard as he held it to the man's head. Frustrated, he swung it around and aimed it at the others. He didn't try to chamber a bullet as his temper subsided. He knew that every man was needed to find his prisoners.

"Take me to the hut."

The oldest one pulled himself up from the beach. Chaniago threw the automatic to him, which he grabbed before it struck him in the chest. He started to follow the path into the rain forest. The others followed Chaniago like a line of ducklings. The captain and his boat hand stayed with the trawler. It was dry, out of the wind and needed protection from the storm. The boat slapped up against the posts of the dock, but stayed in place.

At the prisoners' hut, Chaniago lifted up the chains from the muddy floor. The post lay on the ground. He walked to the rear wall and felt the opening in the bamboo with his hands.

"So, we start here." He looked through the hole into the jungle.

Chaniago paired the men in teams of two.

"You come with me." He pointed to the young boy who had liked the Marine. He drew the island in the sand with a stick and planned the search.

"It is small. They will not have been gone long. Somewhere, there is a hole or a cave. We will find them there."

"What if we find them?" The question was from the oldest one.

"Kill them." Chaniago wouldn't waste any more time with an execution. The Marine had been too smart. And he had been warned that another escape would be the last. "We can take the bodies back. We'll hang them from the light posts in Banda Aceh."

The storm still blocked the sunlight. The day was overcast, offering only a dim glow. They started off with Chaniago and the boy following the shoreline. It was difficult to navigate, with jutting rocks separating the small beaches. In several hours the two came upon what was left of the Gulfstream. Much of the aircraft was below the water and what wasn't was covered by sand and seaweed near the shoreline. The nose of the aircraft was buried deep in the jungle and in just the short time since the wreck the jungle growth had almost made it disappear.

The boy looked into the torn-off cockpit.

"Cobras like shelter like that." Chaniago issued the warning and the boy pulled back. As he walked by the wreckage, he saw the shape of a dead man in the pilot's seat.

They headed farther along the shoreline until they came upon a boulder. Chaniago noticed something bright at the base of the rock.

"Look at this." He held up the brass lock, which had been sheared apart. He followed the rock until he saw several links of the chain sticking out of the sand. The storm had nearly covered up what was left.

"He was here." Chaniago surveyed the edge of the rain forest. There were no other signs. If there had been torn ferns or traces of a trail it had disappeared in the storm. Chaniago never saw the eyes looking down on him at that moment.

Suddenly, automatic gunfire erupted from the north of the island.

"Let's go." He grabbed his AK-47 from his shoulder and headed up the beach and toward the sound.

A burst was followed by another burst.

"Good!" he shouted to the boy.

The two followed what they thought was the direction of the sound. The jungle was silent again. They followed the shoreline as far as they could until they reached a point that the rocks had cut off their path.

"Stop." Chaniago turned toward the rain forest. "It came from in here."

He led the way as they made their way through the underbrush. The vines were thick and the ferns blocked their view of anything beyond a few feet. The jungle was soaked with water and the leaves dumped it on the two of them.

"I hear something." The boy stopped. "Over there." He pointed to the left and beyond where they were. They moved through the ferns until they came to an opening. Several of the men were standing over a body.

Chaniago smiled.

"Did you get the Marine?"

The older one wasn't smiling. None of them said anything.

"What is it? What's wrong?" Chaniago pushed the men aside.

A limp dark shape lay on the ground.

"What?"

"A monkey." The older one spoke. The long-tailed macaque was covered in blood. His body had been riddled with bullets from the automatic rifle.

Chaniago became silent.

"Did you see anything?" the older one asked the boy with Chaniago.

"He found the chain. The one from his neck."

They knew the two were somewhere on the island. They just hadn't been found.

"Tell Chaniago what you saw." The older one turned to another of the hunters.

"We found a freshwater stream."

"Good, good, they must be there."

"We also found something else." The hunter was one of the men who came with him on the boat. "A saltie."

The others shuddered when he spoke.

"Saltwater crocodiles eat people." The boy's voice quavered. It was one thing to hunt two prisoners who were not armed, but another to be crawling through the jungle with saltwater crocodiles.

"Let's go back to the huts." Chaniago needed to get his men to a fire and some food.

"Can we take him?" The older one lifted the arm of the monkey. "They are good to eat."

They walked back to the south, one of the guards who had been on the island for some time serving as their guide. They walked in single file with their fingers on the triggers of their weapons. It wasn't the Marine they were worried about.

Chapter 53

"You did good." Will was at the airport with Hernandez, Retno, and Kaili. Moncrief was standing with him at the wingtip of a Beechcraft Super King Air 350 with IndoJet Charter Service marked next to the door. Hernandez was loading several gun bags, boxes of ammunition, bulletproof vests, and other supplies on board.

"The pilot not worried about this?" Will asked. Loading weapons and ammunition onto an airplane in the United States would have required several days to just make bail.

"Hey, it's Indonesia. Bigger problem was getting into the airport, and she helped." He pointed to Retno. "I told them you only needed one pilot. That you had your hours."

"Yeah. With this weather I feel better being up front." Will had the problem that all experienced pilots had. There was something comforting about having your hands on the yoke. Sitting in the back while flying through zero visibility made for a long day for someone who knew how to fly. "Where did you get it?"

"Old friend at Evergreen hooked me up with them." The airline was no longer in existence, or at least no longer in existence as a company owned by the Agency. For years Evergreen carried cargo to places few others would fly. During the Vietnam years, it was known as Air America. "Amazing what you can do when you got some plastic from Langley."

Moncrief liked the open account that he had with the CIA. It gave him license to scrounge whatever was needed and from whomever had it.

"Got you a boat at Campbell Bay. Pretty fast. Not a local fisherman's boat, but shouldn't stand out too much. This one is pretty quick." The Grand Banks was fully gassed and stocked. "Sure you don't want me to come?"

"You got to keep an eye on the kid." Will was speaking of Ben. "Plus, you look like shit." He smiled at his old friend. "When this is over you are going to go back to my farm and crash for a month or two."

"Yes, sir, follow your orders."

"We'll talk on the net." The communication gear was tied in with a satellite.

"Got moved to over here." Moncrief waved toward a hangar on the other side of BTJ, or the Sultan Iskandar Muda International Airport in Banda Aceh. "We got one more load. Should be fully up before you land."

"OK, Marine." Will climbed aboard and closed the door.

He stepped over the bags, past Kaili and Retno, and climbed into the right-hand seat. The pilot smiled, shook hands, and turned back to the controls. The ground guide signaled the airplane's clearance. Will listened through the headsets as they followed a Boeing 737 to Runway 35 and in a few minutes were airborne.

"Is this the last of it?" Moncrief was just inside the rear door of the villa talking to Ben.

"Got some of that classified gear up top and that will be it." Ben was carrying his hanging bag over his shoulder and a plastic storage container in his hands.

A loud knock came from the front.

"What's that?" Enrico was standing there with his HK416.

"Don't know." Kevin had a semiautomatic pistol in a shoulder holster under a rain jacket he was wearing. "Go to the truck in the back alley and wait." His order was to Ben, not Hernandez.

The two Marines went upstairs to the computer bank, which was still on and which had the cameras trained on the front door.

"This ain't good." Hernandez looked at the camera that showed four men dressed in black with their heads covered.

"Not Army." Moncrief pulled the slide back on his HK pistol and chambered a round.

The sound of automatic fire came from below. Bullets tore through the thick teak door.

"Let's go." Moncrief reached for a gray object from behind one of the computer terminals, pulled on it, then placed it at the base of Ben's wheeled chair.

They made it downstairs. The door had held, as the automatic fire still was hammering away on the wood.

Moncrief led the way to the back door with his pistol in hand. He stopped short, signaled Hernandez to move to one side, and slowly opened it.

Ben was standing a few yards away with another man dressed in black holding him, a pistol to his head. Another terrorist was standing behind him.

Few knew all of the traits of Kevin Moncrief. His ancestry included a line of warriors that were ferocious and feared by the 1870s U.S. Army of the west. He also taught marksmanship to young Marine lieutenants who came through the Basic School in Quantico.

A whap, whap sound came from Moncrief's gun.

The man holding Ben seemed to stand still, not moving, until the gun in his hand fell to the ground. The other man was laid low with a bullet to his face.

The three climbed into the truck and drove down the alley and onto the road that followed the river.

They had not reached the Army's roadblock when the explosion from the Willie Pete grenade rocked the villa behind them. The plume of white phosphorus tore through the wooden structure, destroying the villa in only a few minutes. None of the invaders would be found.

Chapter 54

"You have a phone?" Chaniago held out his hand.

The youngest one sheepishly handed him the cell.

"How do you charge it?"

"Solar," one of the older ones volunteered. He went to the back of the hut they were staying in, reached into his bag, and brought out a black and green rectangular device that was the same size and shape as the cell phone.

"I need this." Chaniago tried to dial the number to one of the people back in the jungle. The phone didn't reach anyone.

"Not good. No way from here." The boy held out his hand.

"Then why have it?"

"Don't know, just have it."

"It's the game." The older one spoke again.

Chaniago was ready to smash it on the rocks, but then realized he needed it for something else.

"Hold on to this." It will serve a purpose. "We need to get back to finding the prisoners."

The search parties broke up again in separate groups. This time Chaniago headed uphill with the older one. He wanted to see the lay of the island from the peak of the rocks. They worked their way through the rain forest until they found an opening that headed up a rocky path.

At the peak, the one with Chaniago stopped and sat down on a rock.

"My sandal." He wore what could be described as a well-worn plastic flip-flop. The rubber had been worn down to a thin wafer. His feet were as tough as shoe leather, but the sandals helped when he tried to cross sharp rocks.

Chaniago looked out over the island. The storm had let up, so much so that the shape of the trees and mangroves could be made out below. He could see the outline of a beach, marked by white sand, and the waves that were breaking onto the shore. He turned back to the other man.

"Let's go down."

Chaniago stopped and stared past the man sitting on the rock.

He pulled his automatic off his shoulder and pointed it to something just beyond the man. The other one stood up and put his AK-47 to his shoulder. The sound of the bolt sliding forward was loud.

The two sidled up to the opening in the rocks. Each took a side. Chaniago pointed to the black hole. The guard took it to mean that he should fire.

The rifle fired off several rounds of ammunition into the hole. The bullets ricocheted about in the bunker. Chaniago held his gun on the opening until the gunfire stopped.

The two stood there for some time. Shortly, several others reached the top of the hill.

"We heard. You got them?"

"Maybe." The terrorist held up his rifle.

"Let the boy find out." Chaniago signaled the young one to climb down in the hole.

"OK." He got down on his knees and leaned over. His legs looked like spindles. Unlike the man with the sandals, the boy was barefoot. His feet looked old and well used despite his young age. He moved slowly, not knowing what he would find. Soon, he disappeared into the bunker.

"What?" the men outside yelled. "What?"

"Anyone?" Chaniago yelled down into the hole. There was silence.

Half of a coconut shell missing the white meat was tossed out of the opening. The boy's head appeared.

"No one, but these." He tossed out several more pieces of shells.

"They were here." Chaniago felt they were getting close.

Chapter 55

The Grand Banks trawler continued up the east coast of Great Nicobar Island after it left Campbell Bay. Will steered the boat from the bridge. He had his automatic HK416 rifle resting next to the wheel. The radar unit was on the console with a multicolored screen of green, yellow, and red that scanned the path of the boat. Kaili came up from the galley with a steaming cup of coffee.

"Here you go."

"Thanks."

"Nice boat." She sat down next to him in the captain's chair. "Like the name."

"Yeah, *Determined* seems to fit." Will smiled.

"I wonder if the Gunny picked it out for that reason?"

"Probably one that was in the harbor or nearby."

The Grand Banks fit the mission well. Unlike many other boats, its color was a flat Navy gray paint. The trawler would be difficult to see in the low light of overcast clouds or at dusk. It had a small, fully stocked galley and the bow bunk beds were stacked with their weapons. It was, however, made of wood and would not take well to gunfire.

"We don't want to engage with them in a firefight." Will held the wheel on course to the north.

"Do you think we will even find them?" Kaili stared out toward the bow.

"Best guess from their plotted path. We'll know more when we get to the west side and the Bay of Bengal." It was a calculated risk and plan, but the best chance for the Marine and other passengers from the Gulfstream. "As soon as this storm clears, we'll get on the sat phone with Ben and see what the satellite says." He held the rudder on a set course.

"Take over. I'm going to get out what we might need." He moved away from the wheel. Kaili grabbed it, thinking that his letting go would cause the trawler to go into the rocks. "Keep it heading north and stay away from the shoreline."

Will went below to find Retno unpacking the gun bags.

"We've got an arsenal here." She held up another HK416 with a banana-clip shaped magazine.

"Used this?"

"No, we have the SS2." Theirs was another automatic assault rifle that used the NATO 5.56 round. "Looks pretty much the same."

"Let me show you." He stood behind her and held the HK with the rifle in her shoulder and the sight up to her face. He twisted a small dial on the mounted sight.

"Look in it. Do you see the red dot?" The laser's light was no bigger than the tip of an ink pen.

Her hair smelled of coconuts.

"Yes."

"It's set for a hundred meters. Within a hundred meters that bullet will go wherever you place that red dot."

"OK."

"This has got automatic fire, but don't use it." He took her hand and put it on the switch on the side of the weapon. "If you use automatic you won't hit anything."

"I understand."

"And when you put the magazine in, give it a slight pull to make sure that it is locked into the weapon." He took her hand and placed it on the clip, put it into the rifle, then pulled down on it until she felt a click.

"How's that?" He smiled. They were close enough that they both felt the warmth of their combined bodies.

"Will!" A voice came from above.

"Shame we have another passenger." Retno's brown eyes were so very close.

"Yes!" Will handed her the weapon. "And don't shoot me."

He climbed the ladder to the upper deck.

"Look at this." Kaili pointed to the radar. A large object was off to the east. It was moving slowly to the south, toward where they had come from.

"The Campbell Bay ferry from Port Blair." Will took a pair of binoculars and stared out into the gray mist. The storm was clearing and the lights and shape of the ship would appear and disappear.

"What's next?" Kaili asked her navigator.

"Fifty more miles and we should see Little Nicobar." He pushed a switch on the radar that brought it out from a ten-mile focus to fifty and then to a hundred. "We can turn to the west and cut through to the Bay of Bengal."

"What's that?" She pointed to a smaller object north of Great Nicobar but short of the little one.

Will pulled out the map and laid it on the console.

"Kondul Island. Nothing on it but jungle and rocks."

"You know we can anchor off the beach here and I can take a swim." Kaili smiled.

"What?"

"In case you two need a room."

Will laughed at Stidham's daughter.

"No, we got to find some folks."

Chapter 56

Chuck Hedges watched the men from an outcrop of rocks near the beach below. The sound of the automatic rifles reverberated off the jungle, the rocks, and under the overcast sky. He watched the men apparently celebrating what they had found. It wasn't what they found that was the worry. It was that they shot first without pause and then celebrated.

The engineer was tucked into a small place between two boulders on the edge of the beach. He seemed to have gained energy from the coconuts, but Chuck knew it wouldn't last long. They couldn't survive on coconuts, and every time they left their hiding place to search for food they risked being caught. The greater worry was when the storm cleared. The island was small and left little room for hiding from half a dozen searchers.

Chuck waited until the sounds stopped. It appeared that they had headed back down the hill on the other side. Cautiously, he waited some more, which aligned with the sniper training he once had with a Recon unit attached to his MEU, or Marine Expeditionary Unit. The best weapon a sniper had was waiting out the target.

Finally, he very slowly moved down the rocks to the engineer, stopping often and waiting for any movement or sound. He snugged in close to the man.

"How's your swimming?"

"What?"

"Can't be a mile from here to that bigger island." Chuck pointed out to sea.

"What island?" The rain and mist nearly blocked its view.

"There's one right there." He pointed with his arm as if he was holding a rifle.

"Oh." The engineer's voice sounded meek and wasted. "Do we have to?"

Chuck knew that some men gave up. He had met a few. Young Marines who gave up from the exhaustion, or loneliness of a combat tour far from home, or just frustration. With them, it was rarely life or death. He couldn't understand a man like the engineer. No one, in his mind, could give up, facing the odds that they did.

"Listen, they found the bunker. They emptied their rifles into it without even taking a look to see if we would come out. If you stayed there, the bullets would have torn through you, ripping you apart as they went in and bounced off the walls and went in again." Chuck grabbed what was left of the man's shirt. He kept his voice down, but looked directly into the man's red, round, sad, exhausted eyes. "On that other island we got a chance. A chance to find some help. A chance that they won't find us."

Chuck let his shirt go.

"What about sharks? Crocs?"

"With a shark you have a chance. Stay on this island and you don't."

"OK." It seemed that he wasn't in agreement as much as he was willing to die by drowning instead of a bullet to his chest.

"Good." Chuck turned into a cheerleader. "We can do this."

"OK."

"Wait here." Chuck followed the beach to the west away from where the men were. He reached a point just below a cliff. On the other side, the beach would eventually lead to the dock and the boat. He was on a mission. Like before, he was looking for a log that had floated into shore. This one had to be bigger than the last, but not so big that he couldn't bring it back to the engineer.

The trunk of a large gurjun tree was caught in the rocks. Its dark brown bark was darker still by its immersion in the salt water for days, weeks or months.

"This is going to be a bitch," he said as he pulled it away from the rocks and pushed it out into the water. It would be difficult to handle, but the engineer could ride it astride. Chuck pushed it around the rocks, followed a beach, crossed past another outcrop of rocks, and finally made it to the engineer's beach. He pulled it on shore.

The sun was starting to break through the cloud cover. The sand was a blinding white as he moved across it to the cover of the rocks. The engineer was sitting up as if he had prepared himself for the crossing.

"Let's go. The sun coming out means we have less time."

The two crossed the sand to the log. They waded out until it was chest high, then Chuck helped him onto it. The gurjun log had no branches so they risked it rolling over on both of them, but it did float.

"OK, here we go." Chuck pushed away from the beach. This side of the island was sheltered from the open ocean and winds, which left little surf. He started to climb onboard but quickly realized that any effort to get on top of the log would roll it over. Once in deeper water, the chances of getting the engineer back on the log would be nil. Chuck held the log with one hand while he used his legs and his other arm to paddle. Soon they were in deeper, dark blue water.

The trip would be exhausting.

Chuck stopped paddling and looked back at the shore. The island's size had become more apparent as he had gotten some distance from it.

"Wouldn't have had a chance," Chuck mumbled from the water.

"What?"

"They would have found us and strung us up."

"Yeah." The engineer glanced back at the island as well.

They moved slowly across the water. A current grabbed them and pushed them to the east, but the island they were heading to was so much larger that there wasn't much risk that they would miss the target. The greater risk was that Chuck would collapse with exhaustion. This was far worse than any marathon he had ever run or forced march with a heavy pack. The lack of food had drained his reservoirs of energy. His head began to fall under the surface; he would stroke hard and raise it up to grab a breath of air. He was fading fast.

He felt a hand on the back of his collar.

"Come on, we got this." The engineer had slid into the water and was helping them paddle. They began to paddle in unison. The loss of weight and resistance on the log helped Chuck regain his strength.

It was getting dark and they seemed so far from the island.

"We got this," Chuck repeated.

They paddled for another hour, during which it seemed the current fought their movement.

Chuck felt his foot touch something. He felt it again. It didn't move.

"God, thank God." His foot was on sand.

The engineer was still paddling, oblivious to what had happened.

Chuck stood up.

"Hey, look!" He was standing up and looking over the log.

"Oh, God!" The engineer stopped and tried to pull himself up but the exhaustion caused him to stumble. He fell face-first into the water, then stood up again.

"We made it!" Chuck fell down on the sand. The engineer joined him and they lay there together. "Looks like we are on a sandbar. Need to get to some land before it's too dark."

"What's that?" The engineer pointed out to the east.

The lights of a ship moved slowly to the south. It wasn't a cargo ship, as there were no cargo masts or containers.

"Must be a ferry." Chuck knew that they shouldn't get up their hopes.

"Can we signal it?"

"No." He studied the ship as it continued to move over the water. Those on board would never see them. If they were on the log and near it, the ship would probably run them over. It would not be a source of help, but it did mean one thing. It was heading toward somewhere and to someone. They were not alone.

Chapter 57

"Can you hold this course?" Will had taken over the wheel but his satellite phone was blinking. Kaili came across and took over the steering.

She was built like a jet fighter, petite but solid as anyone who could run an Ironman. She seemed to have the determination of her father and his mental strength. Shane Stidham never complained. Whether he had shrapnel in his body from an IED or had humped thirty miles through the desert with a full combat load, Stidham never said a word. She appeared to have the same warrior DNA.

Maybe she is a good fit, he thought as he stepped out of her way and onto the main deck. The light was fading as they continued to head north.

"Hello."

"Will?" It was Moncrief. "We've got something." The voice broke up. "We've got something."

"What?"

"Get your laptop. The weather has cleared."

Will went down into the galley and grabbed the backpack with his laptop. He opened it with his code and the password device in his body and pulled up the email from Ben. It opened a picture of Google Earth but this one was through the Agency's feed. The satellite feed was in real time and the lighting was amazingly bright despite the descent of darkness. He quickly recognized the ferry heading south on a parallel course to his, but farther out to sea and behind them by now. He was able to focus the satellite image in on the craft and pulled the picture over his trawler. He zoomed in and the shape of the Grand Banks first became identifiable as a boat, then he could see the fine details of the boat.

"Damn."

Will had worked with these satellites before, but he climbed up on the top deck and looked into the sky. At the same time, he held his laptop and focused in on the man with his computer on the top of the Grand Banks trawler. He waved at the sky.

"OK, Colonel, stop horsing around." Moncrief sounded like he needed some humor. "Look to the northwest."

"What at?"

"Ben, can you show him?" They appeared to be on a shared call and Ben took over control of the picture.

"Here you go." He had moved the screen up to the pass north of Great Nicobar Island. And just to the north of the larger island was a smaller one. It carried the name of Little Nicobar Island. Between the two islands was another smaller one barely noticeable.

"What are we looking at?" Will studied the screen as Ben manipulated the picture. It sharpened on the small island with a name below it: Kondul. The picture showed a small, sandy beach and a dock on the western side. The dock appeared run down and every other board was missing. It wasn't the dock that got their attention.

"See it?" Ben asked.

"Yes, yes." A trawler was tied to the dock. It wasn't the usual fishing boat. As the satellite closed on it, it revealed the metal riggings of a squid boat. The picture became sharper and focused in on the man standing on the deck.

His AK-47 was slung over his shoulder.

"Call in the cavalry?" Moncrief asked.

"What do we know of the cavalry?" They had talked briefly at the airport before departure. It wasn't a random question. It was meant to ask whether Moncrief had spoken with MARCOS.

"I got Scott's help."

"Really?"

"Seems they want one of the passengers back pretty badly."

"Which one?"

"He was the head of Chevron's engineering team."

Scott could be an asset as long as their interests matched. Here, they paralleled. Scott wanted the engineer and Will wanted the husband of a Marine wife.

"Don't need Marcos in right now." Will knew what he was talking about. The Indian Marine Commandos would hit the island with the force of a tornado. The *dadiwala fauj*, or bearded ones, trained to the extreme. If a Navy SEAL swam five miles, they would swim ten. Both were good, but there was too much chance that any hostage would be dead before the gunfire stopped. "Keep us on the satellite and if anything looks out of control, get them in."

"OK, they have a unit at Port Blair. It'll take time for them to get there. These islands cover a lot of miles."

"Yeah, Indira Point. It's the most southern point of India." Ben interjected the lesson. "The point on the south end of Great Nicobar Island is the most southern point of India."

"I've got them on the satellite phone. Told them that we are just looking around right now." Moncrief handled it well.

"There is something else," Ben interjected. "Look at this."

He moved the video picture back to the eastern side of Kondul Island. The cursor moved up the coastline of the small island to the northern end. The beaches seemed to be on the eastern side, while the west side seemed rockier. The satellite focused in on the clear water near the shore.

"I'll be dammed." Will looked at the shape just under the water's surface. The wings of an airplane stood out. As they moved closer, there was what appeared to be a cut in the vegetation of the rain forest that the nose of an aircraft would have made.

"It wasn't a crash. Or at least, not an unplanned one." Will had found part of what he had been looking for.

The Grand Banks trawler headed north at full speed. Will formulated a plan while they moved toward Kondul Island. He needed to know if the men were alive. He needed to know if they could be rescued.

"Here is where we are going." Will pointed the two to the east side of Kondul Island where the ribs of another dock extended out into the sea. At the end of the dock and well into the water was what appeared to be a platform, perhaps made of cement. The walkway of the dock to the platform was mostly under water.

"What was that?" Kaili asked.

"Probably left by the Japanese." Will studied the structure. "We'll pull in at that platform, let me off, then you head south.

"OK."

"I will travel through the jungle and see what I can find. You head south to the pass and I'll meet you there."

It made sense logistically.

"Don't tie up. Don't want you to be within two hundred meters of the shoreline."

"Out of the range of AKs," Retno commented on the plan. "But if we are out of their range, we won't be able to help."

"Got it. Just keep this extra sat phone at the ready. Talk to Ben with his satellite link and the DIVA program." They would be the eyes that helped Will avoid danger. If it all worked, Will would know more about the enemy than they would ever know about him.

Chapter 58

The two walked the length of the sandbar until it neared the beach. There, they waded across the warm, shallow water of a pool until they felt firm land under their feet. The beach where they were at, however, was on the edge of a swamp that went into the interior of the island.

"We need to stay away from that." Chuck picked up a stick shaped like a baseball bat.

"We good?" The engineer stood close.

The rain was stopping, but the overcast sky made the night even darker.

"Just need to get to some land. Something other than this low area." Chuck knew that in this wilderness, a swamp wouldn't be much of a benefit. It was the home to saltwater crocodiles that would eat anything within their range.

"So, inland."

"Perhaps. Need to stay close to the water in case someone friendly comes by." He paused. "At least they aren't going to get to us here."

"Yeah."

"Maybe in the light I can do my Boy Scout thing and start a fire." Chuck smiled. He was exhausted, but felt like a man spared by the governor when walking to the gallows. "Let's get inland, find some cover, and get some sleep."

The sounds of the jungle weren't going to help. Creatures seemed to come alive as if welcoming them to the rainforest. A howl deep inland was responded to by another howl.

"Sleep? Did you say sleep?" The engineer surprised him with the humor.

"Help will come, I feel it." Chuck led him up a sandy hill to a grove of mangrove trees that bordered the swamp. "We'll have something to eat in the morning."

The fruit of a mangrove tree littered the area near the swamp and trees. "How about now?"

"Don't want to go exploring in the dark."

"Got it."

"We can make it for some time with this fruit and maybe a coconut or two." Chuck was laying out a plan for survival. Once they had the lay of the land, they could decide how much risk to take. The others still had a boat and it was entirely possible their captors could reach them.

"OK. Forgot to say thanks." The engineer knew that his survival depended on one man.

"Wonder what my family is doing?" Chuck tried to calculate the time zones and dates. He knew it was just past sunset in Indonesia but had no idea as to whether it was a Wednesday or a Sunday. His mind and memory had been melted down by the crash and following days. "Is it October?"

"No, September." The engineer had that scientific mind that retained details. "Early September."

"So, my boys have started school." Chuck had missed too many starts of schools. "I promised her I wouldn't do this anymore. Only stay with Chevron if it was a desk job."

"Well, after this, you deserve it."

The two leaned up against the base of a coconut tree.

"Get some sleep." Chuck told his partner. "I'll keep guard."

The baseball bat of a stick would hardly hold up against a saltie.

Chapter 59

The men returned to the bunker at the top of the hill. They had fanned out all morning, covering island to the north. From the bunker to the south, there wasn't much left of the jungle or land. They didn't realize that there were other eyes on them during the search.

Will had made it to the edge of their huts and the dock where their boat was moored. As they left the huts in the morning, Will made it to the end of their encampment. Like criminals who don't return to the scene of the crime, they were everywhere on the island but at the huts. He found the chains in the hut where the prisoners had been held. A post lay on the muddy ground. He moved out of the encampment and worked his way back to a sandy trail. He stopped when he heard noise coming from behind him.

Will pulled into the cover of the rain forest. He listened to a group of three men that passed within only a few feet of him. They spoke of the missing prisoners and Chaniago.

"Man, he won't stop." The first one seemed to have had enough.

"Don't say that," the other protested. "You weren't there back in Lhoknga. He cut the man's head off and smiled."

"It was an infidel." He described the death of the man as if one were exterminating a rat. "He was an American. His death was important to our faith." The words sounded like a man in Germany decades ago who said the same thing about another race. Then, the man described the need to eliminate those with bad blood circulating in their bodies whether they be a father, a mother or a child. That leader described his enemies in the same light as Chaniago had. Their prisoner had become an "it" and not a human being.

They also seemed lost.

"Which way?"

"I think they went up that hill."

"Let's go."

"We wouldn't be doing this if you kept a better eye on them."

The accusations flew.

"You had last watch! Chaniago will not be pleased with you!"

"It's that Marine. I will kill him first. If it wasn't for him, we'd be back in Aceh. Then I'll kill the other one." The first one spoke.

Will had learned that only two were left, but two were alive. And the two were missing.

Chaniago stood at the top of the outcrop of rocks. He climbed to the top of the bunker. The sun had come out and drenched the jungle in its bright light. The leaves on the palms glistened with the reflection of the light on the beads of water left by the storm.

"What would I do?" he asked himself. He had survived years of combat and killed far more than his share of men by thinking of what his enemy would do. More than once in Syria, Chaniago had set up ambushes at a spot in the road based on asking himself what the Americans would do.

One ambush he was famous for was an *L*-shaped one on the road out of Raqqa toward Baghdad. He had studied the route for days in the hills above the road, watching the Americans stopping their convoy at the same spot. It was near an oasis and a pool of water. Men had stopped at that spot for more than a thousand years. The American Army would be no exception. The shape of the ambush meant that the fire of the RPGs and machine guns would interlock, forming a thunderstorm of bullets. He watched as the lead driver stopped, climbed out of his Humvee to take a leak on the side of the road, and jammed up the convoy. They bunched up in the curve and the RPGs rained down on them. It was a slaughter.

What would I do? He looked down to the shoreline from his perch. A beach below had something that caught his eyes.

"Come with me!" He barked his order as he climbed down from the bunker and headed down the rocks to the sand. The others followed as some slid down the rocks. Chaniago made it there first. A print, protected from the rain and wind, was at the base of a boulder. A shell from a coconut tree was in the hole between the boulders. The footprint pointed out to sea. Beyond the beach, the land of another island was close by. It wasn't more than a mile swim at most.

"To the boat!" He had found his game. The men reversed course and climbed back up the rocky hill, then followed the path down to the other side of the island. They scurried like crabs on the beach when the wave pulled back from the shore. "Quickly!"

Chaniago had vengeance on his mind.

"First the Marine!" He shouted the words.

Chapter 60

The men ran past Will as he laid low in the dense undergrowth at the base of the hilltop. He waited until the last one passed by, then waited some more to be sure. The last one was a teenage boy. The automatic rifle he was carrying was nearly as long as the boy was tall. He was thin, very thin, and Will wondered.

He'll give his life for this fanatic. Will had seen others like this boy in other battles. It was always the terrorist groups that preyed on the children. It didn't take any military training to load an AK-47 and pull the trigger. The men that Will had killed were that—men. They were soldiers who had made the choice in their lives to put on a uniform. They made the choice and risked the consequences. But the boy hadn't lived long enough to make a true choice. He had been given food and friendship. The price for those gifts was the risk of death. Will let the boy pass because he didn't want to put a bullet in him.

But the boy was just as dangerous and deadly as the cobras that lurked in the jungle Will was hiding in. In fact, the snakes were more innocent, as they only reacted to the search for food and the need to protect themselves from danger. The boy wasn't in danger. He was a part of a group that caused danger.

Will felt the grip of the semiautomatic pistol in his hand. The gun was the best of well-made German machinery. It was dependable. Its manufacturer also had a history. At the end of World War II, the Mauser factory in Oberndorf had been dismantled by the occupying French. Its records, drafts, and diagrams were all destroyed, but the French couldn't destroy the brainpower of the engineers. Edmund Heckler and Theodor Koch built machines that could kill but could also protect. The weapons were, in many ways, the polar opposite of the AK that the boy carried. His weapon was made in a sweatshop in one of the southern islands of Indonesia. It was simple, functional, but just as dangerous as Will's weapon.

Will was well armed with his HK pistol equipped with a silencer. He remained as still as a cobra.

Not yet.

It wasn't the time to engage them. If he had, the first shot had to be the boy at the rear of the line. Then, like hunting game, he would hit the next one up the line. With the silencer and the jungle that also suppressed sound, each one in line would not know that the man behind him was dead. But at some point, a man would fall to the ground and make a noise as he hit the path. His rifle might strike a rock or make a thud. The next one up might turn around and start firing. He would fire blindly into the jungle, but soon the others would be firing. The jungle would be sprayed with automatic fire. And a random bullet might strike its target. It would not help for Will to be wounded. At least not while the two were missing. It was better to regroup and plan his options.

The men made it to the encampment and beyond. Voices could be heard screaming in the jungle. It became clear that Chaniago was taking two or three men with him to the boat and the rest would stay at the encampment.

Will climbed out of his hiding place below a large vine entangled around a tree that stood more than thirty feet above him. He made it back up the hill to the bunker. The expended brass from their automatic fire covered the ground. An empty shell from a coconut was among the spent cartridges. He climbed up on the bunker and looked out over the island.

"So, they aren't here." He studied the water and the beach. The sun had cast a bright light over the channel. Another island was reachable within a short swim. He heard automatic gunfire come from the western side of Kondul Island like a raiding party ready to go to war.

The island to the south was very close.

Will held his sat phone in his hand and called the boat.

"Where are you?"

"We are just offshore and rounding the point." Kaili's voice came through.

Will saw the trawler just as he spoke.

"Stop."

They were below him, off the shore of the island and heading directly toward the path of the terrorists' trawler.

She reacted slowly to the command. Her boat seemed to continue to head west.

"Do you copy?"

The sat phone gargled with static.

The squid boat had turned the corner from the west side of Kondul. He watched as it changed direction. At first, it was heading directly to the other island, but as it came past the last land of Kondul it shifted direction toward Kaili's boat. The two were just below his position on the hilltop and not far from the beach. Will raced to the shoreline. When he reached it, he saw the squid boat pull alongside Kaili's boat. Men with automatic rifles were climbing on the *Determined* like ants from an ant hill that had been kicked. Will heard more automatic gunfire.

Chapter 61

"Well, my surprise!"

Chaniago stood on the bridge of the Grand Banks trawler. His men were holding the two prisoners. Retno was struggling. One of the guards struck her on the side of her head with the butt of his rifle. She went limp and fell to the deck. Kaili pushed back against the guard holding her, but when he lifted his rifle to strike her, she stopped moving.

"Lift her up."

The guard picked up Retno from the deck.

"Tie her up and throw her in."

The guard grabbed a rope and tied her ankles. He took the limp body to the main deck and tossed her over the side. He held on to the rope as she sank under the surface.

"Pull her in." Chaniago didn't want it to be an easy death. The guard dragged on the rope and her feet came out of the dark water. He pulled hard and her legs came to the railing of the boat.

"Get her head out!" Chaniago spewed out the order.

The guard reached over the side and grabbed her by her hair. He pulled her face out of the water and then pulled her body, by her hair, onto the railing and then the deck.

She started to cough, coughing up water, spitting it out and gasping for air.

"Chaniago, come look at this." The other one stood at the ladder down to the bow. Several of the gun bags were open as well as several canisters of ammunition. "The best!"

"Man, this is a problem." Chaniago looked at the arms. "Two women would not be here with this."

The guard realized that he was right. The trawler could not have these arms and be manned by two people alone. Or, even worse, trouble might be around the point.

"Put them on our boat and sink this."

"But, Chaniago?"

"Grab what you want, but sink this quickly." He knew with this type of arms a satellite might be overhead. And an Indian MARCOS helicopter might be following.

The men grabbed the hostages and tossed them onto the deck of the squid boat. Two of them grabbed several of the guns and several containers of ammunition, putting them in the pilothouse. The last man used his AK automatic and riddled the wooden trawler just below the waterline. It took several magazines fired into the boat before it began to list, then quickly slid below the surface.

"Where to now? Don't like hanging out here." The captain's boat and livelihood were at stake. He pulled on the throttle and the boat moved in reverse as it moved away from the sinking craft.

"Over there!" Chaniago pointed to the other island.

"You have these two." The captain's voice was a protest. There wasn't a reason to keep searching for the others when he had his new hostages.

"I want them." The Marine had escaped. He and the other were proof that the aircraft had been hijacked. He and the other were representatives of a major American corporation.

The squid boat turned toward the island and crossed the water. The current pulled it to the west, but the captain corrected course and headed to the center of the beach.

"Tie them up." He ordered the guards to tie both women to the mast pole. "If they get loose, I will cut your guts out and feed them to the sharks while you watch." He meant it.

The boat's bow grounded on a sandbar. It struck the sea floor and the men on board fell forward. They quickly got up and headed to the bow.

"You stay here with them. We'll be back shortly." Chaniago knew that the other two could not have gone far. The island was just as overgrown as Kondul. Great Nicobar's people only lived in the southern part and numbered less than a hundred. The only military was the local police at Campbell Bay, which was nearly thirty miles away through one of the densest jungles in Southeastern Asia. The northern coast of Great Nicobar was a succession of beach followed by swamp followed by beach and swamp for several miles. And the swamps were well stocked with saltwater crocodiles. The cobras, spiders, and dangerous wildlife gave the prisoners little chance of survival.

Chaniago slid off the bow of the boat with three of his men. They headed toward the land and the mangroves. The escapees were not armed and had no food or fresh water.

"Keep an eye out!"

They moved in a single file toward the tree line.

"Shoot anything." Chaniago didn't care whether they survived. He had two live prisoners that could made the video he wanted to record with the cell phone. He didn't need any more. Two recognizable bodies would serve just as well.

"Anything at all."

Chapter 62

The engineer was the first to notice the trawler coming around from the east side of Kondul Island. He jumped up, and as he did, he woke Chuck up. The exhaustion had caused Chuck to fall asleep while sitting at the base of the tree. His eyes followed what was happening as it unfolded.

"Get down!" He grabbed the man, who fell backward. Suddenly, the engineer had more energy than he had seen during this entire ordeal. The engineer turned to him with eyes full of anger.

"This is our way out!" he shouted.

The engineer started to struggle to get up when he heard the gunfire.

The two pulled back into the cover of the jungle and watched as the trawler was overtaken by the other boat. They saw the shape of a woman tossed overboard, and then dragged back on the ship.

"God, they are going to sink it," the engineer cried out. "Those bastards!" It was as if he had made it to the border after escaping the Gestapo only to be dragged back at the last second. The trawler quickly slid into the water as the two watched.

"What are we going to do now?" He was in tears realizing what had happened. Escape had been less than a mile away. If the trawler had only turned toward them and away from Kondul Island, they could be safely onboard.

"Look!" Chuck pointed back toward the water.

The nightmare wasn't over. The squid boat turned toward them.

"We need to get in deeper." Chuck pulled him toward the jungle. "Now!"

They headed south and the rain forest quickly became thick and impassable. The tall grass and fern leaves cut at them. And they had moved no more than fifty or so meters into the undergrowth.

A clearing seemed like it should be only a few yards away. It got to the point that Chuck was pulling the other man along as he moved through the brush.

"Come on, come on!" Chuck pleaded with him.

"Go ahead, I'll stay here." The man was giving up again.

"Come on!" He turned back to the opening only to face the barrel of an AK-47.

The guards had lived in the jungle all their lives. It was easy for them to chase down the two men. The order was to kill on sight, but the prisoners didn't resist. The man thought that Chaniago might be pleased when they marched the two out of the jungle.

Chuck was close to giving up.

Maybe at the boat. Perhaps a guard would turn his eyes away at the wrong moment. Perhaps he could grab one of the men and use him as a shield from the others. The choice that didn't work was letting them tie him up and take him onboard.

If I die, I will take at least one with me. He would choose the smallest he could grab. They were half his weight and if he had the energy, he could toss one into the swamp or water with ease. He would wait for the right moment.

Chaniago wouldn't give him that opportunity. Both would be torn apart by automatic gunfire as soon as possible. They knew he only wanted a picture of their heads.

The two surfaced from the jungle with the two guards who had caught them. Chaniago had returned to the boat when he saw them emerge from the rain forest.

"This is a good day. Allah is great. He rewards the chosen one." Chaniago smiled as the two were marched across the beach. "Bring the other two so we can video them watching the Americans die."

At this order the guards dragged both women to the railing. Retno was still an unconscious lump, but Kaili struggled against the guard holding her. The one holding Retno tossed her onto the beach then jumped overboard. Kaili moved to the railing as the guard pointed his barrel toward the sand. Her hands were still tied, but she swung her legs over the railing and slid to the sand. He followed her, keeping his automatic trained on her. Only the captain stayed onboard.

"Allah is great." Chaniago watched as the prisoners were walked and dragged to his feet. He looked at the Marine and engineer. "On your knees!" It was the same order he had given to Americans captured in Syria. The same order given to the Jordanian pilot who had bailed out of his aircraft and made the mistake of being captured. The same he gave to the other American who he beheaded.

The executioner studied his prisoners.

Chuck noticed it first. He looked beyond Chaniago to the boat. The others' eyes followed his. The boat seemed to move, but not away. It moved up and then down as if an enormous invisible forklift raised it and then lowered it. The water receded. Soon, the boat was on ground.

The fault shifted. The earth moved.

Suddenly, birds in the jungle filled the sky heading to the east. They were moving away from trouble.

There was little sound. A million nuclear bombs were going off just below the surface of the water to the west, but there was no sound.

The Great Sumatra fault slipped underneath the plate of the earth's crust. It was nothing compared to the earthquake of Boxing Day. It was enough, however, for the guards to hesitate.

The squid boat was suddenly grounded. Its keel caused it to list. The captain disappeared. From around the stern of the squid boat a man appeared. The HK semiautomatic pistol was nearly silent as the bullets flew at their targets. The guards dropped, one by one, from left to right. The .40-caliber slugs hit some in their necks and others in their foreheads. Each man collapsed as if a bolt of electricity had surged through their bodies.

Chaniago was the last. Without thinking, he turned towards the others that had collapsed from the bullet fire and then back to the boat. The stranger stood there just to the side of the grounded boat with his raised pistol. No one would be there to save Chaniago from what was deserved.

The man who had killed so many in Syria fell to the sand on a remote beach in Southeast Asia. He was struck by Will Parker's rounds in each shoulder, causing him to drop his rifle. The third bullet struck the center of his chest. He fell to his knees, gasping for air and looked up into Will's eyes.

"Who?" The last words of Chaniago were not answered.

The water returned to the sea. The earthquake was measured at 6.2 by the Berkeley Seismology Lab nearly ten thousand miles away. It caused a ripple compared to the earthquake on Boxing Day years before. But it did save several lives. The rumble of the earthquake passed and the squid boat floated again.

"You all right?" Will asked Retno as she came to.

"Yeah, sure."

The sound of the MARCOS's Mil Mi-17 helicopter nearly drowned out her words. The sand blew up around them as it set down on the beach. Another helicopter was seen over Kondul Island. Gunfire could be heard as a team of MARCOS Marines took out the encampment. The boy never made it off the island.

An Indian Marine ran to those on the ground. His squad followed him and spread out in a twenty-four-point formation. At first, he held his HK MP5 submachine gun on Will until his eyes took it all in.

"You must be Colonel Parker." Again, rank was used. It meant that Kevin Moncrief was behind their being there.

"Yes."

"Happy to see you." He smiled a large toothy smile through his black beard.

Will didn't ask his name. It was known that the names of those in MARCOS were never spoken.

"No, we're happy to see you."

"Let's get you to Campbell Bay."

Will helped Retno to the Soviet-built helicopter along with Kaili, Chuck Hedges, and the engineer. Two of the Marines retrieved Chaniago's body in a black, zippered body bag.

"What's up?" He pointed to the men carrying the body bag back to the second helicopter that had landed on the beach.

"The Chinese have wanted him for some time. We were told if he ever showed up, they would pay a bounty to our government."

"And the others?"

"The salties need to be fed."

The helicopter lifted off and gained altitude as it headed east-southeast over the channel and Nicobar Island. As it turned further east, Will looked back to the islands and saw a flash of flame erupt from the beach. The second helicopter had fired a rocket followed by another rocket into the squid boat. It was in shallow waters and seemed to melt below the surface.

The helicopters landed on the single strip runway at Campbell Bay. Another helicopter, an American-made Chinook CH-47, was already there. A series of white tents had been erected.

Will followed the leader of the MARCOS team into the first tent with the others.

"Medical is waiting. We have plenty of food for you."

Chuck and the engineer followed a doctor in a white coat into another tent. Retno limped along with them to a third tent. Kaili stayed with Will.

"We keep an eye on the Nicobar Islands, but there are many," the MARCOS officer explained.

"Yes."

"Your aircraft is on its way and should be here shortly."

Will was ready for a long nap after eating. The rush of adrenaline seemed to cause the same effect as running a marathon. He heard the Beechcraft twin as it turned for final approach just before touching down.

Kevin Moncrief was the first one to step on the ground followed by Hernandez and Ben.

"Saw it all from the satellite. No fun. Like watching the towers drop. You want to jump in but can't." Moncrief seemed to feel a need to explain himself.

"We need to get to Kuala Lumpur." Will knew that one other person was missing.

"Yep, the CIA's got a C-17 inbound as we speak." Moncrief smiled. "You OK?"

"Oh, yeah. Feel great."

The team boarded the King Air 350 with Will in the copilot seat. The trip to Kuala Lumpur passed over the entire length of the Malacca Strait. It seemed that word had gotten out quickly, as ships dotted the waterway going both north and south. The day was bright and clear. From their altitude Will could see the foam of the fantails of the giant ships as they moved through the sea-lanes.

He felt a touch on his shoulder.

It was Kaili.

Will pulled the headset off. Everyone in the back was sound asleep.

"We need to talk." Kaili was close to Will's ear. He shook his head. The sound of the turboprop engines meant that no one could hear over the noise.

"He's got leukemia," she whispered in his ear.

Will looked into her eyes with a stare like the one Chaniago saw just before dying.

"How bad?"

"Very."

They flew in silence for the remainder of the journey to Kuala Lumpur.

At the Skypark FBO of the Sultan Abdul Aziz Shah Airport near Kuala Lumpur, a woman was standing just behind the plate glass windows.

With sorrow can come joy. Chuck limped across the tarmac to the arms of Margie Hedges.

"I will never leave the United States again!" he mumbled into her ear.

"But I want to go to London." They both laughed and cried. She walked over to Will Parker and gave him a kiss on his cheek.

"You did what you said you would do."

The US Air Force C-17 arrived early the next morning. Kaili, Chuck, and the engineer showered and dressed at the FBO before boarding the jet. Margie and the others joined them onboard. Lisa Kim had come in with the aircraft.

"Will you return?" Retno's eyes were teared up. She stood just inside the terminal.

"For some baung fish in Pekanbaru?" He smiled.

"For whatever you want."

Kim stood nearby, waiting awkwardly, as if the jet was waiting for this goodbye to conclude. Will turned and walked to the airplane with Kim by his side.

"Mr. Scott says congratulations."

Will only smiled.

"I have a request." He took her aside on the ramp. "We need to go back to Houston."

"Change the flight plan?"

"Just do it." Will didn't sound like this was something he was flexible on.

The flight took nearly eighteen hours before arriving at Ellington Field Air Base in Houston. A black Yukon was waiting.

"Let's go." Will grabbed Moncrief and Kaili. "I've got to do something."

"They got me on a flight back to Georgia. I'll call as soon as I get to the house." Hernandez hugged the other three and took off for the commercial airport.

"What we got?" Kevin Moncrief was puzzled.

"Got another mission." Will was very quiet. "Got a friend who needs our help."

The lobby to the MD Anderson Medical Center looked like the lobby to the United Nations. Men in their *thawbs* of white satin and women covered in abayas crossed the lobby with small children. Some wore clothing representative of the upper echelon from Saville Row and Manhattan, their wives in the best of Paris fashion. Others were dressed more simply, fathers and mothers with a child in a wheelchair and an IV hung on the chair.

"What the hell are we doing here?" Moncrief gave Kaili a look at that could stab through the heart.

"I want you to meet a friend." Will led the way to the counter. He didn't even reach it before a tall man in a white coat approached.

"Is this my new patient?"

The doctor stuck his hand out to Kevin Moncrief.

"OK?" Moncrief stared at him.

"Your man here saved my life and said I owed him yours." The doctor smiled as Will looked on. He turned to Will. "Everybody knows what happened on my hunting trip, but I would appreciate it if you don't say anything to my nurses."

"You save his life and I will keep my mouth shut." Will stuck out his hand.

Conclusion

The earthquake did more than shake the people of Sumatra. Along with the death of Chaniago, it took the air out of the sails of the rebel forces. VAT 69 and the Army rounded up other members of JAD, and in a raid on the encampment in the Ulu Masen forest, broke the terrorists' back. The location of the encampment was provided by an Agency friendly to the cause and as the result of the work of a technician from IARPA. Some of the rebels had played their video game on their cell phones for the last time.

VAT 69 also visited the airfield near Pekanbaru. As soon as their Humvees pulled through the gate Iskandar Muda ran. He wasn't given the chance to even reach for his pistol. The machine gun fire nearly cut him in half.

Will returned to Alaska and received a visitor.

Lisa Kim's black Huey helicopter landed just in front of the cabin. It blew up a gust of blinding snow. The pilot shut down the jet engine and stayed in his seat as the door slid open and Kim jumped out. She crossed the snow-covered yard with her hood covering her face. It was an early snow so it didn't cover her boots.

"So, all is well?" She shook off the snow from her gray Canada Goose parka on his front porch.

"Glad you came." Will handed her a steaming cup of coffee he had brought out once he heard the aircraft pass overhead. They stayed on the porch in two rockers. The air was frigid, but it would soon be midday and it was still early in the season.

"Brought you this." Kim handed him a clipping of a news article from the *Anchorage Daily News*. "Didn't think you saw it."

NOVEMBER 400CP IS MISSING 233

The caption read, "Mystery Hero of the Mountain." Robyn had given a detailed story of her rescue.

"Probably ends your spy days." Kim said what Will knew. Exposure was not good for someone who worked for the Agency even as an independent.

"So, the engineer? Scott didn't seem too concerned about Hedges." Will changed the subject.

She didn't answer the second part of the question.

"He is more than the chief engineer at Chevron. He is a volcanologist and knows Sumatra like no other."

"How's that affect the CIA?"

"Indonesia had started to take over its oil fields. The engineer found another deposit of oil and gas, bigger than any other. He predicts it is the size of the Ghawar Field in Saudi Arabia. But Ghawar is fading. Its resources are dwindling."

"And Sumatra could be the next Ghawar." Will put the pieces together.

"But possibly in the wrong hands." Will took another sip of the coffee.

"So, the CIA can't be sure the world needs to know of this deposit. And Chevron can't be sure that if they develop the field that they won't be kicked out of Sumatra." Kim laid out the problem.

"And there is another problem. A smoldering one." Will recalled the steam vent that his helicopter flew over in Sumatra.

"Yes, it is within a few short miles of the most volatile fault line in the world. And near fundamentalist Muslims. All of which adds up to something that could be very bad on many fronts." Lisa Kim outlined the reasons why Scott and the Agency had needed Will in Sumatra. "Yes, until things quiet down over there. Imagine JAD on top of an oil field that could produce more than the best fields in Saudi Arabia? Or an earthquake that caused an environmental disaster that would destroy much of the food supply of Southeastern Asia? So, we needed to get him out of there."

"He did well. He never said anything. And they never knew what they had." Will sipped the coffee.

"I came out here for another reason. There is something else I thought you deserved to know." Kim seemed unusually obtuse in her efforts to share the news. "Mr. Scott wanted me to share this with you. To say it is top secret would be an understatement."

"OK."

"The Chinese had a theory. It was bolstered by the execution of the American held by Chaniago."

"The video? Yes."

"Their intelligence service has followed this for a very long time."

Will's eyes followed her as she slowly rocked.

"It seems that they had gathered some DNA from a visit to an airport restaurant years ago in Kuala Lumpur. The DNA matched the body of the terrorist you killed."

"Chaniago? And they think he was the Italian." Will's words shocked her.

"Yes. You knew?" Kim put down her coffee cup.

"The mystery man on the Malaysia flight MH370." Will continued to connect the dots.

"The Chinese lost more passengers on that flight than any other country."

"And two of the passengers were using fake passports."

"Correct."

"The man who stole the passport of Luigi Maraldi and was on that airplane that night." Will put the clues together.

"Exactly."

"So, it's out there? Somewhere."

Keep reading for a special excerpt

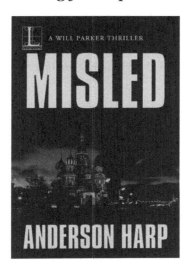

The greatest thriller authors alive have praised Anderson Harp's books as riveting, authentic thrillers. Now read for yourself: a prescient novel of interference with American lives as Russia targets the CDC...

Marine recon veteran and small-town prosecutor Will Parker became a bush pilot for two reasons: a love of flying, and Dr. Karen Stewart. Years ago in Somalia, Will saved the dedicated CDC researcher's life. Now he may have to do it again, under even more challenging conditions.

Two Marines have died under suspicious circumstances, and Will is the only person who can get to the truth. Even if it means an off-the-books mission that will take him thousands of miles away to remote Russia. Both of the dead had in common a fellow student at the Maryland Cyber Security Center. He's missing, but his trail leads Will to a small village outside Moscow known for worldwide hacking—and ultimately to an American financial institution with a shady multi-trillion-dollar secret to which the Marines and their classmate held the key. That key compelled certain executives to unleash killers to ensure its concealment . . .

Because of her importance to Will, Dr. Karen Stewart is once again a target. The enemy knows if they get to her, they get to him. Now, with her research taking her into the far-flung Yukon, Parker's arctic-combat training and skills as a bush pilot will be his only hope of saving her, not to mention himself . . .

Look for MISLED *on sale now*

Chapter 1

Deep in the Yukon

The arctic fox did not move when the aircraft narrowly cleared the tree line and crossed the open field. The animal was caught in the open, far from the protection of the tall pines and spruce, paralyzed by fear and sickness. His nearly pure-white fur blended perfectly into the blinding sunlit snow of the Yukon. The air had a sting in it from the subzero cold. His breath caused the faintest vapor cloud to form as he panted, his white-frothed tongue hanging from his mouth. The exhaustion had overtaken him. He was dying.

In a daze, the animal tracked the airborne object above, head canting left and right as if he were drunk. As the engine's throaty sound grew louder, he jumped and fell back into the snow. He tried again to run, but at a tilt, stumbling as if his internal gyroscope were off. He recovered his balance and made a desperate break for the protection of the trees.

The DHC-3 Otter's pilot circled the field, lining up what had once been an Army runway, putting his flaps down, and landing softly on the single strip buried under the snow. The sleds of the aircraft barreled through the drifts as the aircraft's propeller churned the dry, powder-like snow into a cloud of white that followed the bright yellow Otter to the end of the runway.

A lone person waited next to the runway with a backpack and a rectangular object next to her feet. The shape of her parka gave a clear impression that this was a woman, petite, not nearly tall enough to reach up and touch the aircraft's wing. She held up an arm to shield her face from the blast of icy air from the propeller. A black, canvas-covered rectangular object near her feet shook as the aircraft approached, seeming to wobble on its own. Something alive inside moved the covered cage.

The aircraft stopped at the end of the runway near the passenger and her cargo. The old Otter had black oil streaks across its yellow engine cowling. The tall propeller blades came to a stop and the engine silenced. With the motor halted, the sudden silence of the outback weighed heavily until movement in the airplane broke the quiet. The sound of metal echoed as the door handle was turned. The pilot's door swung open and a man climbed down. Tall and built firmly, he jumped down from the cockpit with a subtle air of confidence. It didn't seem to be his first trip to the backcountry.

"Did you see that fox?" Will Parker glanced toward the other end of the runway.

"Did it have two black-tipped ears?" the woman asked, carrying her backpack to the airplane.

"Yeah." He leaned against the cargo door. "Didn't think he was going to move."

"Surprised he moved at all. That's George." She took off her mitten and pulled the strings on her backpack at her feet to ensure it was closed.

"Another infected one?" He had already seen a few types of animal in the area infected with the rapidly spreading rabies virus. Mostly, the small varmints were the targets of the dreaded disease.

She nodded.

What a way to go, he thought. As a Marine who had served in special operations in some of the most dangerous places in the world, William Parker knew all about "ways to go." Having spent much of his time in the arctic prior to leaving the Marines, he also knew that rabies was rare in such cold climates. Will had been a member of a small band of experts that instructed Marines in how to survive above the arctic circle. He knew what eighty-below could do to the human body. But brutal cold was an old and well-known threat up in the north. The rabies epidemic, on the other hand, was new. And growing.

To pick up his cargo, Will had flown to this remote, abandoned airfield in Snag, Canada, deep in the Yukon and well east of the Alaskan border. Snag was an abandoned outpost of the Royal Canadian Air Force from World War II and it no longer hosted regular visitors, instead becoming a backcountry ghost town.

Perfect for my Otter, Will thought as he walked around his aircraft, performing a post flight check. The Otter aircraft was designed to get down fast and land hard in a very short space. But flying in the arctic required much of a bush pilot. Something as simple as a slightly damaged strut could, in extreme, subzero temperatures, easily snap off as the airplane landed. Yet the unusual demands of flying in the bush were what had brought Will here. He'd long ago passed the ultimate challenge for a bush pilot: landing a Super Cub on a riverbank no wider than the wheels of the aircraft. But winter was something else again. Regardless of season, though, Will had found no place on earth that had flying like the Yukon.

He had also come for the cargo.

Dr. Karen Stewart visited Snag on a regular basis. Lying to the east of the Saint Elias Mountains, the flatlands ranging north and south drew a variety of wildlife to the local habitat. Karen had left Médecins Sans

Frontières to take a position with the CDC's unit in Alaska, monitoring zoonotic infections. Zoonotic diseases followed the movement of animals, and the most dangerous of the zoonotic illnesses was rabies. Alaska and the northwest had gradually become warmer each year and, as they did, the rate of rabies had increased. The rabies virus burned through the brain and progressed relatively quickly. But as winters became milder, the sick animals were able to move farther north before dying, thus interacting with more animals and continuing the rapid spread of the fatal disease. In joining the CDC, Karen Stewart had followed in her father's footsteps, but by studying the spread of viruses among the animals of the extreme north, she'd blazed her own trail in this relatively new field.

She and Will Parker had some history—he had saved her from a kidnapping by Al- Shabaab in the western frontier of Somalia. The purpose behind the raid on the Doctors Without Borders camp had been simple: Capture those whose families could pay the ransom. Like her father before her, Karen had worked with Doctors Without Borders in the meningitis-stricken Horn of Africa until it and terrorism caught up to her. After her close call in Africa, she'd taken the CDC job and been posted to Alaska. That's when her father had called in a favor from Will Parker.

"Just keep an eye on her," was all Dr. Paul Stewart had asked after hearing that Will was flying as a bush pilot out of Anchorage.

Will had agreed gladly. He owed the man who had saved his life.

"Did you get one?" He hefted Karen's backpack and fitted it into the Otter's cargo space.

"Yeah."

He walked to the canvas-covered cage, slipping on his leather gloves. "This one have a name?"

"Juliet."

"She going to make it?" He managed to fit the cage in the rear seat of the cabin.

"No."

Karen had been in the backcountry for several days already. Parker had wanted to join her, but she'd refused. She was fiercely independent and he respected that about her. Having been a prisoner of a terrorist group in Somalia and living face-to-face with death every day, Karen had plenty of reasons to take a nine-to-five in Atlanta. But, like Will, she'd had enough of being walled in by an office.

"We need to get out of here." Will glanced west at the Saint Elias Mountains and the darkening skies above. "A bad one's coming."

She nodded, hauled herself up into the copilot's seat, and pulled back her parka hood. Her short, shaggy haircut and well-tanned face made for an attractive, athletic woman who could live in the outback with no makeup and look no worse for the wear.

He climbed into the pilot's seat, buckled in, and started running through his preflight checklist. "You know, that's a good name," he said as he worked.

"What?"

"Juliet."

She gave him a false frown.

"Dr. Juliet." Will smiled, knowing it was her middle name.

The Otter's engine roared with a throaty growl. Will spun up the turboprop to a deafening roar, turned the aircraft into the wind, and sped along the runway until the sleds started to leave the surface. As the plane lifted, he banked to the southeast, heading away from Anchorage.

"Why this way?" she asked through her mike.

She had donned earphones to hear Will above the guttural sound of the engine. The radial Pratt & Whitney engine on the Otter was as old as the 1967 aircraft, but more than once it had been taken apart piece-by-piece and rebuilt. An engine like this was meant to be overhauled. Its parts were made of heavy castings for repeated use until it ended up in a graveyard or short of a runway in a bad crash. No matter how it died, the Otter's body would be cannibalized for its knobs, handles, and gauges like a transplant donor. In that way, it would keep on living for decades. But for now, it had thousands of landings to go and many years of flying to come.

"We need to skirt the storm." He pointed to a dark line that crowded the tops of the peaks that stood between them and Anchorage. "There's a valley to the south that we can pass through." Some of the mountains in the Saint Elias range topped out at 19,000 feet. Will's Otter was not made for such high altitudes.

Suddenly, the cockpit's electronics panel shuddered. At the same time, the aircraft's engine sputtered.

"What?" Karen's voice betrayed her fear.

"We're okay."

Will knew immediately what had occurred: A solar flare. The weather report that morning on takeoff had mentioned a risk of the flare's arrival. The sun had unleashed a magnetic shockwave that had traveled millions of miles through space until it collided with the earth and overloaded the electronics of the airplane. Like being knocked down by a wave, the avionics on the cockpit's panel sputtered, then went black.

It shouldn't have affected the engine, Will thought as he loosened his grip. A nervous pilot only made matters worse. He kept the yoke steady and the wings level, going through the mental checklist that an experienced pilot would use to check each system quickly. He looked at the fuel gauge, then tried to turn the engine over, but the big radial simply coughed and went silent again.

Probably some bad fuel. Will scanned the panel again. He had landed at a small airport to refuel after crossing the mountain range. It didn't take much water in the fuel to cause havoc, especially when combined with an electrical failure.

Will Parker knew one thing about the Otter: It was made to land in any condition and on any surface.

Give me the space between home plate and first base...that's all I need. Ninety feet and he could put the airplane safely on the ground.

He scanned the terrain ahead for that much room, keeping the nose of the aircraft tilted down to maintain his airspeed. Without power, some airplanes can glide for miles as long as a calm hand can keep the nose down.

"Hand me that radio." Will pointed to a small handheld in a storage pocket next to her seat. The battery-powered radio was a must for flying in the bush. It could serve as a most important backup.

He radioed air traffic control. "Anchorage Control, this is November one-one-two." He hesitated to use the word *mayday*. A quick landing, with an equally quick passing of the solar interference, did not qualify for a mayday.

The SP-400 radio only crackled.

"We can land this...no problem." His voice was intended to calm his passenger—and himself. He looked straight ahead for a likely landing spot, as a turn would only cause the plane to lose critical airspeed. Air slowing down as it passed over the wing meant the loss of lift.

Easy, Will thought as he relaxed his hands again. It never helped to fight an airplane, even in a situation like this. He scanned his panel to make sure that something obvious was not missing. Engine failure in the arctic didn't happen every day, but this was not Will Parker's first.

Nothing.

He looked across the horizon. A ridge stood in front of the nose. There was no telling what was on the other side. It didn't matter. Their situation required commitment without hesitation. He steered the plane steadily, holding on to as much altitude as possible and for as long as possible.

"Altitude is our friend." He spoke the words unconsciously, forgetting for a moment that he had a passenger. It was an old pilot's saying that went back to the most basic instructions and first flight lessons.

"What?" Karen was turning pale.

The Otter's sleds brushed the top of the trees at the crown of the ridge.

"There you go." He pointed to a small, ice-covered pothole lake just to the left of the nose. The pothole lakes of the Yukon were Mother Nature's version of the same small, deep holes found in the Yukon's road surfaces. These were filled with ice and water. If he could hold on to a gentle turn, they had a chance. The Otter slowly slid down the hill as it lost altitude. The crown of a pine tree brushed the strut. Lower, lower, finally reaching the lake.

The aircraft slammed down on the ice and snow, the banking turn having caused the airplane to lose all of its remaining lift. The speed rapidly bled off as the skids scraped across the frozen lake until Will saw a log sticking up out of the ice.

"Hold on!"

The crunch of metal echoed through the woods and all movement stopped. The right skid had been sheared off, and the remaining sharp point of the landing gear had gotten stuck in the ice. At least the airplane had come to a stop.

"Let's get out of here." Will pointed to the door on his side. The aircraft was tilted with her starboard side angled down, causing the cargo to slide to the right. He pulled Karen across his seat and helped her down onto the ice, which seemed more than adequate to hold their weight.

"You okay?" Will was still holding her on the ice. She'd felt so small and light in her parka as he'd helped her out. He'd forgotten what the woman he'd saved in Africa felt like.

"Yeah." Her face remained ash-gray, but she seemed steady enough on her feet. Suddenly, she jumped at a noise from behind.

The cargo door on the other side had popped open; they heard another sound.

"Watch out." Karen shielded him with an arm and backed away from the wrecked aircraft.

Will saw motion on the other side as a white form crawled out of the wreckage and scurried away across the ice and into the woods on the far side of the lake.

Juliet had escaped.

"This storm isn't going to be pretty." He looked back to the Saint Elias Mountains. "We need shelter."

He knew that the clouds would bring a blizzard; after that, the temperature would drop precipitously. The clear Siberian air that followed a major front could be deadly. He pointed to a space in the timberline on the other side of the aircraft across the lake. The gap in the trees made an oddly straight line from the edge of the lake deep into the woods. In the center of the timber cut was what appeared to be a rock formation covered in deep snow. Will pointed at the outcropping. "Let's go there. We need to get out of this wind."

A cold breeze swept across the lake. The tail of the Otter squeaked as the rudder was pushed from side to side by the wind. It was the only sound.

"Whitehorse is south." He pointed in the same direction as the swath of broken trees. "But no one will come." He calculated the process. The airplane would not be missing for some time, and air traffic control was likely overwhelmed with others affected by the solar flare.

"Even though we crashed?" She looked up at him with eyes that seemed larger than normal.

"Not a crash." He smiled. "A landing." He looked back at the storm coming in. "Anything you walk away from is a landing."

"Great." Karen gave him a sarcastic smile like the teenager told about a curfew. But at least he got a smile.

They were several miles from Snag and a massive, thickly forested hill deep in snow stood between them and the airfield. Although the pilot-training strip had closed decades ago, pilots still recognized the name Snag. It had a distinction in Canada that Will didn't choose to share with Karen. Gasoline froze at forty below, but Snag was known for temperatures that turned oil into fudge. Metal would break off in your hand when the mercury hit seventy or eighty below zero, like stale icing falling off of a leftover cake.

"Follow me," he said, taking her arm. "We need some shelter, Dr. Juliet."

Printed in the United States
by Baker & Taylor Publisher Services